A RICH MAN
AND OTHER STORIES

a way, and that I soon did; for being a quiet and stirring laddie wean, folk took notice of me and many a bawbie I got by my glegness in running errands. Other less thoughtful callans would have wared them on marbles or played at the unthrift of pitch & toss, but I had a natural propensity all my days for saving, and told mother to put my bawbees in a teacup, for she was obligated in course of nature to keep me till I came to years of discretion.

My mother was a pawkie carlin, I mind her well, and she said often I spoke of gaining, that I was ordained to be long a cuff on her for my speech, either wi symptoms that discretion was not far

Letter ~~chapter~~ II

4

Although it is not to be ~~expected~~ looked for in the course of nature that a man can have a very clear recollection of the hour he was born, yet he is seldom long in the world 'ere he learns whether he is cast into the lot of Dives ~~and~~ or of Lazarus. For my part I was not left to consider which was ~~to be~~ mine, for ever since I could like a cold — chunky stone from a hot ; laughing potatoe I have had a notion that man is ~~the~~ ~~born to trouble~~ the heir of afflictions

Facsimile of a page of Galt's MS. of A RICH MAN.
From the original MS. in the Editor's possession.

A RICH MAN

AND OTHER STORIES

By JOHN GALT

EDITED WITH AN INTRODUCTION
BY WILLIAM ROUGHEAD

T. N. FOULIS, Ltd.
London & Edinburgh

Published in June
Nineteen Hundred and Twenty-five

PRINTED IN GREAT BRITAIN
BY PILLANS AND WILSON, EDINBURGH

TO

J. M. BARRIE

THESE

GLEANINGS

FROM

"THE FIELDS WE KNOW"

CONTENTS

LIST OF ILLUSTRATIONS

INTRODUCTION

WELL-NIGH ninety years ago John Galt, long broken in health and fortune, died at Greenock, a disappointed man. He had experienced in larger measure than the common lot the victories and the reverses of life; but the curious thing about him is this: that to the end he belittled his triumphs, while bitterly magnifying his defeats. Few men—certainly no man of letters—ever had so variegated a career of literary and mercantile adventure as the author of *Annals of the Parish* and the founder of the city of Guelph.

There were in Galt two persons: the story-teller and the pioneer. Sometimes they joined forces, and the issue of the unhallowed union is painfully visible in the later books. The Jekyll partner had rich and priceless gifts: knowledge, observation, a whimsical and peculiar humour, a quaint and individual style. In his own original line he is unapproached and unapproachable save by the very greatest—Sir Walter Scott. Hyde, on the other hand, unfortunately the dominant member of the co-partnery, was a publicist and an administrator, indefatigable in affairs, diligent in business, but constitutionally incapable of appreciating the artist with whom he was so incongruously yoked, or of recognising the unique quality of his genius. He it must have been who held the pen in those remarkable passages, which read so strangely in the *Autobiography* and more strangely still in the *Literary Life*, that depreciate the profession of letters and disparage its followers in a way that surely no other writer has dared or desired to do since the art of writing first was practised. Authors there may be who set small store by their wares from the artistic standpoint, content if they prove remuneratively vendible, and we should be the last to question the soundness of their judgment; but here was one who could and did produce work at once of singular merit and of high success, yet put no value on it whatever.

The evil genius of the firm had from the beginning the whip hand: he was, as has been observed, " at one time or another law-student, researching historian, voyager, playwright, and contrabandist "; and his last lamentable speculation in the Canada Company brought the business to bankruptcy and ruin. But midway in their devious course the junior partner managed to assert himself. The year 1820 saw the publication of *The Ayrshire Legatees* in Blackwood's popular magazine; in 1821 appeared the unfading *Annals* ; in 1822, *The Provost* and *Sir Andrew Wylie* ; in 1823, *The Entail* and *Ringan Gilhaize*: six masterpieces in four years. No wonder that his practical colleague protested against such waste of time and energy, and roared for commerce! But meanwhile, as the other had the bit in his teeth, schemes and projects must be laid aside: there was nothing for it except literary collaboration. So with Machiavellian subtlety Hyde pointed out to Jekyll the resounding fame and prodigious profits accruing from the Waverley Novels to their fortunate begetter, and urged his partner to enter the lists against " the Great Unknown." *Rothelan, The Spaewife*, and *Southennan* are among the unhappy fruits of this insidious counsel. Thenceforth, with one bright exception, Hyde had it all his own way. The whole capital of the firm was embarked in the Canadian venture, to the disastrous effect we know. Yet despite worries innumerable, failing health, injustice, ingratitude, and grievous disenchantment, the victim of colonial enterprise contrived to add to his former achievement two excellent examples of fictive tragedy and comedy: *The Omen* and *The Last of the Lairds* (1826): which in their so disparate manners are as fine as anything he ever wrote. Thereafter the collaboration was resumed in *Lawrie Todd* (1830), in subsequent " didactic " fictions, and finally in the *Autobiography* and the *Literary Life*, of which the less said, the better; until in 1839 the partnership was dissolved for good. Verily is it written: " a man's foes shall be they of his own household."

. . . .

Appended to a list of " The Separate Works of John Galt "—extending to upwards of sixty volumes—with which he concludes his *Autobiography*, is this characteristic note : " *N.B.*—These are all I recollect." And in his curious " Estimate of Myself " at the end of the *Literary Life*, he writes :—

Enough, however, of literature is before the public by which my station as an author may be determined. But I shall not be justly dealt with if I am considered merely as a literary man: all that I have done ought to be taken into the estimate. . . . But when my numerous books are forgotten, I shall yet be remembered. . . . I contrived the Canada Company, which will hereafter be spoken of among the eras of a nation destined to greatness. That project, flourishingly carried into effect, I not only projected, but established myself.*

Alas, the pity of it is that of all concerned, the founder was the only one who reaped no benefit by the undertaking. Again, in the *Autobiography* he complacently remarks :—

At no time, as I frankly confess, have I been a great admirer of mere literary character; to tell the truth, I have sometimes felt a little shame-faced in thinking myself so much an author, in consequence of the estimation in which I view the professors of book-making in general. A mere literary man—an author by profession—stands but low in my opinion, and the reader will, perhaps, laughingly say, " it is a pity I should think so little of myself." But though, as the means of attaining ascendancy and recreation in my sphere, I have written too much, it is some consolation to reflect that

" I left no calling for the idle trade."

This I assert with confidence, for, in looking back through the long vista of a various life, I cannot upbraid myself with having neglected one task, or left one duty unperformed, either for the thrift or fancy-work of letters.†

Surely no more amazing apologia for the craft of fiction was ever penned by mortal novelist!

Such being his literary creed, I doubt whether Galt would have thanked me for what in this, and in a form-

* *Literary Life and Miscellanies*, I, 357-358.

† *Autobiography*, II, 200-201.

er volume,* I set out piously to accomplish: the rescue from bygone magazines of his uncollected tales. But as few of his readers would subscribe to these " blasphemous fables "—I hasten to add that I mean, of course, Galt's beliefs, not his fictions—there is little fear that the " acute and honourable minority " who relish him at his best will fail to appreciate the result of my endeavours. The three stories here first published in book form will, I am confident, prove a welcome and ponderable addition to the sum of his achievement. Of the history of the first and second I can find no trace; Galt himself does not mention them, nor are they referred to by " Delta " in his *Memoir* of his friend. I am fortunate to possess, however, some pages—one of which is herewith reproduced—of the MS. of " A Rich Man." They are entirely and throughout in Galt's beautiful running script, which shows that he wrote the story with his own hand, before he was disabled by the paralysis that compelled him to dictate all his later work. The earliest symptoms of that evil, as we know from Dr Moir,† manifested themselves in 1830; from that date Galt suffered repeated attacks, which nine years later brought about his death. It would therefore appear that, although not printed till 1836, " A Rich Man " was written while Galt was yet in the full exercise of his powers. And, indeed, apart from the evidence of handwriting, the matter of the tale suffici-

* *The Howdie and Other Tales.* Edinburgh: 1923.

† *Biographical Memoir of John Galt,* by D. M. Moir (" Delta "), p. lxxxv. Edinburgh: 1841.

ently attests the fact. Why, seeing that it is so good, he did not include it in his *Stories of the Study* (1833), or in the *Miscellanies* (1834), which contain much inferior stuff, and were both dictated, I cannot tell. Doubtless he overlooked it, for he had already forgotten the existence of two full-length novels—" an illustration of the kind of forgetfulness to which I am subject; perhaps I should say, of the little heed which I give to my own works "! *

" A Rich Man " is, in my judgment, a fit companion to *The Provost.* This is a high claim, but an examination of these twin studies of civic magisterial proficiency and " pawkiness " will warrant it. Both are autobiographic—Galt's happiest form, so long as he did not apply it to his own case—and allowing for the difference in scale, the self-portraiture of Archibald Plack, Esq., is as good a likeness and as admirably drawn as that of Mr James Pawkie himself. The vocabulary of the London-Scot has suffered nothing by reason of his long tarrying in the court of the Gentiles; it has all the " birr " and " smeddum " of his Ayrshire colleague, whose days were passed in the royal burgh of Gudetown (Irvine), and whose peregrinations were limited to a trip to Glasgow. Indeed, so racy of his native soil is the language of this expatriated Scot that I have been constrained to concede a glossary for relief of his adopted countrymen. Galt's vernacular is the Scots of Burns: a purer, stronger spirit than the blend used by

* *Literary Life*, I, 349.

Sir Walter, and still further refined by Stevenson; it has, in Mr Crockett's just phrase, " the rich tang of the mother-earth." A sad reflection that speech so vivid, nervous, and expressive should come to be regarded as practically a dead tongue.

In " A Rich Man " Galt was able to realise the intention he had formed for *Sir Andrew Wylie*: " a view of the rise and progress of a Scotchman in London." No particular story, he tells us, was engrafted on his original idea for that work, but by the persuasion of some egregious friend he was induced to make it " more like an ordinary novel "—with the dire result of spoiling his conception. Fortunately, this pestilent adviser had no say in the fashioning of Archibald Plack. The appellative Plack—a copper worth one-third of a penny sterling or four pennies Scots, approximating to the Widow's mite—is chosen with Galt's unerring flair for names, as suggestive of the inconsiderable beginnings of his hero, who, like his forerunner, Sir Richard Whittington, from a poor 'prentice rose to be Lord Mayor of London. His only child, a daughter, has married a nobleman, and to the issue of this patrician alliance, the Hon. George Spend, then an undergraduate at Oxford, the grandfather's letters are addressed. We do not know the motto of the house of Plack, but Hamlet's "Thrift, thrift, Horatio! " might serve for one. The lad, who is of a different breed, has outrun the constable, and has asked for a remittance; this " replenishment," together with his extravagance, form the burden of the old gentleman's complaint. But, as he himself says, his bark is worse than his bite; and his grandson, having had to endure much good advice, receives in the end the necessary supplies.

For the young man's improvement and instruction the letters set forth, with delightful naïveté, the senior's experiences of life: his early servitude to an irrascible, wooden-legged captain; his sojourn in a chemist's shop; as an "errander" or messenger boy in Glasgow; as a porter in Liverpool; and his removal to London, where in due season he embarked "in the provision line," which proved the foundation of his fortunes. From these humble origins, by dint of native shrewdness, industry, and luck, aided by an unromantic but prudent marriage with a sail-maker's well-dowered widow—who had the good taste shortly to rejoin her former lord, "leaving me with the meal, though the basin was taken away"—Mr Plack's position was so improved that he added money-lending to the provision business, with excellent results. His second matrimonial investment proved equally sound; he espoused the sole and "sonsy" heiress of a wealthy merchant, who soon after obligingly "coupit o'er off his seat in a 'poplexy," leaving behind him to mitigate his loss no less than fifty thousand pounds. Mr and Mrs Plack were now able to take a fine house, to keep a carriage, and to give their daughter the best of educations. By skilful dealings on the Stock Exchange at the time of the French Revolution he contrived to add to his fortune and to his growing reputation as a financier. He became successively sheriff, alderman, and Lord Mayor, but to the end he elected to remain a commoner and " eschewed a bawronetcy "—both on account of the expense, and " because it was not an inheritance which I could bequeath to Clemy, that was ordained to be the heiress to my bit gathering." When that young lady came home from school her parents took her on a " jaunt " to Scotland. Edinburgh, proud, cultured, and historic, did not appeal to Mr Plack, who esteemed it but " a cauldrife similarity to a city." He found Glasgow more congenial: " everybody in Glasgow is busy making money in the best way he can "; the folk were modest, too, in their prosperity: " there is nae rifting in a neighbour's face, when they have gotten a fu' kite." At Cheltenham, on their way south, the travellers made the acquaintance of a young lord, who, " casting a sheep's eye at our Clemy," presently became a suitor for the damsel's hand; and though her practical sire looked upon lords as " a kind of canary-headed cattle, having, for the most part, a want," he was induced by his wife's exhortations to consent to the match, settling on the bride a sum of five-and-twenty thousand pounds. Such, in brief outline, is the simple " plot "; but Galt's best stories really have no plots. Their charm resides, as here, in the consummate quality of his humour, the blandness and humanity of his wit, his rich faculty of representation, and his exquisite fidelity to life.

In the second of our tales* we have for hero a complete contrast to the capable, worldly-wise man of affairs. The Reverend Cowal Kilmun, minister of a small Argyllshire parish, is a divine of the school of which Mr Balwhidder of Dalmailing is the palmary exemplar: a simple, kindly, childlike soul, whose knowledge of human nature and acquaintance with life are bounded by the narrow confines of his rural charge. His " tribulations " have their rise in the celebration of the mysterious nuptials of Mr Ettles and Miss Sylvia Graham. The couple part immediately after the ceremony, the bridegroom going to America upon his affairs, while the bride remains behind to perish of consumption. Her husband returns, only to find that she has just died; and it is to be presumed that the shock accounts for the aggravation of his pristine eccentricities. He forms a friendship with the sympathetic pastor, and introduces to him one Mr Roslin, an elderly man who had made a fortune in the States. Mr Ettles marries again, not happily—the misfortune in this instance being that he does *not* lose his wife: some people are never satisfied. Mr Roslin, intending to take passage to America, being wind-bound at Greenock, crosses the Firth to visit the minister, and on his return finds that the ship has sailed, not only without him, but with his trunks and money.

* I once examined in a bookseller's hands part of the MS. of the " Tribulations," which, like that of the former story, is in the handwriting of Galt himself. The point is important as bearing on the date of composition.

In these circumstances he applies to Mr Kilmun for a temporary accommodation. The dilemma in which this places the prudent man, divided between his disinclination to lend and his desire to live up to his principles, is most diverting. He goes reluctantly to Greenock to discharge his Christian duty; and so appreciative is Mr Roslin of his "apostolic simplicity," that he promises to leave him by will one hundred dollars to buy a mourning ring. The testator is taken off suddenly that very night, and next day the minister is faced with the charges of the burial. A will, however, is found, leaving to Mr Kilmun, in addition to the promised bequest, a legacy of five thousand dollars, "because he is a worthy character, overflowing with simplicity and truth." The residue is left to Mr Ettles, who writes that he is going to Edinburgh "to settle everything," and asks the minister to meet him there. The good man does so, though he has little faith in the legacy, and "it was a certain loss to come into Edinburgh." His fears seem well founded, for Mr Ettles announces that the deceased had a relative named Junor, who has a claim upon the property, and whom to discover is their present business in the city. In quest of this retiring beneficiary he drags the long-suffering divine up and down the wynds and closes of the old town, their adventures providing much matter of entertainment. Finally, he discloses that Mr Junor is, in fact, akin to the immortal Mrs Harris, and that the purpose of the deception was to indulge his own charitable impulses and to enlarge the minister's mind. Over and above this experience, however, Mr Kilmun is a gainer by the amount of the legacy, which Ettles duly pays him. The expedition furnishes Galt with an opportunity for a further "dig" at Auld Reikie, which plainly was not the city of his affections: "one of the most self-conceited Babels that ever the Lord put the breath of life into; and certain it is, among the residenters, there are some who would give more for a forbear in a stoury kist than for a living preacher of the gospel." Here, as in the case of the reverend hero of the *Annals*, the art consists in the naïve self-revelation of the amiable pastor's little weaknesses and foibles, and in the blend of innocence and "canniness" of which his character is so cunningly compounded.

For the third tale I can give chapter and verse. In a letter to his friend Dr Moir, written on his return from Canada, and dated London, 14th July 1829, Galt writes :—

> I have brought here with me a great mass of book materials, the fruits of my solitary *noctes* in the Canadian wayside taverns. Part of the "Landlady" I have sent to Blackwood, leaving it to himself to publish in the "Magazine" or otherwise. This has been forced upon me by the manner in which the fair copy and rough draft have been made up by my clerk—the series of the chapters having been broken in such a manner that I shall have many pages to re-write.*

Fifteen chapters were duly printed in the four following numbers of *Maga*. The tale, as published,

* *Biographical Memoir*, pp. lxxvii-lxxviii.

would seem to be incomplete, but I can find no further reference to it or its fortunes. Probably it was never finished, which, in view of his loose literary habits, is more than likely.* "Delta" tells us that Galt, shortly after arriving in London, was arrested for debt, and the next we hear of his literary activities is the creation of *Lawrie Todd* in the depressing *milieu* of the King's Bench.

The opening chapters of "My Landlady" read like a record of facts; I find that the author's first visit to London was in the spring of 1804, and that he alighted from the mail-coach at the Bull and Mouth.† If the subsequent doings of the traveller are imaginary, the quest for rooms and the personality of Mrs Winsom appear to be the fruits of real research and observation. Doubtless it was Galt himself who gazed awestruck at the august person of the Prince of Wales, walking, like a mere mortal, down Pall Mall.

The amiable, loquacious landlady of Mortimer Street, Cavendish Square, like the great Mrs Lirriper of Norfolk Street, Strand, is a matron largely versed in the knowledge of human nature, as exhibited by the nomads who pitch their temporary tents in hired parlours, and is endowed with a similar gift for communicating it

* For example, he writes to Moir on 11th December 1833, when preparing his *Miscellanies* for publication: "In looking over my papers, I have found a batch of MSS. that I did not think existed. They were written prior to my going abroad for the first time."—*Biographical Memoir*, p. cii.

† *Autobiography*, I, 62.

to others. Her character is developed with surpassing artistry, as she tells the story of her life, and recounts her so varied experience of her fellow-creatures. The combination of keenness and kindliness which she exhibits in this connection is typically Scottish. While she has a professional preference for such lodgers "as those wha hae the handling of public money or the rooking of Hindoo Rajays," she is capable of leaving more than five weekly bills unpaid by the impoverished Melbourn. Her powers of observation would do no discredit to Mr Sherlock Holmes, as witness her diagnosis of Mr Flowerfield's linen: "His ruffles were of delightful French cambric, but the body of his shirt was of that Glasgow duplicity for linen commonly called calico, but which every sensible and frugal woman better knows by the name of steam-factory flimsy." Wonderfully true to life is the disenchantment of that unfortunate nabob, in returning after many years to the scenes of his youth. The comical episode of the rebellion of "his blackamoor man, Jugurtha," and the trouble to which it leads, are described in Galt's most hilarious vein.

The Paisley Bailie, "with a pawkie whirly in the corner of his eye, that shewed, if he wasna a sinner, he kent what a pleasant thing sin might be," and his good lady, "not of a genteel habit of body, being short, and of a protuberant corpulency," are genuine creations. Their "gallantings" in London, including a dinner "at the Talbot Inn at Richmond, on a Sunday, though the bill for eels, a duck with green peas, and a grosette tart, was enough to make the hair on the head of any man to stand on end, far more that of a Bailie, who is reputed to get his dainties from the common stock" ; and the "diversion" of witnessing the execution of a forger— "for, as Mrs Seeston said, if it was not sae dreadful a thing as a murderer's, yet it was an edifying curiosity of its kind," are conceived in Galt's happiest humour.

As a contrast, he gives us the story of the tragic loves of the fair Fatima and Captain Rampant. We share the narrator's wonder at the "dramatic propriety" of Mrs Winsom's relation, and appreciate the quiet power of the death-scene. This is noteworthy as an example of Galt's fine restraint in pathos: unlike certain of his successors, who have graduated in the kailyard school of which he was the founder, he is never falsely sentimental, nor does he "squeeze your body for the briny drops," after the fashion of more popular exploiters of the pathetic. His kail are cabbages, not brier bushes.

Kenneth Macquirkie, Esq., W.S.—"he was as greedy as a trap, and as gair as a smiddy vice"—is an acquisition to Galt's admirable gallery of legal portraits, and the "kittle question" of the controverted lobster forms an amusing incident. He "presents" the diverting humours of the rivalry between the neighbouring towns of Blackbirch (Greenock) and Port-Punchtown (Port-Glasgow), and the fate of the Bailie's Bill—"a thing they called a Committee took hold of his Bill and tore it all to pieces." Greenock had for Galt an inexplicable attraction. He lived there as a lad, he returned to it as a family man, he elected to die there and there to be buried. But his attachment for that uninviting seaport did not blind him to the peculiarities of its inhabitants, as this sketch of their municipal manners shows.

The remaining lodgers to whom we are introduced include the Drury Lane prima donna, Miss Cymbal, with her pet guinea-pig, and her conquest of a peer; the mysterious mother who attends the Sessions, and brings back from Newgate the body of her son—she came, appropriately enough, in a dead season, "for the French Revolution was then rampaging like a drunken man with a drawn sword; and I had nightly fears anent dethronements, and the casting forth of every man of substance, so that lodgers should come no more" ; and Captain Monsoon from Calcutta, with his native servant " in an Indian dress, and a turban like a puddock-stool; an extraordinary well-bred thing it was, and it aye made a low boo, with its hands on its forehead"—who suffers so much by the deceptions of London that at last he " would scarcely believe the sun was in the firmament on the sunniest day."

Here, with the conclusion of the Captain's troubles, the tale abruptly terminates. Although ended, it is not finished: Mrs Winsom's fund of anecdote, her richness of reminiscence, and her engaging garrulity are clearly not yet exhausted.* But either Galt tired of

* *Cf.* the opening paragraph of the last chapter.

her, or he forgot her in the press of his affairs, and she remains a torso. *The Last of the Lairds*, of which its author wrote to "Delta" on leaving England: "Perhaps a sentence or two may be wanting at the conclusion of the *Laird*. If you think so, supply it,"* contains much of his finest and most characteristic work,† yet he was too careless to round it off himself, and deputed the task to another hand! Devoid of conscience in matters of art as he was scrupulously precise in matters of business, Galt, in a literary sense, was the chief of sinners. But despite his shortcomings in that regard, he has by these three tales increased our debt of gratitude. The figures of the shrewd, self-made magistrate, the guileless old minister, and the likeable, gossiping landlady, are, I venture to think, no unworthy addition to the goodly company of whom in other of his books he has so generously made us free.

. . . .

There are superior persons who will tell you that they can't read Galt. There are also people who advocate Summer Time and those who favour Prohibition. These matters (especially the last) being questions of taste, it is proverbially idle to dispute about. But just as there are still some obsolete souls who enjoy a con-

* *Biographical Memoir*, p. xli.

† *E.g.*, the splendid description of the old laird's death, at a sederunt of the Langsyne Club in Luckie Gawsie's public, as chronicled in Chapter III, which for grim humour and admirable Scots, is surpassed only by "Wandering Willie's Tale" in *Redgauntlet*.

vivial glass, and prefer to dine by candle-light; who do not like to "have to go to bed by day," or to get up an hour earlier than usual, by Act of Parliament; so are there divers old-fashioned folk who love the good-natured, warm-hearted author of the *Annals*, and all—well, nearly all—his works; who savour his delightsome humour, and revel in his quaint conceits. For such have I taken the trouble to set forth these three forgotten stories, in the belief that they will be received no less kindly than was my former gathering of his tales—as, indeed, they deserve to be, in that they are much more attractive and important. But if not, and should they meet with the cold reception commonly accorded to *revenants* in other than spiritualistic circles, then blame not their begetter, but the officiousness of the misguided medium who has thus unwarrantably disturbed their rest.

WILLIAM ROUGHEAD.

I

A RICH MAN; OR, HE HAS GREAT MERIT

BEING THE

AUTOBIOGRAPHY OF ARCHIBALD PLACK, Esq.

LATE LORD MAYOR OF LONDON

In a series of letters to
his grandson, The Honourable George Spend

A RICH MAN;
OR, HE HAS GREAT MERIT

BEING THE

AUTOBIOGRAPHY OF ARCHIBALD PLACK, Esq.
LATE LORD MAYOR OF LONDON

Letter I

MY oe and heir, ye kenna-what, how can ye think that ganging a gey gait is the way to turn the penny, unless it be out of your pouch? It wasna, my lad, by such gavalling that I gart the bodles whelp in mine; and, therefore, instead of sending you " a replenishment " at this time, I'll send you much better, being an account of the different come-to-passes in my creditable life. They'll maybe serve you as well as Latin books, which are only things that may do good to doctors, and others that follow the poor trade of philosophy; which, with God's help and my bit haining, I hope you are never ordained to take up: no that I make an objek to birkies of a pedigree—as surely you are, by the father's side—to get a slaik of college lair; but it's no to be feart that ye'll ever be dour at your books.

It's very true that my Lord, your father, that's married upon my only dochter, your mother, is a discreet man—and there was a good because he should be so; for the auld Lord, his father, was a canary-headed sorrow, and didna leave a crumb or moulin of his patrimony out of the coomy clutches of the lawyers and Jews; so that, had he no forgatherit with your mother, my dochter, he would just, in a sense, have been going from door to door, with a meal pock about his neck, and a rung in his hand—no living at heck and manger, as he is now doing, in yon Castle Folly, in Vanity Fair, as the west end of the town ought by rights to be called.

But, before I get all the rift off my stomach, it is needful to remark, that, although I dinna intend to be as mim as a May puddock with you, yet I'm no of an overly virgos nature, even in my displeasure about your galravitching and keeping of an eating horse; on the contrary I'm of a most natural mild temper, as in the end you may experience: indeed, if I'm no so to my only dochter's kitling, I wonder to wha I should be so. But what I have to say is all for your good; and I redd you no to take it ill, for I have my will and testament to make; and all I have is of my own conkesting, which frees me from leaving a doit to your father's get, unless it pleasure myself; and yet there is not a living Christian that better kens that blood is thicker than water than I do. And, Geordie, although ye were not a Lord's offspring, I cannot but recognise you as my only daughter's affset—my bark is mair dauntoning than my bite.

I dinna mind if ever I told you anent my ancestors; and I am sure my dochter Clemy, your mother, never would, for she was aye an upsetting cutty; it therefore behoves me to let you know whatna brae I have had to climb, that ye may see riches are no gatherit like sclate stanes, to the end that ye may consider well of writing to me letters anent replenishments, keeping, as I am creditably informed you do, an eating moth of a horse of the hunter speshy—maybe two, one for a flunkie. Geordie, Geordie, ca' canny! Hunters and racers are genteel creatures; and I would have as meikle hope of a ne'er-do-weel with a laithron, as a young man with such gambolling cattle: the very whisk of their tails is an evendown outrage among decent folk. From this you may learn what is in my breast concerning this wastry; and, by the next post, I'll make a beginning, which is all at present from your auld daddy,

ARCHD. PLACK.

LETTER II

Although it is not to be looked for in the course of nature that a man can have a very clear recollection of the hour he was born; yet he is seldom long in the world till he learns whether he is cast into the lot of Dives or of Lazarus. For my part, I was not left to consider which was mine; for, ever since I could tell a cold chucky-stone from a laughing het potato, I have had a notion that man is the heir of afflictions; accordingly, I felt it soon to be my duty to ettle what I could to get into a way. And that I soon did; for, being a gair and stirring laddie wean, folk took notice of me, and mony a bawbee I got by my glegness in running errands; less thoughtful callans would have waur'd on marbles, or played at the unthrift of pitch-and-toss, but I had a natural appety all my days for saving, and told mother to put my bawbees in a tea-cup, for she was obligated in course of nature to keep me till I came to years of discretion.

My mother was a pawkie carlin—I mind her weel; and shesaid, when I spoke of haining, that I was no ordained to be long a cess on her; for my speech kythed wi' symptoms that discretion was not far off when I was near—and so it was seen; for, when I was scrimp six, her dead-ill fell upon her, and, being a sailor's widow, she departed this life, leaving me an orphan to an old aunty with few teeth and of a cankery inclination; having but her spinning-wheel for her bread-winner.

However, aunty did her duty; and, as I had ninepence halfpenny when I went to domicile with her, she sent me to the school; for which every week I paid a penny, and every day read in the Mother's Carritches; so that, before I had won through the Sixpence, I was accounted, by her and the minister's leddy, a deacon of a scholar. The minister himself patted my head because of my profishency.

But, although it couldna but be said that I learnt to read like a bailie in the course of the first winter I was at the school, yet there was an outcoming of fortune in the spring that detained me from learning any more till the next winter; and this was the coming into the clachan of a soldier officer with a timber leg and a fashious temper, who needed a gleg callan to do his turns.

By dint of speaking well of me, aunty, through the

minister, got Captain Sash to give me a preferment; but I had a sore time o't in attending to his yeas and nays, specially in the warm months, when flies are bloody-minded, and, as he often said, most damnable.

How long I might have bided in the servitude of Captain Sash is not to be rehearsed; but, towards the hinder end of har'st, we parted; and the chief because of the amputation was his wooden leg, with which he was in the scowry nights, by habit and repute, in the way of riping the ribs. Thus it came to pass, that he came home one evening, and the fire being low, and he being cauldrife, lifted his timber toe and gave it a powter.

Gude kens how it came to pass, but in so doing he staggers, his wooden leg was among hands broken, and he wytes me with the exploit; which I would not thole, for it was not true; whereat he called me a mutinous vagabond. My corruption rose. I replied he was a scarlet tyrant; he lifted his hand, I jouked the blow, and he, having but one leg to stand on, swung round and fell on the coals, which it was a mercy were not kindled. He paid me, howsever, my wage; for, though of a frush temper, he had a modicum of honesty about him. Nothing, however, would persuade me to come again within his reach; for even then I was a spirit.

With the wage, aunty put me again to school, to learn to write and cast 'counts, for I had learnt, as I have told you, to read; but in this political economy I was not cordial; for, understanding that the session was obligated to do something for me, I was loath to part with my penny-fee, for no other end, that I could see at the time, than to draw crunkly effigies on paper and a sclate. But I soon came to discern the good that was in them ; and before Candlemas, the dominie said I was a geni—telling aunty, though, it was kittle to say for what. I think myself it was a geni for making money, as, before the Candlemas, I had hained, from going errands, two shillings and five and a bawbee; and when the thought came into my head, that my capacity was of the peinor-pig order, it is not to be told what a revelation I had. I was, in sooth, a pawkie wean, and kent a mite by its mudging from a moulin.

But of that blithe and heartsome time—it may be of scant and want—I have not much remembrance. Like others, I have a pleasant recollection of my ramplar days. The summer was warmer then, and surely winter brisker. Oh, the pretty moonlights! Surely Time has grown aulder, and a thought tavert since syne; and I think Nature now is wersher of the smeddum than that she then sowed into the young heart. But I was never one that neglectit a turn for daffin.

Letter III

When I had perfited my edication, which was afore Beltane of the next year—I being then weel through my eighth year—it behoved me to think of some gaet of going into the world to seek a living; for it was not thought I was of a proper habit of body for a trade, as I was short-sighted, and very ready to take the cold, which shewed that herding would never do for me. Some calling of a sheltered nature was, therefore, to be thought of. The neighbours of aunty considered, however, I was still young enough; but there was a confabble among them anent me, which made it manifest that there would soon be an outcoming.

In the May after, the laddie who kirned James Junor's, the druggist, medicaments, took the kingcost; and, being of a weakly constitution, paid the debt of nature in no time. Thus there came to be a vacuity in the druggist's shop, and I was elected, by James, to the office. It was, indeed, as aunty said, a blithe upcast to meet with; and I thought so, too, and often thought so, when dunting the pestle on the bottom of the brass mortar; for I hope ye have gotten a sufficiency of learning to understand that kirning drugs is braying in a mortar with a pestle, similar to the utensil which, as I have heard the one called, that stood above our door, gilded, the effigy of a doctor.

With Mr Junor, I was the best of three years; and it cannot be said, at the end of the term, that I was even then owre old to take my foot in my hand, to see what the world was like ayont the dyke. But it was a pleasant, sober time—the remembrance of it is lowne in my bosom, like a bonny April morning, when the buds biggen, and the birds begin to sing. Nor was my being in that odoriferous shop (as I heard the schoolmistress one day call it) without profit, in a sense; for, at my work, I thought but of such a nice thing it must be to be rich, and used to lilt, in a cutty-crumb voice, keeping time with the pestle—

> The king sits in his parlour,
> Counting o'er his money;
> The queen sits in her garden,
> Eating bread and honey—

thinking his Majesty's duty was the pleasantest vocation of the two.

Nor, though Mr Junor might be an exact man, was he an Egyptian task-master, requiring bricks and giving no straw; for he was very considerate—which is more than can be said, as my experience teaches, of every one that has the repute of honesty in the world. Accordingly, he sometimes, of his own voluntary motion, gave me the play; and was sorry he could not do it on the Saturday afternoon, when the schools were skailed, as Saturday was, of a' the seven in the week, the throngest day in the Doctor's shop.

This James Junor, the druggist, though he lived among dry mint, thyme, and camomile, like a dead and stuffed alligator, was no an every-day body, but something by ordinar, and my heart warms yet when I think of him; for, though he lived by selling odious trash, his nature had no broo of any such commodities, he being a genteel man, and born, you would have thought, to be an ostentation in the world. But, now that I am well through life, I may say nothing is more common than to meet with a man whose nature is at war with his luck. The master was of this kind.

His father was a barber-man, in the High Street of Glasgow, near the College, and had the dressing of two Professors and the Principal, by which he acquired all the knowledge he had; but learning had little to do with it. In time, James got in, free gratis, to the classes, where he ettled so well that he was egged on to be a doctor; but when, however, he was in the middle of the strive, his father died of a sore income, and he was obligated to quit the College and to implement on chins. His heart, however, having a preeing of the light turns of doctoring, aye lay to that trade; and, in process of time, he got the druggist that then was in our town, to take him intil his shop, where, after mony a year as helper, he ripened, in the course of nature, to be his successor; and such he was, well stricken in years, when he took me on.

Besides being a druggist, James Junor was a good man; and one of the few I have ever seen that money was no required to make better. His wife, Mrs Junor, was not, however, either the yolk or kernel of womankind, but a mere woman—which is not saying a great deal in her behalf; but it's an auld observe, that the best of men have often the worst of wives, which, in my opinion, must be somehow a cause of their goodness; for, if they can thole the devil in the house, they'll no be overly fashed at any of God's creatures on the causeway. But, anent this head of discourse, however, I may as well keep a calm sough. Poor woman! she's long gone to her rest—and I'm sure she was not out of the need o't.

LETTER IV

When I had been two years and a half with that gospel-hearted saint, Mr Junor, tholing as well's I could with his Jobish conjugality, and being nearing on the time to do for myself, I had some wiselike confabble with aunty.

It was agreed between us, that, as I had no prospect of being a robustious man, I should spouse my fortune as an errander in Glasgow. But the easiest trades are no without their craft—as may be seen by looking at watchmakers making faces at spectacle-eyes, as they keek by them into the bowelry of their commodities; so I could not set up as an errander in Glasgow till I learnt the outs and ins of that royal city. But, in this, Providence, as in all cases, was large; and the willing-to-do-well will never want a friend as long as there's a God in the Heavens.

It happened that aunty had a far-off cousin by her guidman's side—a well-doing weaver in the Gorbals; and he had a wife that was spoken of for that couthy kind of eidency which foretokens thriving; indeed, the truth of the saying has kythed on them, for, in the fulness of time, he was gathered to his fathers, in a bien way, and a bailie.

Well, it so happened that aunty got the schoolmaster to write a bit scrape of a pen to her kith, John Douce, and sent it by the Glasgow carrier, to tell him what I would be at, and how well I had behaved with James Junor. John was not long of making a response; for, when the carrier came back, he brought two lines from him, saying, he would do all in his potentiality to help me; and telling me no to be blate, but to come away and bide with him, making a recompense out of my earnings as I could afford it. Thus, it came to pass that, on my eleventh birthday, I went with the carrier to begin the world as an errander in Glasgow.

I cannot say I was very vogie on that morning of the venturing, when I bade farewell to aunty, and looked o'er my shoulder from the braehead at the town below. But I was so boun to be rich, that everything else was secondary; and the thought that I might be so in time, hampered the tear that was fain to creep into the corner of my eye. Still I could not but think of the times that were past; for, let our youth be never such a moil, there is something in the mysteries of the spirit that aye makes us look back upon't as on a blithesome morning.

Ye may think that to say so is rather more like a safthorn than ye believe I am; but they look for trout in a shallow burn who dinna see that a man with an earnest intent has deep feeling. Do ye think I would ever had my dochter married to a lord, had I no got the upper hand of my human weakness, which was more than many would have liked to own? Na, na, my lad; ponder well, and warning take. I cared nae mair for wealth, for its own sake, than others; but I saw it was the key to all comforts, and to have my own will of them I in a sense coveted; but it was not the covetousness forbidden in the tenth commandment, for I never grudged no man his having. I only longed for the means by which I might conquest such havings. It was that power I sought to gain, by gaining riches—well knowing that with them I would get the potential; so dinna think I was either daft or doited, for I was no miser, but a man that saw gold ruled the world and only thought to make it a friend.

This observe is needful, now that I am telling you of what happened to me on the threshold of life; for, although ye maybe think, like many others, that I had never a right purpose, be ye assured that there is none without some aim—for, although we are not all alike in strength of will to do, we have the same likeness to each other in mind as we bear in body. And I dinna err in saying this; for, if ye didna jalouse me to be of the niggarality order, you wouldna have been so bird-mouthed in the way you have asked for a " replenishment." Gair, Geordie, however, as you may think me, I never ettled for wealth but as a means; and, if you had the ee in your neck that I wish ye had, ye would see that. I had an early notion, that an onedicated man like me wasna the fittest to make a solid choice of the best butts and targets of fortune. I saw, however, that I couldna be far wrang if I got the means to win at any of them. So, if ye see, now and then, a bit glaik of fancy about me, no very like what ye thought, ye shouldna be surprised, or think in my auld days that I am putting on a new man, for I was aye the same; only, having long since conquered all my wants, I have grown slacker to make money in my age; indeed, my bairn, to tell you the truth, I have long made as much as I feel in myself capacity and fitness to use—and more would be fashious. As an earnest that I'm no at the grounds so foul as ye think, I send you enclosed a " replenishment," as you call it, on Tommie Coutts, to make good what I say, and to reprove your thoughts of me, if they need it.

Letter V

I weel mind the welcoming I got from John Douce and his wife. It couldna be said he was unjustly a narrow man; but he was, maybe, a thought hard. His wife, however, was a handwaled woman, and had from the womb been ordained to bless the man she was made for.

We had some solid conversation anent what put it into my head to think of being an errand porter rather than a tradesman; and I replied that he might see I wasna of the right cut to be a prime tradesman, which was an admonishment no to try.

" Ay," quo' the mistress, who had sat for some time before silent, " guidman, he'll do weel, if that's his ain thought; for there's nothing helps on a man like a right knowledge of himself and what he's best fit for. The failures we meet with happen oftener from the man not knowing what he's fit for, than from want of ability. I aye doubt the thriving of those that itch for more than they seem to require."

From less to more, we began to discourse together; and Mrs Douce spoke to me as if I was an experienced man, no only an auld-farrant wean, which was the most that could be said of me at home; and when I told her how I intended to make myself acquainted with the town before I set up in business, she said mony a pleasant thing about my having inherited a discerning spirit.

The outcomings of that night I have never forgotten; for John Douce himself was a canny far-forecasting man; and, as for the mistress, I wonder how Nature was so thoughtless as to drop such a pearl, for the clutes and hooves of the multitude to tread on. Her heartening was a cordial that cheered me long, and made the dooly of my first night in the world as blithe as the banqueting of a baptism.

The next morning I rose betimes; and having covenanted with the carrier lad on the road, to shew me some of the town, we went hither and yon together till eight o'clock, in a very satisfactory manner. John Douce, after breakfast, having gone to the looms, his wife said that, as she was not very throng, she would go about with me, adding, it was aye to her a pleasaunce to help them that were so willing to do well. She was, indeed, a prudent woman, and very wisely thought that to make money was the true substantial way to do weel in this world.

I have often thought since that it was a wonderful thing how a woman of such sagacity had so much earnestness for a perfect wean; but she had none of her own, which partly may account for it: the promptings and spiritings of her own active nature was, however, no doubt, the main cause. Largely I profited by her pains; and, as we walked along the streets together, all her discourse was advices and admonitions. In short, my lines at the first with her fell in pleasant places, and she was a mother by common to me.

When I had learned myself well in the wynds and turns of Glasgow, I took my station aneath the pillars forenent the Tolbooth; but when I gaed home at breakfast time, a thought dowie because I had come no speed, Mrs Douce said it was not the right side of the street.

" One," quoth she, " should aye endeavour to begin the world on the right side of the causeway. It's no doubt a very creditable stance ye have taken; but it's no so good by a degree as the plainstones on the other side where the gentlemen congregate;—and, besides, ye must change that Kilmarnock bonnet. It gars you look of a country complexion. Do in Rome as they do in Rome; and mind never to make yourself kenspeckle unless it's in snodness; for maist folk, though they cannot tell why, have no broo of them that has onything out-o'-the-way about them."

In consequence of this advice, I niffered after breakfast with another laddie for his hat with my bonnet and twopence, and took up my stance at a closs mouth wester the Tontine, which was then bigging; the gentlemen, provost, and magistrates making then their houff at where the cross used to be, as I was told.

Good luck was in the change; for an Englisher soon after hired me to take a letter as far west as Madeira Court, and I made such nimble speed with the errand that he gave me a whole sixpence, the first white money I ever had received; in short, before the day was done, I had made a rough ninepence—that is, a bawbee over; and Mrs Douce, when I offered the half to John, would not let him touch it, saying that all I made the first day ought to be my own; for it was the luck arle of a fortune. It could not, therefore, but be said that I had a prospect in the very beginning.

Letter VI

The second day of my erranding, I mind weel, was not splendid; saving a twalpenny job to the Broomielaw, for a scrimping shopkeeper, to a Greenock gabbart, with the bundle of a Highland tartan plaid, belonging to a nauby that was going to Tobermory, I had but a scrimpit measure of luck. To be sure, towards the heel of the evening, a bailie, with a red north-west countenance, being vogie from his punchbowl and the funny stories of his cronies, hired me to go to Ruglen with a letter, on some 'lection ploy; for there was a great sough at that time of a Parlimenting, as it was called, which I have since learnt meant a general election. This achievement caused me to be in the gloaming before I got to John Douce's ; and a weary wean I was, both with the length of the road and its sliddiness, caused by the forepart of the day being showery. Mrs Douce, seeing me so scomfished, took pains to hearten me, when I had rested myself, saying that there was no profit in running lang errands, and, therefore, I ought to eschew them.

" When ye're out o' the gait," said she, " far afield, like as to Ruglen, you may miss a shorter errand in the town, whereof the pay would be better, on a calculation; it would be hard, indeed, if the wage for twa hameart jobs were not as good as a runagate exploit to the country. Besides, there's a weariedness in a journey of one long continuance that's no to be coveted; one errand in the forenoon to sic like as Ruglen, does the best up for the remainder of the day."

Thus she made it plain to my ordinary capacity, that the errand trade was, no more than the weavers' or the souters' trade, one of instinct, and that it behoved me to exercise my judgment in it as well as any other; for it had its craft as well as cabinet work. In a sense, the Ruglen 'lection job was thus no without its profit; for, after that day, they would have needed gleg een to see me on a toll road in the way of business.

But, although the erranding canna be said to be an ill ready-money business, when rightly followed out, it has its fasheries, as well as merchandizing; and I soon made an observe anent the same, which seems to shew what a wonderful regularity there is in all the works of Providence; and that was, that, counting by the days, it had a degree of uncertainty, proving it ought not to be trusted; but taking the earnings by the week together, it was more of a dependance; and, by the monht, it was as good as a stated income, which you of the genteeler orders have no notion of. In short, before I was anything like half a year on the pavy of the Trongate, as I once heard a playactor man call the planestanes, the jingle of my peinor pig told, in sterling language, that erranding was an effectual calling, though, maybe, no just a coining of money; nor did I repent I had taken it up. As the winter, however, came on, with short days and long nights, I had my experience, that, like everything of a human nature, it had its blemish of onagreeables—particularly in the dark days of November, on which I discerned, that, although the morning and the forepart of the day could not be objected to, the hinder end and the evening was always obstrapulous and showery, when porters, and erranders who are kind of 'prentices to them, are fain to howff and harbour in close mouths and other places, that, at times, would not be the waur of a souping, cuddling themselves with their hands in their bosoms or in their pouches.

Nevertheless, for all the wind and the sleet that we

were exposed to, the first winter was won through, with an ettle; and when the fine, sunshiny spring mornings came round, there was mirth in my veins; and the skies, taking off their cloudy fause-faces, looked well pleased on the earth, new-washen with the growing showers.

In short, I cannot complain very sincerely of the time I spent in Glasgow; but, when I had got the upper hand of my fifteen year, I left it; and, ye may be sure, I would never have done so, had I no been wiled away by a glaik of hope that promised to make me better; no, maybe, of a bible betterness—I'll no say that—but in the circumstances; and the cause of the come to pass, I will presently rehearse.

In the meantime, speaking of my departal from Glasgow, it is but a duty incumbent to say that I staid the whole time I was there, with John Douce and his wife; for baith were kind, discreet folk. The mistress, however, was the honey bee; for, although John was an eident, gair creature, he had never the gumption of his rib; and he would have been content to moil on in mediocrity, had she not been blest with a discernment past common. Afterwards, when the thrive of the late war began to sprout, and I heard how they were topping, well I knew wha put the spunk to the peat, and snodded the heartstone. It was the mistress. Oh! she was a managing woman, and a sorrow for egging on her guidman, who would have been content to have gotten through life with an insignificance, but for her, who was really upsetting, and saw the right ways o't. In short

I had a peinor pig full of dollars, and, had there been a Saving Bank in yon times, I'll no say but what I might have found the way to it; for, besides a silver watch, to tell me what o'clock it was, I had mair than seven pounds to the fore for a sair foot, when the time ordained was out at Glasgow.

Letter VII

Never being of a strong make, I was not made for hard work; and having, by the time I was in my fourteen, seen that, one year with another, I could not expect to make gold in gowpens at the erranding in Glasgow, I began to cast about for a new line. A sturdy porter I could not be, by reason of my weak back, for that with a careful man is no an ill way; but an errander, which, though for a callant it has a feasibility of a competency, is, upon the whole, for a grown-up man, but a cold coal to blaw at; so, seeing that I must soon deval from the erranding, and couldna be a porter to carry heavy trunks and boxes, I made up my mind for a change; and thus I soon had an experience of what I have often since noticed in life—namely, that it's never long till the chance casts up of getting the thing the mind's set on.

As I entered my fifteen, there was a family with their chattels and chairs going by the Liverpool traders from

Greenock to Manchester, where trade was brightening; and they, jalousing that the Englishers could not be so good as our own sober folk, wanted a man of the lad speshy to go round with their things, offering good pay for the turn. Thus it came to pass that I got a preferment. I had indeed the repute for being an obligatory creature, with a willing heart and a pawkie blithe tongue.

The going to Manchester did not appear to be such a very desperate going out of the Christian world as John Douce thought when I first spoke of it to him. His guidwife had very rational notions on the subject, saying that " surely Manchester couldna be so kittle to a hobbledehoy of fifteen, as Glasgow had been to a foreign laddie of ten, with bare feet and an innocency." And thus it came to pass that I covenanted with Mr Nichol Spreul to go with him and his plenishing to Manchester, he paying me days' wages.

When the gear was on board the gabbart, and the master and the mistress away with the fly, me, and the servan lass, and the four weans went down to the Broomielaw and took shipping in the same gabbart, from which we were landed safe at the mid-quay of Greenock, nigh to the Liverpool packet ordained for the family; when, without any great ettering of fash, we got all our rickle of things put on board, a full day before the " Perseverance," as the trader was called, could be ready; by which I had time to look about me and to make observes on Greenock and the inhabitants thereof ; or rather feuars and sub-feuars, as I saw them spoken of in a proclamation on the corner of a house, which one Sir Michael Stewart, Bart., had put out, to admonish them anent something concerning a steeple then about to be biggit on a kirk that the bailies had put up for one Sir John Shaw.

Greenock, it cannot be honestly said, was in yon days, whatever may be said of it now, just a marrow for Glasgow, though it had a Bell entry that was not ill-faured; but, if the streets to the westward were not paved like those of the new Jerusalem, with precious stones, it must be allowed that there was no want of herring heads to be seen on them; and as for rain, there was a sufficiency for a calamity to every other person but to folk accustomed to make their living by the sea, which the Greenock folk surely are. I observed that it was not true that the childer, as was said of them in Glasgow, were all and every one web-footed. Na, the Glasgow bairns are more web-footed, their fathers in general being weavers.

It was not concerning the oddities of the place, however, that, in my day of idleness, I was chiefly taken up with; for I got a new light from what I saw there that was as precious ointment to me among the Englishers.

It seemed that a seaport was a real fine place to set up as a porter in, so many strangers coming by the shipping behoving to have help because of their strangeness. And this notion barmed and worked in my noddle all the voyage to Liverpool, and was of a great outcoming;

for the first thing I did, when we got afterwards to Liverpool, was to look with a scrutinizing eye about me, regarding this very thing, insomuch that, before Mr Spreul got his commodities off to Manchester, I had made up my mind to make a trial of Liverpool, as a place of bread; for I had seen that an inward town would not be so expedient to set up in, for the line I intended, as an emporium. In landward towns, like Manchester —which was like Glasgow, as I was told—every creditable concern had its feed porter; but the like of Greenock and Liverpool had more of a dishevelment.

This was a thought of wisdom, for out of it grew all the kything of my fortune that I want you to learn the particulars of, and for which I am inditing these epistles; for the moral I would make, is, that a man should well consider things before he makes his downseat. Not, however, to tire you with outs and ins, ye see that my capacity was growing as I grew aulder, and that I was not without an understanding before I even got so far into the world as Liverpool.

Letter VIII

When I had gotten Mr Spreul and his perafarnals, as I maun call his family and fasheries, weel housed at Manchester, I came back on shanks' naggy to Liverpool —for I had no thought then to cess myself with a boutger of a horse, like you, no having a grandfather that I could write to for a " replenishment; " and I set up in business there as I had weel before devised.

I had not, however, been long in a way till I was led to make an observe, that the Englishers, compared with right Scotch folk, are a desperate set for being het and fu'. It is weel for the poor amang them that they have the parish pockneuk to gang to.

What led me to make this notandum, was a fatty sort of man that was a porter on the quays and wharfs. He had a swelled muckle toe, by reason of the gout; with which there never was a man that bore a burthen fashed, it's my belief, in all the ancient realm of braid Scotland. Indeed, it's no a malady that messes or mells with hard-working folk, but is a gentle distemper, rife only among them whose wives paint their faces as if they could thereby scog their sinfulness; for it is well known they have much need to hide their shame, if all tales be true.

This man with the sore toe was an object to me which I narrowly and 'cutely scrutinized; for he seemed to have the gleggest and weel-doingest laddie weans for a family of the male gender I ever saw—wonderfully, as I thought, all of an eildens. He himself did nothing but sit on a stone from morning to night, and take orders for errands, on which he sent his gets, as I thought them; by which I could see he made a power of money, really siller like sclate-stanes. By and by, however, I began to come to the rights of it, and learnt in time that the

the callants were not of his own clecking, but taken on as servitors, 'cause of his being a lamiter; and that he paid them a wage, making a bein living of the owercome.

When I had reached the depth of this mystery, and had thought with myself of taking up the same way of business, there came an Irish gentleman from Limerick—a wee he was of the flaunty order; and was going to London town to set up a trade of selling pork in barrels, beef in tierces, and firikens of butter, to say nothing of neats' tongues. Seeing me of a composed stature and a creditable complexion, he offered to take me as his porter, and I agreed to go; for I had ever a forethought that London was ordained for me. To be sure, it would have been far from a sober Scotsman's hand to have hired an Irishman on the quays of Liverpool for ony sic job; but the Irish have their own ways—that are, perhaps, no ill for those that ken how to make them serve their turn. Thus it came to pass, that, before I had long sojourned in Liverpool, I was taken to London to see Mr O'Gommarel's kegs o' provisions; and there began my fortune to lay golden eggs, like the goose that I mind reading of at the school in a history book.

Mr O'Gommarel, being a gentleman, went in a coach, and I, being only a porter, coggled on the top of it; but we fell in with no accidence—only an Irish wife was there that would fain have made up to me, so that I jalouse she was of the clans of the city of Dublin.

However, in course of nature, to London we did at last get, and homolgomates ourselves in Ratcliff Highway, opening a warehouse for Irish provisions, with every prospect of doing great things. But long we were not there when Mr O'Gommarel took a calamity intil his head which proved a brain fever; and, from less to more, he became a useless man, and for a time I knew not what to do. At last, he was taken away, clean daft, home to his friens in the city of Limerick, and I was left like a knotless thread ganging hither and yon in London for a time.

What might have come of me in that strait of fortune, is not to be told; but it happened that, in consequence of Mr O'Gommarel's by-set, there was a gentleman that took charge of the store; and he, seeing me a wiselike lad, elected me to take charge of it and sell off, as soon as I could, the cargoes that Mr O'Gommarel told me himself would help to make his fortune.

This trust I performed with a sincerity, accounting for every doit to the gentleman that the provisions brought, learning myself the first cost of the commodities, and what could be made by them in the way of profit and loss in Ratcliff Highway.

Thus, without any divination on my part, I was led cannily into the provision line. But I have something to tell of my traffickings before I ripened into full bloom; for the summer was warm, corbies might have been seen shooting out their tongues, and the fairings for sale on my staun being salt, the traffic in them ebbed down to a naething in the warm months.

A RICH MAN

Letter IX

Hinging on in a sort of idleset all day in the store with Mr O'Gommarel's provisions, I had more time than was just profitable for to make a meditation anent the nearest way to take in going to Lucky Fortune's tabernacle. While I was in this posture, the labouring men of the neighbourhood sometimes daunered in for a crack now and then; by the which they got an inkling of the nature of my business, learning that I bout to have now and then a pound or two no wanted; as I had but to sell, and to buy nothing, for I did not, in the slack of the season, settle every week with Mr Boyle, the gentleman that had the doing, as was my wont when trade was lively. Thus it came to pass that a new light broke in upon me that was truly a godsend. The way of it was this :—

There was a weel-doing man, who used to get his wage by the half quarter, who had eight dochters, every one of whom had a brother, as he told me. He was, however, a thought pawkie; for the dochters, and their having each a brother, made but nine children; whereas I, of a naturality, fancied that there was sixteen of them —eight laddies and eight lassies; and had, by consequence, a sore compassion for his small family, and used to think often with dolorosity concerning them even in the kirk.

One day he came to me, and said as how his employer

was gone to Hull, and would not be back for a week; by which he was put to a pinch, as his wage was due and he knew not what to do—begging of me the loan of a pound note, saying he would pay it back, with a shilling for the accomodation, next week, when his employer came home.

Being wae for the poor man, with his heavy handful of eating moths constantly devouring, I gave him the pound note on tick; telling him he need not be particular about the usury, but only to be sure and pay me the pound. Weel, when the master came home, he paid the note like an honest man, and the shilling likewise, as a gentleman should; whereat I was not ill pleased. This was the mustard seed that grew in time to be the great tree; for, when I was at my meditations in the cellar, thinking of this and that, the thought of the pound and the usury came uppermost; and I considered with myself that, if I could so lend, I would soon make my plack a bawbee; so, by littles and littles, I creepit into the banking line, as usury is called by the genteeler orders. My dealings, however, were at first with those in an ordinar' station of life—working tradesmen, and such like. Thus it came to pass that, before Mr O'Gommarel's provisions were all sold, I had made, as ye may say, a penny more than my wage, having weel on to thirty pounds over and aboon hainings.

In the time I was thrang with idleset at the salt provisions, in warm weather, I made another prime reflection, which was of vast use to my prosperity; and I beg,

Geordie, you'll take tent of the same—and that was, I lookit weel about me at the conduct of those said to be doing weel in the world; by which I discerned that there was a something no man could weel thrive without.

They were all sober, prudent, and honest folk. Hempies, I saw, might cut a galore for a season, but they sooner or later proved peoies and pluffs in the pan; whereas your real, sterling, cut-and-come-again characters were discreet men, who kent full well how many blue beans it takes to make fivc, and made a conformity thereunto.

I saw, likewise, that they were all harnisht in the conjugal yoke; though some of them, maybe, didna count marriage a matter of money; but those that did best were methodical lads, married upon elderly widows with a nest egg, whereon they clockit to some purpose: so it was from them that I resolved to take a pattern. I'll no deny, however, that there were decent weel-doers among them that werena just so particular, taking up with lassies for a fancy; but all, both the widow-mongers and the tender-hearted, were most extraordinar' fond of their own firesides; which led me to conclude that, if a man ettles to do right in the world, he maun learn to think that hame's aye hamely; as I shall shew forth by the example of James Hobart, who was a nonplus among the acquaintance of my threshold days, for so I accounted the green strivings of my youth.

Letter X

James Hobart was a lad from the country; and, by reason of no other trade being in his village, was naturally a wheelwright. In his 'prenticeship, he foregatherit with one Harriet Lees, a weel-faured lassie that did turns about his master's house, by which it came to pass that he took a notion of her long before he was out of his time; and so it happened that, in the summer gloamings, him and her used to walk Damon-and-Phillising about the dyke-sides. In this jeopardy, it so fell out that an auld aunty that bonny Harriet had on Tower Hill, fell ill of an income in her legs, by which she was obligated to have somebody with her; and, no approving of the loup-the-dyke cattle of London, she, this frail woman, sent for Harriet—and Harriet came to her.

James Hobart was, about this season, on the finishing of his 'prenticeship, and knowing that he would soon have the upper hand of his 'denture, he made a preparation to follow; little thinking but London was a town for wheelwrights as good as Clearbrook. But he was mistaken, for there are no wheelwrights in London; and, for that matter, though I have been so long in it, I never saw a wheel or a reel for lint or tow therein. So, when James came and had seen his jo, ne'er a turn of work could he get to do; and he wandered about like a demented creature, ae bawbee going out of his pocket after another, as if they were trying how soon he could be brought to beggary.

One day, while he was very waeful, with nothing but the barren street before him, he happened to pass a blockmaker's shop-door; at the sight of which he had an inspiration. It seemed to him that there was a fitness between blockmaking and wheelwrighting that might by a little pains be brought into fellowship; so he went in, and confabbled with the man before he came out; and the upshot was, that James was taken in, and from that day and hour the world never gaed back with him. So, in process of patience, the fractious aunty departed, as she hoped herself, into Abraham's bosom, and James espoused his darling dagon, Harriet.

They had, as need not be told, only a cauld coal to blaw at; but they had a fine bleezing ingle of mutual affection: so they set to and warsled with the world, which they at last got the better of, and had sons and daughters. They were not, however, just marigolds, shining far and aye kenspeckle, but douce folk; and I had great satisfaction in sometimes, on a Sabbath night, drinking a dish of tea with them, for we sat in the same pew at the meeting.

Thus was I led to make an observe, that all who do well go regularly to the kirk; and James and his winsome marrow never missed a day. So they came into prosperity; and when he died, last year, soon after his wife, he was far ben in the world, having been all his days a credit both to his kith and kin, and his three buirdly sons masters of vessels.

Taking by times James Hobart for a patron, I soon

saw that, if I expected to prosper, there was no help for it, but to marry a wife; and I began to cast about for a good one; but for a season I came little speed at the fishing. Howsever, I had learnt, by Mr O'Gommarel's provisioning, that, with a thought of canniness, I could turn a better penny on my own pock-neuk in the banking line than by being subject to the hither and thither of any master; so, when the store was toomed, I grew more intent to get an equal than a superior; which was the cause of my becoming a guidman; by which, as you shall hear by and by, you are the son of my dochter, and in the land of the living, seeking a replenishment, and keeping devouring horses at the College, where it would be more to your advantage, maybe, if you read the Scriptures.

However, Geordie, as ye cannot but be interested to hear how it came to pass that I got lawfully a dochter, the whom in time came to have a kittling, whilk was you, I will let this letter go by the post mail, and in another rehearse more particularities.

Letter XI

Being in a way of trial, and seeing that the way to thrive was to be happily married, and to go to the kirk regular, making my home at my own fireside, I had a meditation thereanent; and I saw that, although there might be a cosiness in the lot of siclike as James Hobart, there was likewise a peradventure; so, not being overly likely to be taking to a maiden's ee, I resolved on making a prudent choice. It's wonderful how Providence helps a man, when he has wrought himself into a resolution, especially if the drift o't be weel-doing.

I had not been long matured in the thought that I ought to marry, when there was an upcast from Providence, shewing a good-will towards mine intent. Going now and then on the Sunday to take a dish of tea with James Hobart and his helpmeat—for she was truly that—it fell out one night that a decent woman of the widow gender, not too well stricken in years for me, also was there at her tea. Her guidman had been a sailmaker in Liverpool, and she was sib herself to Mrs Hobart, which was the cause of her apparition there; for he being dead and gone, she had come to resident in Ratcliff Highway, and was very lonely, being new in widowhood; for which cause she was invited to make a passover of her weariness, by coming to take her tea.

As soon as I saw Mrs Canvas, though I was more than seventeen years younger, I had an instinct, and said to myself, Please God, this shall be my commodity. And really we passed a very conversible afternoon. Towards the gloamin, however, the skies began to gloom; but as it turned out, that was the way Providence blithened on what it had ordained to come to pass; for, about the time for Mrs Canvas to go home, there was an evendown pour, and it rained and better rained, as if the windows of heaven were opened, and the angels had been washing their dwelling; so that it behoved me to go home with her, to scog her from detriment with an imbreley, which was covenanted. But, as we crouched along, the waters were none assuaged, and there came on such a pour of wet, that if, in mercy, an entry had not been opened to us, into which we sheltered, it's no saying to what shifts we would have been driven. However, into the closs-mouth we went, and long we stood together there; but not a dawn of hope kythed. Wet, wet it was, and Mrs Canvas thought of home, giving me to understand that, if I had been her guidman, she would not have objected to go with me to rest ourselves intil a public.

Hearing this, I said, in a consolatory manner, that truly a woman who had been married, was, by reason of widowhood, in a lanerly condition; and, from less to more, we thickened into an understanding; insomuch that, when it faired, I saw her safe home, and called the next morn's morning to speer if she was none the worse of the blattering. In short, having heard from James Hobart, that Mrs Canvas had a something, I made her my polar star; and, no to waste words, we were by and by married. But, for all that, she was not your grandmother; for she had not been my guidwife scarcely a twelvemonth and a day, when she took a kittling in her craig, and departed this life at her appointed time with a sore heart—a kink as it were—leaving me all her residue, which was a good penny, more than double and aboon for what I married her; but she said I had made the best of husbands, and needed a consolation for the loss of her: so saying, she died, leaving me with the meal, though the basin was taken away.

Letter XII

Seeing myself, by the blessing of God, and the removal of my wife, in a state of mair business than I ever thought to be in, I again began to think how I could best cast my bread upon the waters; so, having learned something of how to do in the provisioning, I set myself —for, as it were, a pastime in my doleful widowhood— once more among the casks and kegs of a store of beef and pork; and for more than twelve months, if I didna make gold in gowpens, I turned the penny; which, with my banking, made it no an ill trafficking I had taken up.

It was then I had a preeing of the world; for, as my means grew, and my profits kittled both by the store and the lending of money for a consideration, I had an insight of men's bosoms. Many's the Nebuchadnezzar of the Royal Exchange that has had his ain straits, that, in my day, I have helped. They used to gang by me on Cornhill with a dry civility in their looks, and a pawkie fearfulness in their secret eyes, that told me, though they hid it from the world, how much they were beholden to my wife's residue. The seeing of this made me gleg; and at last I could tell, by the way of a squint, whether a man was going up or stoitering down the hill. It's really wonderful to think of the key ye get to men's bosoms when ye lend them money. Mind this, and think weel of the consequence, my man, Geordie, when your pouch is yawp for a "replenishment."

However, it wasna in learning just the ways of the world that I was industrious, for I was a thought maybe commendable in all things, especially as, before the second year of my doleful widowhood, I began to see that my purse could bide to be shaken in the teeth of an ordinar gale of wind, and that even my superiors once, were, if not inferior, maybe no better than equals.

In this tining and winning there came a to-pass of which it's right I should set down a make mention; for, in the beginning, it did not kythe to my advantage: but it is ordained that good shall come out of evil.

Being, you see, thriving in the provision line, I thought I would enlarge; for, by this time, I had made an observe that, whomsoever in London dealt in eatables and drinkables, and is well-doing in the ways of private conduct, is sure to fen; so I gave an order to my correspondents in Limerick, Cork, and Belfast, to send me an augmentation of their articles in the fall of the year. The reason of my having correspondents for the same things in different places, was this, that they might not be led to think of making their conjectures about the stroke of business I did. Thus it fell out, that, about Martinmas time, which is the season for slaying bullocks and stots, my neighbours, seeing I was getting cargoes, and having a high opinion of my canniness, resolved to get cargoes too, by which the market was glutted, as the saying is, like a churchwarden eating the bastard child of a married man that can afford to pay for it; and thus it came to pass, that some of these speculators, no having their pockets so well lined as mine, were put to sad shifts for the needful, as their bills payable came due. I jaloused that this would be the case, but waited on, keeping a calm sough. No, howsever, to simmer and winter about it, I got many a sappy bargain from them, both of salt beef and pork, in the spring of the year, to say nothing of what I had laid in myself—the cause of all. Indeed, I began to have compunctions of spirit that I was beguiled to my undoing, by reason of so many bargains; but the Lord aye prospers the well-doing with prosperity, and just in the nick of time there came out a rumour of war anent the Falkland Islands, by which the price of Irish provisions was increased, and I got off all I had briskly, without a detriment, maybe with a bawbee of profit. Well it was that I had shewn such a sagacity; for, in a short time, the news of the war diminished away, and those who bought my goods were pushed what to do with them, although they were accounted sicker souls.

By this affair I got a repute that was as good as much profit. It was seen by the handling I made of the job, that I could see as far into a nether millstone as most people; and thus it came to pass, that I grew to be in much esteem with my neighbours, some of whom thought they were of the seed of Isaiah the prophet, and prognosticated that there were signs about me of one ordained to gather the residue of the fruits of the earth as they kythe in the bit rags of bank notes.

Letter XIII

By the time my Falkland Island job, as I call that rehearsal just mentioned, was turned into sterling, there was an elderly decent man, of few kindred, with an only dochter, that I fell into some acquaintance with. She, as you shall be told, came to be your grandmother.

This Mr Marling was a discreet man; and having few down-draughts, his bit gathering was not the worst thing in London town. It therefore attracted us into a cordiality; and I saw that his sonsy only dochter had many points of haivins that showed gumption. In short, in a reasonable time, we were married; and she, being of a genteel turn, I did not make an objeck to her taking a genteel house, because, with her prospect, and what I had in the foot of the stocking, we could afford it. So, thus, I came to be transported into a sphere of life that was not thought of in the days of erranding at Glasgow.

But, saving the exploit of the marriage, and the getting of a child, which was your mother, and which we were not very long about, I cannot say that there was much variorum in my way of life for several years. I saw that, with canny handling, there was outcoming in the provision line: so I keepit on for an ostentation. But the best spoke in my wheel, and it made little cheeping, was the discounting, after all; the beginning of which, as I have rehearsed, had only the chance of a shilling.

By my clecking with what I had, and old Mr Marling's frugality at gathering, before your mother, my only dochter, came to be six, there were not wanting fools who said that I was a warm man; and, surely, it would be an onthankful acknowledgment to deny I had not prospered in all things by my judicious circumspection. At this juncture, however, it was ordained in the councils of eternity, that a golden tree should surely shoot for my behoof; and, accordingly, it so fell out. Mr Marling my guidfather that was, one day coupit o'er off his seat in a 'poplexy, and left to your mother, that was his oe, twenty thousand pounds, and a residue to me and my wife that was worth the lifting off the midden with a pair of tongs. The fact is, that nobody had a notion he would cut up to the tune he did; for it was on the right side of fifty thousand.

There had been a graduality of respect towards me for some time—I was sensible of that—but really the outcoming of reverence that followed on the death of Mr Marling, was just extraordinary; telling me that, let your men of poeticals say what they will, there's no endowment of nature equal to the dripping roast of a fat legacy. But, Geordie, mind now what I say.

Riches I never thought of but as the means to get the mastery of the good things of life; and, therefore, I saw when Mr Marling's hoggart fell among us, it was no longer required of me to be so methodical in my 'conomy as I had been; so I gave consent to my wife to take a fine house; and, as she then began to complain of the rheumatism in her legs, it would not have been Christian to have stood out overly dourly against having a carriage of our own, 'specially when the doctor gave it as his advice that it would do her no harm.

But, although, from our flitting intil that house, it couldna be said that the warld gaed back with me, there was an increase of fasheries that I did not expect. But, in those days, mony a braw man kent what it is to be powdered; and so it was with me. I could complain of no ail; but they little ken what the calamities of life are, that have never felt a youky head because of mity powder.

Letter XIV

Your grandmother was a by-ordinar woman for natural sagacity—in that way, she might have been the marrow of Mrs Douce of Glasgow; so, as soon as we were well settled in our new house, she said to me, one night, as we were in our bed, talking composedly of this and that—the weather being very warm, by reason whereof we could not sleep—that she thought there was a prudence in making use of the means God gave, as well as in gathering them; and that, since we could afford to act as well as our neighbours, we would be looked down on if we did not.

I said that that was my very opinion; and, therefore, while I looked after the traffic, I would trust to her eidency to see to the house. Thus a sort of a silent 'pact and covenant grew up between us; and she went, and came, and said, and did, in all manner of matters of householding, as seemed good in her own eyes; by which, she being a woman of commonsense—which I understood, from some of my friends, is a very rare thing in wives—we had a lowne time o't.

Thus it happened that an exploit came uppermost, that well deserves a place in the chronicles; for there was an instance in it of great prudence, the which my wife often thought was just extraordinar, considering my natural parts, as they had been brought out by an yedication no particular. It concerned our only dochter, Clemy, your lady mother, at that time little better than a playoc bairn.

You see, when, after my guidfather had won away, with a direck circumbendibus, into Abraham's bosom, I made a count and reckoning with the wife, of all that we then had in the hoggart; and the upshot was, that we thought we might take, as I have set forth, a new house; and, as a carriage is surely a great saving to shune and clothes in wet weather, to say nothing of the solacium of it at all times, we resolved that we might do a waur turn in our time than set up one for an economy—which, at the flitting, we did: it gied, however, to my heart to use it, save when the lift was high, the sky blue, and the sun clear.

When we had gotten the chaise, I had a meditation with myself; and I saw that my wife, owing to the straitened way she had been brought up, and likewise that, as my own schooling was not college lair, our get might ettle at a better refinement; so I said that, as the Lord had blessed our basket and our store with a moderation, we ought to take the sanctified use of things. The guidwife cordially agreed with me that it would be a becoming testimony of thankfulness so to do; and I accordingly hinted to her, that, being sensible of our own deficiencies, we should put Clemy into a boarding school, to learn manners and to play on the spinnet. To this there was a most pleasant assent; but the guidwife would not allow that she herself had been educated in a straitened circumstance—though she could not but see that I had not been brought up at the feet of Gamaliel. Anent this, however, there was no controversy; for I had often observed that leddies schooled to narrow breeding, are aye the most logive, and make up for being scrimply thought of by the rest of the world, by thinking muckle of themselves; so, for peace in the house, and glad to get Clemy in a way to take on a pedigree education, I minded the auld guess, that what the rich put in their pouches, the beggars throw awa; and I made the affront a pocket napkin.

Boarding schools for bits of lassies that have a prospect are no that ill to find; therefore, we soon got a very prime one; but I would not hear of it; for there was in it a lord's daughter, and I was a thought blate to let a bairn of mine rampauge with a cutty of nobility. So we gave it the go-by—and well it was that we did; for we got an inkling of a capital leddy in the country, an offisher's widow by lot, and a dean's dochter by nature, forbye being a woman of a share of mother's wit, and a most accomplished character.

To her house, after some negociation, I took your mother, in our own vekle, and were well pleased with Mrs Mortimer, who was surely a most particular leddy, and had all in her domicile on chandler pins. My wife gave her many directions concerning how she thought Clemy should be brought up. In this, however, I thought she was rather inordinate, and said, maybe a wee shortly—

" Mrs Mortimer, ye see we're hamely folk, and it has pleased Providence to give us something for our dochter; so make her, as well as ye can, fit to use it discreetly, and we'll never say ye were slack."

The leddy was confounded; and she looked at me with an inquisitive eye, and replied—

" Sir," said she, " I do not wonder that a man who thinks so well has prospered in the world."

When my wife heard a lady of such breeding say so, I could see a change, and, maybe, more respect for my opinion, on her part, than was very kenspeckle before; for, like other married women, she certainly had not, till this time, always a gospel reverence for her breadwinner's condescendence and discernment.

Letter XV

In the meantime, there was no backwardness in the world with me; for I, being accounted to have elbow-room, had a nerve for an advantage. On one settling day on the Stock Exchange, I made a rough penny on all the best part of my gathering, as well as on Clementina's legacy, for which maybe a puirer man would be more thankful. It was thus—

For some time before, there had been a sough from the parish of France, anent convention doings there, by which men of a discerning spirit saw a hobbleshow barming—and so I thought too; and in consequence gave out that I had a something to lend on mortgage, not thinking the funds the best of investments.

This notification caused many a right honourable and others of landed pedigree, to make application; and, in short, I saw a way of laying out every plack and bawbee I had scraped together, over and aboon my dochter's gratis gift, by way of wadset for a time, to good advantage. Seeing this, without thinking of the French convention, I made up my mind to sell out. No other thought had I but to raise the needful for my own ends. But it was soon known, to the consternation of bulls and bears, that I was turning all my stock, even my dochter's, into money; then everybody thought I had got an inkling of something no canny, and the hobbleshow that was the consequence was dreadful, after it was known that I had really sold all. Some said the King of France, that afterwards got his head chappit off, had been obligated to drink aquafortis. In short, the Stock Exchange was in a commotion, like as it sometimes is; down fell the stocks, down, down, and up flew many a broker's eye, till ye could discern only the white thereof, all owing to me and the wadset intention.

As the fall took place after I had sold out, I had a great plant at my banker's. I began to think—especially as, at the close of the market, it began to spunk out that the latest news from France were rather of a "healthy tint"—that the panic might be from my operations. I said, however, nothing, keeping my own counsel even from the guidwife, for there are things that wives at times should not be conjunct in.

Next morning, I was down at the opening. All looked well; but there was now and then a little waver, shewing, it maybe, a shade of difference upwards.

Then was my time—I bought a few thousands. No sooner had I done so, than the tidings flew that I had made a spec. In came buyers on buyers, droves on droves, as well informed as a flock of sheep louping a dyke; up jumped the stocks, like merryandrews on the slackwire, and before twelve o'clock the reaction was full one and five-eighths above what I had sold at; so I bought in for money, and sold for the account, whereby I got creeshy paws to lick without any outlay of mine. But it was not so thought; and I was, of course, reckoned to be one of the slyest fox-paws in the city; it being the whole sprose of the day, how cleverly I had managed; of which there can be no doubt, as those that said so were considered guid judges. In short, I became into such repute, that divers brokers came from Lombard Street, bowing and cringing, asking me to join their old established firms.

LETTER XVI

From the time I had entered into the banking line, when my chance was only a shilling, I thought it necessar to look weel into the characters and capacities of men; and I soon discerned that it was a custom of bankers to hold their heads higher than merchants, and to snuff the east wind with round and wide nostrils. But I likewise saw, although they were as the golden images in papistical kirks, muckle-made-o' things, yet that the merchants, after all, were like the priests, using them for their own advantage, and, in short, were the bees that made the honey.

I cannot say, however, that their gesticulation, in the way they shot out their snouts, gave me an inordinate conceit of their judgments as human creatures; indeed it's the nature of banking operations to spawn small ideas; for the tradesmen themselves have only to think if their customers be of an ability to endure a certain time.

This consideration of durability breeds a constipation

of the understanding; and no doubt it is because they are so afflicted with it that nobody who can help it likes to see the front of them at a board where any measure of understanding is required.

As for the merchants, poor dependant things—for even when they get their bills done, the inward gladness of their hearts is aye mollified with a humiliation—they are much to be pitied. I never see one of them guffawing, and eagerly kilfudyorking with a banker, saying the craw's white, as he says it, without being duberous of his credit. Catch me, Geordie, melting the bills of such nichering cattle, though I may be wae for their extremities. But, to make an end, however, I never greened to be otherwise than on a guid-e'en and guid-day footing with my banker, for fear of my credit; as I jaloused others in the world might see with the tails of their een as well as me. Nevertheless, my exploit on the Stock Exchange made some noise; and it's wonderful to think how wise I grew: as everybody said, I was just in a sense a wee Solomon.

And thus it came to pass that I ne'er was a partner in an ostentatious banking house: at which many marvelled; but I minded what I had heard aunty say when I was only saft in the horn:—" There's no telling," quo' she, " when twa heads are on the bolster, by whilk the guid or the ill luck comes." In like manner, thought I, there's no telling who is the cause of making the siller in a partnership. Therefore, all my days I eschewed to go marrows with anybody, 'cepts the guidwife; and with her, ye ken, I could not help it, being ordained from the foundations of the world to the conjugal yoke.

But, although I had no broo of your company concerns, there was an outcoming in my prosperity that weel deserves to be noticed, especially for the heartening it gave the guidwife, who, like all helpmeats of thriving characters, liked to have a share of the gains. And it fell out in this way. Just on the back to my Stock Exchange exploit, the alderman of our ward took the gout in his belly, the day after the 9th of November, and was, on the 10th, in Abraham's bosom; by which there came to be a vacancy in the court of aldermen.

As soon as it was known that he was departed, several gentlemen came to my door and finding me not at home, they said they would pay their respects to Mrs Plack, who had a good repute for sagacity in the neighbourhood; and being let in to her by the flunkie, they told her, with a dolorous voice, what a calamity had befallen the ward, inquiring if she thought I would allow myself to be sheriff, as it was minded to make one of the sheriffs his successor. She thereupon answered and said, that, as it was an honour, to be sure I ought to accept, and that her endeavours to persuage me would not be to seek. So, when I came home, I heard of the deputation, ye may be sure: but it's necessar to tell you all about it, for Mrs Plack's heart was set on it, and therefore she thought it was a case needful of a particular cooking.

A RICH MAN

Letter XVII

Coming home to my dinner that day, as I was telling, after the deputation had been seeing how the land lay, I could discern that there was a gale in the cat's tail. Mrs Plack was going up and down, speaking loud and often to the servants, and had seemingly a great turn in hand, though I could not see't. She never, however, opened her lips to me, but had dinner served in less than no time and a jiffy; and I could see, for I have a discernment when onything's gaun on by common, was most instantaneous to have the lad out of the room, and ourselves, in the secrecy of cabinet ministers, as was seen when the table was drawn.

" Mr Plack," said she—which was the more remarkable as her use and wont was to call me only Plack—" Mr Plack, I have been thinking that life is but in our life, and that we are all life-like and yet doomed to die. There's Mr Alderman Gravy—he is released from the troubles of this world, and his place must be filled up. What is your opinion of the accident? "

I, being as innocent as a lamb of the cabal, but having heard when I was out of the Alderman's calamity, replied that it was indeed a hasty warning to be moderate.

" Moderate! " cried she—" I was saying nothing of that; but only observing it was a thing to be considered."

" No doubt, my dear," quo' I, " it cannot but cause a reflection."

"Snuffies!" said she, tartly. "It would not ill become a man of your substance to think of some one fit to be his successor. London, depend on't, cannot do without an Alderman; and Sheriff Stew, it is said, will be his successor; so that there will be a vacancy in the sheriffdom."

Still in perplexity, I said, not knowing what I said, "Do you, my dauty, say so?"

"I never heard," she answered, somewhat gaily, seeing I was dumfoundered, "that Job was a provision-merchant, or I would have an excuse for his wife's railing, having such a husband; but not to say too much about it, what do you think of letting it be known you intend to offer yourself in the room of Sheriff Stew?"

"Me!" cried I, in a consternation—"I would as soon think of evening myself to a kenna-what."

"And, why not?" was her sober quest; "surely ye might be that. You know, you know, my dear Plack, that we are not now as we were."

Then, after some more ambulation, she told me what had been the purpose of the deputation in the forenoon, advising me to consent to the proposal. But I told her that, although I maybe had a bit sleight at turning the penny, it was far from my hand and capacity to be a sheriff, whose duty it is to see rogues stretched, "which," quo' I, "it is weel known, is a most kittle part to play weel."

"Nay," she said, "but you are not the first that did not know his genius before it was tried. As for the trouble, a tureen of turtle soup might be either a sheriff or an alderman. No, no, Plack; leave the matter to me—first sheriff, then alderman—and afterwards I know who will be Lady Mayoress;" in saying which, she gave me such a bewitching look, that I could not but keckle. So it came soon to a bearing, that I was to come forward; and, in the course of the evening, Deputy Spice, the grocer, was sent for to know particulars.

Deputy Spice was not at home, and Mrs Plack was frightened when she heard it; but he had gone to hugger mugger with some other person. But, while she was in the middle of her dolorosity anent this suspecting, he came to the door, and with him another of the common council, that had not been of the morning party, which shewed I was growing popular.

Hearing what was come to pass, Mrs Plack went away, leaving us to our ain confabble; and then we had all the outs and ins laid open. But just in the crisis of our discourse, there arose a shriek and a blast your eyes in the lobby, which took us all to the room door, when we beheld Mrs Plack lying on the floor, as it were in a cold swoon, and Jacob, the footman, limping as if his leg was out of joint.

It seems that she had, somehow, not being used to it, put out the lamp in trying to snuff it, and Jacob, soon after, coming up in the dark, stumbled against her at the room door, by which arose all the hobbleshow. She, however, utterly denied, even to me, that she was in a listening posture at the keyhole.

Not, however, to spin out particulars till they grow tedious, when peace was restored, I consented to let the gentlemen think I was not sweert against being a sheriff, which made them both most content; and, thus, next morning, it was bruited about that I was to be the new one; so, in process of time, on the appointed day, I was chosen; to the great contentation of Mrs Plack, who was maybe more vogie of the honour than me. No that I was just heart-broken with the thought of being a sheriff of London, whilk is a higher post in the goverment than the Lord Provost of a city that shall be nameless.

Letter XVIII

But, although I say it that should not, having been myself one, the trade of magistrating is not one of great profit. There is no telling the outlay Mrs Plack was at, to pave the way, as she said, with splendid expectations of what would be our mayorality: 'deed, a dignity is not the ways and means to make a fortune. There was, however, an outcoming in being a sheriff, which I did not forsee so clearly as my wife. In short, it behoved us to be more circumspect in who we entertained in our house; no that we were by nature overly given to gavalling, for I did not like that way of life, and Mrs Plack made a conformity. Public stations, however, must be kept up; and there is a moral obligation on every titled citizen of London and elsewhere, to have a spit and raxes, to say nothing of a gawsy kail-pot and a winsome fish kettle—all which Mrs Plack provided of a prime quality. 'Deed, many more preed our trenchers than the flies.

At first we were lavish enough; and, thinking so, I spoke quietly anent the same to the wife, which set her on making a selection, shewing in it her wonted discretion; for she made no change till the year of my sheriffdom was out. Then, however, she was so scomfished by galravitching, that we went to a watering-place; from which, when we returned, we lived a douce life, seeing only a few particular friends now and then; so that, by the time I was leeted to be an alderman—for a vacancy soon happened in the court into which I was chosen—we had the ball at our foot, and played it in a most genteel manner; which causes me here to make a notandum. Surely those ancestors were long-headed folk, by whom our glorious Constitution and Protestant ascendancy was framed, to obligate a man to be a sheriff before he comes to be an alderman, and an alderman before he is Lord Mayor. For sheriffs, being nearer to the commonality than aldermen, are more furthy among all classes—elbowing in slily with the gentry. Then, after having served, they can be most judiciously so fatigued, as to long for retirement, in which they need only visit and receive their betters. By the time they rise to be aldermen, it would be very extraordinary if they had not made a choice circle of friends, to garnish their mayorality. After their mayorality, they naturally come, you know, to be among the great, and may do as they please, if they can afford it.

This I say here, that you may understand me as I go along; for, if the arcana were not explained, it would not be easy for you to think, how, after my sheriffry, I came to pass so lowne a time, or how, when made an alderman, I was accounted one of the select—I might say the elect—only I do not like to construe that word to a profanation. The sheriffry is, indeed, a kind of purefaction, a leave-taking, or payway, given to the citizens in general; but an alderman enjoys a higher station of life, and a Lord Mayor is a real dignity. Aldermen who have passed the chair are no less, in my opinion, than a wee sort of nobility for the remainder of all their days.

Letter XIX

Anent my savoury mayorality, which came to pass four years after I had been made an alderman, it becomes not me to speak, especially as it may be read of in the newspapers of that victorious year. And, by all accounts, it will be no edification to you, Geordie, to read of it; for maybe it would instigate you to buy a third gelding, and ask for another replenishment; so I will go on to talk of doucer matters.

Being, you see, the father but of a dochter, your mother, it did not consort with my notions to lay out money for a vanity, as I count certain kind of epitaphs to be;

and, therefore, when it was said to me, after I had been Lord Mayor, that I might be a Bawronet, I eschewed it, because it was not an inheritance which I could bequeath to Clemy, that was ordained to be the heiress to my bit gathering; accordingly, I was most obstinatious on the point. I'll no deny that, maybe, had there been a male get in the case, I would have seen things in another light, and both bought a pretty estate in the country, and a bawronetcy forbye, to transmit my name to the latest posterity. That, however, not being ordained in the councils of wisdom, it behoved me to look at baith sides of the bawbee before I wared it, and I made up my mind not to faik a farthing for such a balloon matter as a teetle—not, I am sure, that, after having served mayor, it would have cost me much more than the fees; but the fees were a penny, and I have aye thought that a penny hained is a penny gained. In fact, I'll no say that a bawronetcy, got for doing weel in the magisterial line, is just a disgrace to any man; and it's surely far better than laying out thousands for sic like, as certain country gentlemen have done, whom I know, with high heads; but they, poor feathers, shall be nameless. Howsomever, a bawronet I would not be, for I thought it a concos mentos job to pay for a nickname; as I told Mrs Plack a bawronetcy surely, though of a genteel kind, was. She said precious little, and I never let on that I saw her glunching and glooming with the tail of my ee; but being rather of a kindly nature—as you know I am, Geordie, or ye would never ask me for a replenishment

—I grew wae to observe the effect, for she waxed wan and dowie, and became greatly given to yawning, which the auld proverb notified to me was a bad sign—

> Them that gaunt, something want—
> Sleep, meat, or making o'.

And, being fashed thereat, I said to her in bed, on a Sunday morning, when she had reason to be well pleased, that I was of opinion that she would not be the worse of a jaunt somewhere in the warm month. "Indeed," quo' she, "I have had a notion of that myself." So out of this rose that great come-to-pass which led us to forgether with your lordly faither, then in a straitened circumstance; but of the particulars I shall speak in my next. So no more at present.—Yours, &c.

Letter XX

But, before I tell of our jaunt, it is needful to relate a few particulars that came to pass ere we set out.

When our dochter had been five years under the wing of that most discreet woman, Mrs Mortimer, and had learnt more than I can tell, it behoved us to bring her home.

By this time she wasna an ill-faurt lassie—as comely as a red cheekit apple, my wife would say; but she was a thought given to outing when onything pleased her. Indeed, with Mrs Mortimer's connivance, to say the least o't, Clemy had grown a credit baith to the school and her parents likewise.

A RICH MAN

She came home at the Midsummer holidays; and it was proposed, as she could not be " brought out " till the winter, that, in the meantime, we should take the jaunt to let her see the world, and particularly that part of it which is in Great Britain called Scotland. Against this I was not sweert; for Scotland, ye ken, was my calf-country, and I had an inclination to go to Glasgow and see if it was as pleasant as ever; for I minded the blinks of daffing I had when in it a poor barefooted laddie, and I aye thought that surely it was a land of much blessedness—that scant and want could in it be almost heartsome. So it was agreed, towards the latter end of July, that we should set out, and travel easy, hoping the weather would be fine, with an elderly woman on the dickey with the footman. The woman was well recommended to us as a sedate motherly character, with an experience that my wife would find most useful in inns and places where a lightheaded maiden would need looking after.

I was the more consenting to hire Mrs Snod, because she was a Scotch woman born, and could 'terpret for us in the language of that country, my long residenting in London having naturally made me no to understand it aff hand, or to speak it without an accent. To tell the truth, this consideration anent the tongue had its weight for some time with me, and I could not make up my mind, by reason of it, to go all the way to Scotland, till that god-send, Mrs Snod, made me set a stout heart to a stey brae.

But, although I had my own prudente about going to

the northerly land of Canaan, I'll no take it upon me to deny that I had now a wish to go thither; for I had a very strong wish. Indeed, everybody kens that it is as natural for a Scotchman, who has done well in the world, to shew his testimonies among his kith and kin when he grows old, as it is for him to eat parritch for his breakfast, and to go about barefooted when young, especially those that have been of my degree. So having, by reason of Mrs Snod, gotten the whip-hand of difficulty, we set out, as I have said; and here it becomes me, my man Geordie, to make an improvement for your behoof.

Having, as you have seen, raised myself by my own merit and geny into maybe a bein way of life, there could be no solid obstacle to my shewing I could come in my own carriage among my auld friends; and so I let my wife understand; saying that I would put on no sauce, but go among them with a blithe guid-day here, and a couthy good-e'en there; therefore it behoved her to make agreeable faces, to shew we both could carry a full cup. Clemy, our dochter, I did not think it was inevitable to instruct; for she was a real fine thing, mim as a rose-bud and sweet as a plum, and had mair politess and pleasantry in her wee finger than baith her parents had in their whole bouks. This your mother, however, would not allow, and therefore I have no need to flatter her to cause you to love her; but she was, if I may say it, in my eyes a golden creature, in so much, that a minister of the gospel, whom I fell in with in Scotland, where they much abound, said of her to me that her gentleness and modesty certified to him that her parents lived according to the evangelists—nor did I gainsay him; but I may tell you, for ye have a kind of an e'e in your neck, ye sorrow, that now and then I thought her mother was a wee condumacious, which is the original sin of all wives, especially when they are in the right—that, however, thanks and be praise! they very seldom are, or there would be no living with them.

Letter XXI

But now to begin about the jaunt. When a'thing was put in an order, me and the guidwife, your grannie, with Clemy, your lady mother, after an early breakfast, steppit into our own carriage, whereto, behind, divers trunks were strappit; and we trintlet awa down the north road, taking the airt of the south wind that blaws in Scotland. At first it was very pleasant; and as I had never been much in the country in a chaise, I was diverted to see how, in a sense, the trees came to meet us, and passed, as if they had been men of business having a turn to do.

After various observes anent this comical movement, a sleepy thought came over me; and the guidwife, who was fain to be a leddyship, not being in a talkative inclination, I lay back in the chaise, and had a most conneck and comfortable visitation to the land of nod for some time; in so much that, when we came to an inns where it behoved us to take a chaise, I was as fresh as a newly shelled pea, and felt an admonishment I had an appety; so we made there a consolatory dinner, the mistress being well pleased with the cold lamb and the lettuses, which she judiciously said was as cool as a cucumber.

After our solatium at "The Frightened Mouse," which was the name of the arms, finding a long evening before us, we took a dish of tea, and bidding the coachman get his horses ready, renewed our jaunting; and, at a reasonable hour, about nine o'clock in the gloaming, alighted in another public, where they sold strong ale that was just a cordial; which, to tell no lees, put such smeddum intil me that I was heartened to go a stage farther. Lucky it was that I did so and I was so courageous; for it was a far better house, and in it there was everything to be had that the heart of man could have a notion of.

We passed a pleasant night; but I was a thought troubled with the nocturnals, by reason of the strong ale of the predecessing public.

The day thereafter was more of a moderation in all things; we journeyed on with a sobriety that was heartsome without banter; for really the parks on both sides of the road were salutary to see. The hay was mown, and the corn was verging to the yellow. The haws on the hedges, though as green as capers, were a to-look; the cherries in the gardens were over and gone; but the apples in the orchards were as damsels entering their teens.

When I was nota-beneing in this way, your grandmother consternated a great deal to Clemy, saying she never thought I had such a beautiful taste for the poeticals, and that I was surely in a fit of the bucolicks. But I, hearing her, told her I had aye a notion of the country; only that I had soon seen fallen leaves were not coined money, which, if a man would gather, it behoved him to make his dwelling-place in the howffs and thoroughfares of the children of men.

This led us on to a very conjugal crack, which, with the lowne influence of the air, led us into what may be called paths of pleasantness; in so much that the guidwife said it was a sore pity my geny had not been cultivated, for that I had surely a nerve.

This commendation of my parts from her drew me into a confabble concerning divers matters which I had noticed in my life; and I told her I had seen that all great men of my kything were just wanton when they could stretch their tethers and gambol in the country, the reason whereof I could not tell; but it was a proof that the stoury minds of town folk, and of those who sit maundering in offices, have only their vocations, as it were, in cages, and ken not the beatin in the breasts of the birds that make blithesome the boughs.

It is indeed a jocose remembrance to think, in my auld age, of that jaunt and the pleasant day thereof—the primest, I may say, till then, of my life; for, till then, though I had been in a sense a thriving man, there was yet, maybe, now and then a seasoning of fashery in my lot. Thus it came to pass, in the course of the second day after we set out on our journey, which we intended to be for only a fortnight, that we came to a resolution to make a desultory job of it, and to go hither and yon, if the weather was good, as might seem comely to ourselves; and so, when we stopped for the night, I wrote to my head clerk and told him no to trouble me with anything pertaining to the lucre of gain till he heard of my return to the earth; likening London to that region, and the scope of our journey as a tea-drinking visit to Adam and Eve, naked in a state of innocence, in the garden of Eden.

It was in this way, coming afield, and having nothing to do, that we made sport and pleasantry to ourselves; the upshot of which, as I have already let wit, was the matteromonial connection of your father, that was born a lord, with my only dochter, whereof I shall speak by and by. In the meantime, let me rehearse the uncos we fell in with.

Letter XXII

At this distance of time, I cannot undertake to say that all our carouse along the king's highway was alike pleasant. We had no doubt our own ups and downs, to say nothing of showery days, and cod fish of the sea that were very high in inland towns; but of a certainty we did not stint ourselves in feasting on the fat of the land, going to the right and to the left, with sundry sojourns in good inns; the which, in my solid opinion, make it an obligation for a man well to do to take sometimes the door on his back, the staff in his hand, and speer the way to the well at the world's end. In truth, that jaunt gave me both pleasantry and insight; for I soon discovered how it happens that men who wax bien, and are yet neither rich enough nor sufficiently upsetting to be made magistrates, are so given in the summer time to jaunting. They dinna very well know, nor their wives likewise, how to keep companies at home; but having the natural longing for flesh pots that all those in a state of prosperity have, they surely have a right to gratify themselves by going to and fro like roaring lions, seeking where they may devour. But not to digress about them, it's just necessar that I should give a bit inkling on the matter, to let you see that I make observes; for it was by so doing that I found out the reason of genteel jaunts in po'-chaises, when shadows are short and days are long, by decent folk that live soberly at home. Having done so, I will touch on them no more, but resume our charioteering.

Having resolved, as I have said, that, for a while, because we could afford it, we should take our foot in our hand, we told the coachman that we would trust ourselves to him and Providence, so that he was free to go where he pleased, and take us to any place that he thought would entertain us, and we see uncos; so being thus 'mancipated, he drove us to a town which we knew could not but be to the right, for the sun, which had hitherto been on our backs, came to our left, and was, by course of nature, in our e'en before setting—a certain demonstration.

However, there was a Providence in our going thither; for at the house where we put up, Mrs Plack had a confabble with the landlady in secret, who told her that we were not far, not more than a stage, from Addleborough; which caused us to make a deviation, for good and substantial reasons best known to ourselves, respecting which I will let you into the secret in my next. Be ye, therefore, content with this curt letter till then. Patience is a fine thing for a young man to learn, being, in a certain sense, better than all the lear of Oxford, whereof no deacon of men is a worshipper unless he thinks of making his bread by the wind of his mouth.

Letter XXIII

When my wife heard we were so near Addleborough, she remembered a cousin, who was married and settled in that town, with a merchant for her guidman, and said it would be friendly to give her a call; so we went there, never thinking of staying aboon ae night. But the ways of nature are most mystical; we staid the best half of a whole week, so weel pleased were we with our cousin and her acquaintances, for they were all the topping of the town. It would be too tedious to mention them by name; but one of them was a great litterally character, who sent into the newspapers every month something about the tides and changes of the moon, with other lunaticals most kittle to understand, and had, moreover, on the outside of his bedroom window, a weather glass, screwed up in a 'stronomy manner, perplexing to ordinary folk, wherewith he held a secret wark; for all that, however, he was a genteel man, and no without commonsense, knowing something of Christianity in a degree.

But, Geordie, it may not be plain to you, though I dinna despair of your understanding, what good it could do to me to be with philosophers. Howsomever, I'll tell you.

You know that, in my beginning, I did not cleave to riches, but as a means; mind that—as a means. I saw that the rich commanded the earth; and I thought if I could get near unto riches, I could not be far off from every other thing; and so to get near to them was all my ettle. But, as I began to get up, sidy for sidy with them, I got an inkling that there was the use of riches needful to be learnt, as well as the way to get them, and that in striving for them, I had thought too earnestly only of them. I missed use altogether; in so much, when my hogger was of a condition to bide being shaken in the teeth of the wind, I was no quite sure how best to lay out my talent to the usury, which is real profit. I am now speaking seriously; so give ear attentively.

The first of this suspicion I had during our sojourn at Addleborough. Hitherto in London—with my bit jobs on the Stock Exchange, melting of bills in a canny way, and with one thing and another—my hands were held full and thrang, so that I had no leisure to make *nota benes* about mankind; but at Addleborough, though we bided there but four days, my eyes were opened, and I saw it was not enough to make money—that was not difficult with God's blessing, though men that can only make money, think muckle of the talon, and have a notion that those upon the thrive have great merit; but to know what to do with money is the craft of life. Many, no doubt, make a sight of money by hook and by crook, and think they thereby do well; but I do not think so of them, being in all things of the notion, that honesty is the best politicks; having noticed, at the mention of some rich men's names, that decent folk wag their heads with a scrupulosity.

Among hands with our gavalling at Addleborough, I had leisure enough to have justified me in thinking long; and had I no been one that had ever a turn to do, surely the time in the forenoons would have gone dreichly; but while my wife was confabbing, anent this and that, with her cousin, I went about the doors, spying the nakedness of the land; by which I soon saw that a borough's town was not the New Jerusalem for me, though maybe it's no unlike that city which, is said, in the Psalms of David, to be compactly built together; in short, all in a borough's town strive for themselves, whereas in the metropolis, some work for the public. No that in a sense that's neglected in provincials either; but there the vista of advantage shews the recompense nigher at hand for what is done, than in the capital, by which maybe a disinterestedness is seemingly caused—I say seemingly, for I am no sure, after all, that men are egged by better feelings in London than elsewhere; though sure and certain it is, that there are men in the metropolis that are actuated by other look-tos than folks, decent though they be, in a country town.

Letter XXIV

Having surfeited ourselves with Addleborough, me and Mrs Plack had one morning in bed a great controversy about what we should do next. I was for going right on to Glasgow; but she would not hear of such a thing, being intent to see Edinburgh, and especially the writers and poets there, whom she said were, to a moral certainty, the primest, according to their own opinion, in the whole 'versal world; putting out books in shoals and nations, and making such to do, with a Review, whether of soldiers or cavalry I know not, that was fearsome to hear; so, in the end, to keep peace in the house, I was obligated to make a capitulation, the upshot of which was, that, leaving Addleborough, away we came to Edinburgh; which, after divers pleasing inspections of curiosities, we reached by the end of the week, and tabernacled in the Royal Hotel, where all thing is very orderly.

It is not to be contested that Edinburgh has a certain similitude to London; for, if the one has the tower, the other has a castle; and provice, it is well known, is just the Scottish word for mayor, as it is the proper English to call a bailie an alderman. Upon the whole, Edinburgh, although this was the first time I had seen it, is not quite as big as London; but well does every Scotchman ken that it is a most fine place; if there should be a doubt that in greatness, it's no just a match for the metropolis.

But, Geordie, a word in your lug, and let it go no farther: yon is a very cold place, especially when the wind is easterly; and all the merchants thereof, together with the rest that make money, are in the main, shopkeepers. As for the writers, I was just confounded; we have nothing like them in London. Poets there are no better than stacks of duds; but in Edinburgh, man, if ye forgathered with some of them, they would gar you believe that spade-shafts would bear plumbs.

One piece of wastry I noticed in Edinburgh—if it be wastry to be negligent, but it no doubt comes of their gentility—and that is in their state of the streets, in that blaw-thorough, their new town. The streets there are dreadful, having on them the very finest grass sward that can be, whereupon a whole flock of sheep might fatten, to say nothing of black cattle. Really yon is a shame, especially when, in the country, commons, as I heard, are everywhere on the diminution. I think the 'conomists of Edinburgh would shew gumption, if they had but geese on yon commons. I was told, however, that those quadrupeds were not liked there, because the Edinburghers are not cannibals, fond of eating their own speshy. However, it does not do to be overly particular about the causes of anything, when, like me, a man sees but as it were a blink. So, to make an end, I got my wife, your grandmother, in three days, to leave yon cauldrife similarity to a city, and to come to Glasgow, which is a town—as everybody knows, who has ever been within the four corners of it, and at the Broomielaw—where they load coals in gabbarts, with other manufactures, too tedious to mention. It behoves me, however, to be a little more on the sprose with Glasgow; it being the place where I first set up in business, as I have already rehearsed to you.

Letter XXV

Glasgow was mair to my liking than Edinburgh, for the people there are all in a stir, which gladdens me to see. Only, they are greatly given to coomy work, and have an overplush of foul lums and steam engines. Still they are braw, hearty, and ettling; and have, as the sailors say, "the weather-gauge" of the poor thread-papers of a town that's easterly.

Everybody in Glasgow is busy making money in the best way he can; nor is he looked down upon that thrives, though he may not be topping. This is kent by them all; and there is nae rifting in a neighbour's face, when they have gotten a fu' kite. But they are no without a sense of difference, though they dinna account a dealer in cauk and herrings by retail a merchant as they do in Edinburgh. For a' that, however, it cannot be said, in justice, that they are void of upsetting; and now and then, it must be allowed that one perishes the pack among them without bigging of kirks, though they do manufacture kirks there, and it's a thriving branch of business. On the whole, they are an eident people, and maybe there is some hidden way of thrift in their outing; but our stay was not what we intended, and we were, in a manner, constrained suddenly to turn our faces to the southward; the reason whereof is this :—

Ye'll mind John Douce and his wife, whereof, about my outset, I made mention. Well, by this time, with God's blessing, and his wife's council, John had thriven into a bailieship; and, as they were the first folk after our arrival that I went to see, they were just out of the body, and nothing would serve them, as I had been a Lord Mayor, and was rich, as some said, than that we should all bide with them; which, to say the truth, was like forcing us to put on pumps of a narrow capacity. However, as they would take no denial, especially the mistress, we were obligated to go to their house. Long did we rue that rash action.

John Douce, as I have said, being high on the tree, could not be complaisant enough; accordingly, as lang as we continued to stay in the royal city, he resolved, because I had been a Lord Mayor, to have all the big wigs of the town, with the Principal and Professors of the College, to see what would come out after his long corks were drawn. And thus it came to pass, that, day after day, we had a banqueting at his house.

At first, nothing could go off grander; and it was a visibility to me, who knew something of the auld, that the bailie's wife had, every night, no been blate with her curtain lectures, which partly accounted for the heck-and-manger treatment that we received. Every day, for example, we had a brave cut of a fresh salmon, boiled with the scales no taken off, which Mrs Douce, at the head of the table, shoveled about, as if to shew how well-used she was to the dividing. But, no to be particular, I should here make mention that this daily cut-and-come-again of the salmon was a ministering means of our sudden evasion from the het and fu' roof of Bailie Douce's; and, as we could not, in a sense, go from it to an inn, we made a *parley-vous* departure from Glasgow.

Now, you'll be licking your lips, Geordie, to hear how a very nice cut of salmon at Glasgow could be a cause of a London alderman to eschew that corpulent city; and, for an edification, I will tell you.

It was not because we had it every day, but because we once had it not as it ought to have been. The particulars whereof are surely most comical, as I shall presently rehearse—not, however, so much for an instruction as for an entertainment, and as a touch-and-go hint that ye may turn to profit when ye have a house of your ain; for, mind, though ye may be a Lord's son, the French anarchy and confusion at Parish has taught us that to siclike Miss Fortune has long arms and heavy hands, longer than kings'—and theirs, we all know, are not short; nor are ye ayont her reach—the cankry old maiden.

A RICH MAN

LETTER XXVI

Had the whereof anent the cut of salmon come to pass in these Radical times, it would have been no unco; but to happen when the bailies of Glasgow were drinking their cool punch, every one under his own vine and fig-tree, was surely judgment-like—and the rough of it is this: Mrs Douce had ordained, that every day we stayed with them, as Leven salmon were then very nice, we should have a cut at dinner, fresh and fresh; and every day there was somebody at the table just out of the body with the fish, especially when they held out their trencher for a second sample, saying how fine it was. Thus it came to pass, by the Saturday, that the bailie was very vogie to think of the renown he would acquire for his most excellent fat Leven salmon.

But, when Saturday came, there was a catastrophe.

The weather, it being the eye of summer, was very warm, which everybody knows is not salutary for keeping of salmon, especially when they have to be brought in an open cart from Dumbarton in the sun; in consequence, when the bailie's serving lass, with her bare feet and her red arms, went with a basket to buy a salmon, all that were in the market were high, and if she had not taken one of them she would have gotten none; so it happened that she brought home a salmon that the bailie said, when he smelt it at dinner, was surely in a bad way. A professor of the College, however, sitting by, told him that the fish was not to blame, had it been rightly cooked; but " the Devil sends cooks," &c.

John Douce (I mean the bailie) heard all but said nothing; only, as the salmon smelt like Billingsgate in the dog days, as Mr Deputy Creesh, the tallow-chandler used to say of high fish, it was sent away from the table. However, at night, when the company broke up, the bailie went flying with passion into the kitchen, and an angry man was he at the lass for no boiling the salmon in a Christian-like manner; the which word nettled madam, and she gave him a salt answer, really so provoking that he could do no better than nip her arm with very little loving kindness, insomuch that, on the Sabbath morning, next day, she could not be found.

Once away and aye away. She was gallanting with a clerk, who put her up to summons her master, the bailie, on the Monday, afore the Court, where she shewed the stends of the nip, black and blue; and he was glad to compound for no small sum; which so soured his temper, that me and my wife consulted in conclave about taking the door on our backs;—indeed, we were tired of travelling and wished to be at home again. To have gone instanter would not, however, have been well-bred for folks in our station of life; so we covenanted to say we were going to Cheltenham to drink the physic water with Clemy, and really could bide no longer; and, to make no breach of the truth, we resolved to go straight thither, as fast as many wheels could take us, for we both hated to the uttermost detestation not to keep our words.

Having bade adieu to Glasgow, we set out betimes in the morning, and taking the canny town of Paisley in our way, we breakfasted there, and syne gaed up and down the streets, for it was a fine day. Afterwards an accident befell us most comical to hear; for, among the other manufactories, Mrs Plack, your grandmother, heard the Paisley bodies were famous for making dressing, and she resolved that her and Clemy should have a gown of it. But, och hone, poor Lucky! When we came to send for a swatch, saying we just wanted to see it, they sent us a cog of sowans—dressing being but the reform name of sowans; for I knew them again, as such, outright, when I saw them.

From Paisley we went to Kilmarnock, which is a town, but what it is remarkable for I do not know; only I remember in the days of my youth they made orthoxies there, and shoes of all denominations.

We then went to Ayr, where we had a chack of dinner, and were minded to have gone farther that night; but, being out of Glasgow, we thought better o't, and staid there, not leaving it till the morn's morning, for it is a genty place, and well worth an investigation; only the eggs in it are not cordials, as we found at breakfast, for I tried three of them, and they were the progeny of a hen that surely had a complaint, and were a main cause of our hurrying on to Cheltenham; for they were dreadful.

Letter XXVII

Cheltenham is a most fine place; and there it was that we forgethered with my Lord, your father—a decent, well-behaved lad, but sorely pinched.

It happened that we put up at the " Plough Inn," where he was biding; and, the morning after our arrival there, when I had gotten my breakfast, I went down to the coffeeroom, before me and the wife would go out with Clemy, to see the bill of fare, in which I saw there was to be a roasted lion, with sweet sauce, for dinner.

" Bless my saul! " quo' I to the waiter, " can that be a true lion? "—whereupon your father, who was sitting in a box hard by, rose and told me, with a pleasant smile, in a very couthy manner for a lord to do, that it was only a hare which had been shot by a ne'er-do-weel poacher; and from that time we sidled into acquaintance, till, from less to more, I invited him to take a cut of the lion with us, which was the cause of your being born upon earth, and may be the reason how you came to write to me for a replenishment.

After this introduction, I soon could see, by the e'e in my neck, that the young lord was casting a sheep's eye at our Clemy, who came, in time, to be her ladyship, your lawful mother. At first, for a convenient season, I had no broo of this; for I have aye had a notion that lords were a kind of canary-headed cattle, having, for the most part, a want; but, in the end, I was in a sense constrained, by your granny's exhortations, to make myself no unreasonable; so, at length, I consented to covenant that I should shell out my bodles for an inducement; so, without summering and wintering more, the upshot was, that your father espoused my dochter, with five and twenty thousands of pounds, and wadset, as it may be called, of twice as mickle more, at my becoming functy offishy, which is the law for departing life in a Christian way.

Your father being, by course of his father's extravagance—which was awful—a needful lord, was thus set up among the nobility in a genteel way, especially by his to-look at me; and I having earned, by my ettling, all that it was ever in my wish to do, thought it was but right to enjoy the outcomings of the merits of my talons.

By and by, when ye came to be a most provoking plague, I had you for a pastime; which I jealouse is the cause ye tell me that horses have yawp appeties, and that grumes are eating moths at the college of Oxford.

Howsomever, ca' canny, my lad, Geordie; for ye see that, if I had not been a man of discretion, I, who was not come of a pedigree, never could have been in a way to write to for a replenishment. In short, take tent, and eschew racing cattle, and ponder well the o'ercome of my experience, making your home by the chumla lug, and going to the kirk on the Lord's Day.

But, Geordie, no to be overly on you, I will now make an end; and maybe ye'll find in the corner enclosed a bit slip of paper, with the which, and what I have said, trusting you will never rax your arm farther than your sleeve will let you, I subscribe myself your loving gotchard,

ARCHIBALD PLACK.

Tait's Edinburgh Magazine
June–August 1836

II.

TRIBULATIONS OF THE REV. COWAL KILMUN

JOHN GALT, *from an engraving by* R. GRAVES
after a portrait by J. IRVINE.

TRIBULATIONS OF THE REV. COWAL KILMUN

CHAPTER I

IN the tenth year of my ministry, a very pitiful thing came to pass, the upshot whereof only ended last year, though many, since it happened, have rolled away into the fathomless past.

I was sitting by myself one evening in my study, pondering on the uncertainties of worldly things, when my sister, who was the mistress of the manse, being abroad, one of the serving lasses came in to me and said that a young lady and gentleman were in the parlour wanting a word with me. I rose forthwith, and went to them. They were, Mr Ettles and Miss Sylvia Graham. Of her I had no knowledge, though I had heard of whom she had come, and she was not just an unknown stranger.

He was the fifth son of a creditable bonnet laird, not overly well off, by reason of a small family of nine children, and he had been for some time a clerk with his mother's brother, a merchant in Glasgow. The young lady was the dochter of an officer's widow who dwelt in the next parish, and held in much repute by all to whom her excellent qualities were made manifest.

After some short conversation concerning the weather, and the prospects which the kingdom had of a good harvest, Mr Ettles broke the ice of the intent of their visit, by telling me that his uncle had an establishment, somewhere in America, to which he was appointed to go, a junior partner, and that, as he and Miss Graham had long been trysted, they had resolved to be privately married before he went abroad.

I said that there was no reason to be so hidling about it, which led him to mention that it was not just then expedient to take a wife with him, but that, as soon as he was settled, he intended to write for her.

Something in his manner, when he told me this, made me look at him—I cannot say how—with an eye of compassion. He was a gallant looking youth, maybe short of one and twenty, with a generous countenance.

Without, however, making him any answer, I turned to Miss Graham, who, if ever I saw a perfect beauty, was surely one. She was younger than him, maybe the best part of two years; but she had the air of a crowned queen with a diadem, and was, in short, a lassie that the Creator had taken pains on in the making of.

I cannot say how it fell out, but the sight of that young and pretty pair made me sorrowful, and I told them they had time enough before them, and that to go through the marriage ceremony then was needless. But Mr Ettles told me many things that bespoke my pity for a sincere and tender heart, and, in short, so persuaded me that I pronounced the blessing on their union, after which I wanted them to stay till my sister would come back, and take tea with us; but they evaded, for he had to go as fast as he could to reach a vessel that night at Greenock. In short, there was nothing in what had been gone through but the making of them one in the eye of God; for, when he left the manse, taking the road to the ferry, Miss Graham went up the glen; and, saving what I had done, they parted seemingly maiden persons.

Why I was dismayed, and boded no good of this mystical marriage, has never been in my power to explain; but the thoughts of it settled down on my heart, and I was sad, and given to meditation concerning it, for many days.

Chapter II

About three months afterwards, one fine day, when the hills were purple and the heavens blue, Miss Graham came over to the manse and gave me, with much satisfaction in her manner, a hint that her jo had reached America, and hoped not to be long of sending for her. The news was very gladdening; and, as she was blithe and spirity, I would not let her away before the gloaming, nor till after she had drunk her tea with us; but the skies became overcast, and the clouds black and lowering, and she was hurried with the apprehension of rain, which came on, as it were, with desperation, long before she had reached her mother's dwelling: the result was a wetting to the skin, insomuch that, before getting home, she was ineffectual with cold, and took that night a sore income.

This very great calamity being, in some sort, owing to my blind kindness—for we are erring mortals who know not what we do—I was much troubled about her, and could not think enough of her mysterious marriage, to which I had so innocently, by my tender-heartedness, been led to be art and part.

By and by she seemed to grow better; but still the weight that was on my spirit was not removed; only I had a kind of rejoicing of the mind when I heard she could sit up again. Nevertheless, though I was darkened about her, I should mention that my conscience was very quiet; for surely there was no sin in marrying a handsome young couple that bore God's mark of being made for one another.

During her convalescence, as we thought it was, a letter came about every month from her lawful husband, containing heartening news and blithe encouragements; and before the half-year from his departure was out, he mentioned that he hoped, in the course of the next summer, to be in a way to send for her. Everything was as well as could be expected, only she lingered in her languishment. Still she was in good spirits; for his letters were written in a cordial vein, the free effusions of a heart full of hope, and happy with bright prospects.

I went over to see her every week, and had a satisfaction in conversing with her, for she was of a most mellifluous nature; sometimes, however, I was not quite pleased, for the cold she had taken was very wilful, and in my fears I thought now and then an alteration could be seen upon her. But I did my best to stifle my apprehensions. Alas! they were ordained to prevail; for as the spring came on, there was the visibility of a change that was not manna to my anxieties.

She grew, if it were possible, more and more lovely; but there was a cast in her beauty that was not of this world—a heavenly benignity somehow not delightful to see—that used to make me think sometimes that she was only the vision of a creature " wearing awa to the land of the leal."

Her skin became of a purer innocence, and the hue of her beautiful cheeks as the dawn of a nearing glory, not yet disclosed to the living children of men. I was often filled with a solemn admiration, when I saw her sitting at the window, in her mother's easy chair, brightening in the setting sun, which seemed to have enjoyment in shining in upon her; but there was a cold sadness, tempering that pleasure, which whiles prompted me to silent prayer that the Lord would be merciful to the flower he had adorned with more beauty than was possessed by the rose of Sharon or the lilies of the field.

At last, one day I went to see her, she complained of not being so well, and was obliged to keep her bed. She said, herself, with her natural sweetness, that she was not very ill, but only wearying for rest.

While she was speaking, a letter came from Mr Ettles very dolorous for her illness, but rich with glad tidings, stating that, instead of her coming to America alone, he had obtained leave to bring her himself, and would be across the sea in the course of the summer.

Such a letter was delicious to her heart. She got up,

and was pleasant with gay thoughts; but, in the midst of her joy, I heard, as it were, her conscious spirit give a hollow sigh, and its echo in my bosom was like an unavailing sorrow, in so much that I was soon after constrained to come away, to hide the despondency that had entered into my inward parts.

Chapter III

But though, for three or four days, her health was refreshed by that letter, and the vivifying hope that it inspired, the languor again returned, in so much that she was confined all day to bed. Her worthy mother became alarmed, and my very night's sleep was molested because of her condition; for it was soon seen that she was in the skeleton embraces of a devouring consumption. She did not, indeed, think so herself, but spoke of Mr Ettles as of a coming joyfulness.

To know the truth and to hear her gaiety was very pitiful; for it was soon seen that the measure of her part and portion in this life was nearly full. But not to dwell on a melancholy without hope, suffice it to say that she suddenly departed into Abraham's bosom one forenoon, leaving the arid wilderness of this world to those who knew her piety and worth, and to the millions of afflicted creatures wherewith it abounds.

In the afternoon I had a thought of going over to sympathize with Mrs Graham, her mother, and dressed my self for that purpose; but before I was just ready, who should come to the manse door, inquiring for me, but Mr Ettles himself from America!

When I heard his voice, for I knew it well, my very living heart lap out of its place, and I was constrained to sit down, and let my tears flow.

Fortunately there was no one in the parlour into which he was shewn, my sister being with Mrs Graham—for her duty as a Christian woman obligated her to be there—and the serving lass that let him in, being of the Celtic tribes, was, of course, not overly sagacious; so, not knowing who he was, she said nothing of what had come to pass, telling him only that I was putting on my clothes, by which I got time to compose myself.

When I had wrestled with and overcome agitation, I went down the stair to Mr Ettles with a fause face, as to hide the worm that was gnawing at my heart.

Of course I was well content to see him at first when we met, but said little, and he thinking all was as he expectit, appeared in a manner just carry't; but he stung my heart with an agony, when he said, that for some time he had been haunted with an awful fear, lest any harm had befallen his wedded wife.

I could make no reply; and he continued, saying—"Ever since I was here that terror has disturbed me; for, when we were standing up receiving your blessing together, I beheld, as it were, the sudden glare of death look out from her bridal beauty, and I have never been able to away with the omen."

The very faculty of speech passed from me, which he observing, said—" There is no accounting for these coincidences."

At that moment a vehement rush came over my spirit, and I outright burst into sore weeping. The truth indeed of what the Lord had been pleased to do, could be no longer hidden; so, that, after some time spent in solemn preparation, I told him that, on that day, at eleven o'clock in the forenoon, Miss Graham, as she was called in this world, was with her Maker in paradise.

Chapter IV

He staid at the manse with me that night; and I did what I could to awaken him to a right sense of the disappointments of this life. Next day, instead of going on to Mrs Graham's, he went back to the ferry, and I heard no more of him till some weeks after, when he was on the point of sailing from Liverpool to America, with, as he said in a letter he wrote to me, " a withered heart and little wish for the continuance of prosperity."

For twelve months and more, in the douce solitude of the manse, he was as dead to me. I heard nothing of him; Mrs Graham had not the heart to inquire; but my melancholy concerning him, however, was beginning to be bleached by time; and, at last, when the Occasion was in the neighbouring parish of Demiquiagh, Mr Sprose, the minister, having been newly placed, there was a great gathering of folk from ayont the ferry to hear him; by one of whom, from Greenock, a godly captain, I was told that Mr Ettle's uncle was much spoken of, and that it was supposed, he having already stopped payment, that the whole tot of the concern would be sequestered.

The news was not to me glad tidings; for I remembered poor Mr Ettles, and how sore displeasure had fallen on the spring of his life with the shadow of death, in the removal of his virgin wife; and I was as grieved as if I had been a creditor for more than a hundred pounds—ay, much more. But, saving that sorrow, I had little cause to think of him for a long time.

One day, however, as I was taking a stray by myself, meditating on my sermon, and the nothingness of all things in a world of sin and misery, I sat down on a stone on the loch shore, and ruminated of the sun and the seasons, the mysteries of Providence, and the presumption of the narrow discernment of man; marking the gentle flowing in of the tide, as if there was a spirit of love and fondness in nature, willing to embrace all things.

While sitting there, I saw, afar off, a genteel man coming from the ferry, which was no uncommon thing; but there was something in his mien that made me look at him particularly, and, in the end, as he drew near, I discerned it was Mr Ettles. He was coming to see me before, as he said, he would again go abroad; and he then told me that, after his uncle's failure, which caused him to come from America, he had been in a hanging-on state till he had gotten his discharge.

"I am now again clear," said he, "and I have formed another connexion with a respectable house." But he added, with a sigh that dinnled on my heart—"To me the wine of life is drawn, and I have now but only the lees left."

We had then some serious conversation anent the same, sitting together on the rocks on the calm sea-shore, with the ancient mountains looking austerely upon us from the other side of the loch, as if taking tent that we deviated into no light discourse.

He then told me that men of the world, who had never been tested with adversity, could not understand the feelings which he felt. "You," quoth he to me, "may, by the help of fancy, have some notion of my bridal blight, and see in it a rational cause of grief; all, too, that might have heard of it would, in some measure, be indulgent to my regret; but the coming on the back of that misfortune, the shipwreck of all the scheme of my endeavours, is what no man can understand, who has not himself had the experience; for there is a searching feeling bred by such events, that goes into the recesses of the bosom, and is as irksome there, as if it were the remorse that waits on a guilty action. They are only able to endure the calamity properly, who reap it as the fruit of endeavours to overreach—a consciousness of having deserved blame mitigates to them the sense of ruin. Yes, let an honest man try what he may, he never can overcome the taint that he has incurred, by being thought to have been either unlucky or imprudent."

Much of what Mr Ettles said, related to things in a sphere of life whereof I had no knowledge, and I could only exhort him to put his trust in God, and pray for a continuance of his early integrity.

After a considerable sederunt, that was not overly jocund, I rose, thinking he would go with me to the manse; but he said that his time was limited, and having seen me, he would say farewell, and go forward to Mrs Graham's, where he would sleep that night. So we parted; but I was very sorrowful, for the tenor of his discourse made me feel that he was a vessel selected to hold the sour and bitter of life.

What passed with Mrs Graham I never heard: but he staid there all night, and early in the morning was at the ferry, with a sad countenance, as the ferryman's son told me; for he had seen his aching heart manifest in a melancholious look of contemplation, as he rowed him over. "He was," said he, "like one going to a parent's burial."

CHAPTER V

For some years after, I heard nothing of Mr Ettles. He was, in a manner, to me, swallowed up in the ocean of mankind, like a drop of the bucket in the great salt sea. But, though where he was, and what he was doing, were hidden from my knowledge, I sometimes thought of him; especially when I heard from the war of neighbour lads among the wounded, and of brave spirits cut down in the bloom and pride of their manhood. In those moments, I saw an afflicting similitude in the lot of the courageous in battle to that of those that are untimely cut down with misfortune.

At times I was grieved at the grief of this thought, for I thought it often unchristian; but a better knowledge was at last vouchsafed unto me, and I was made to discern that valour was a gift implanted for a purpose, though the gifted knoweth not its use; and that even the bloody field of guilty battle was a mean devised by Providence to exalt the human heart.

At first, I was not content for thinking this charity, fearful it might come of my fallen and corrupt nature; and, really, I was angry at myself when I one day saw coming from the ferry an armless soldier, who had gone to the cursed wars in America, then beginning, a proud, glorying creature, perfect and sound as he came from the hands of the Maker; for I could not but see he had only earned, with all his bravery, but a stock for the poor trade of begging.

I called to mind the desperate courses of his youth, and tried to persuade myself that war ought to be forbidden by kings and the mighty men of the earth; but, in spite of all, my heart warmed to the visible bankrupt, as I thought him; and I mused of whirlwinds, unmerited humiliations, and the pestilence that walketh in darkness, till I could only say to myself—" There is a wisdom in the dispensation of war, though we see it not, as there is in all the evils wherewith we are in life afflicted."

The o'ercome of all these sort of meditations was Mr Ettles. I saw him as an instrument the use whereof could not be found; and, hearing nothing of him, I often marvelled if the purpose of making such a man had yet been revealed; for he was one that could not, somehow, be seen without awe, like an idol of old when it was not in its shrine. The more I thought of him, I thought thus; for, although surely his abortive bridal was a romance of the heart, and his failure a melancholious affair, there was something about the lad himself that made one, like me, unskilled in crafts of the world, think he should have been a grand man. But we are fallen from our sphere, and are struggling amidst uncertainties.

It happened one night, when I had been reflecting much in this aimless manner, seeing mercy where in other times I could only perceive at best but mystery, I went out of the house and stood by myself on the green in front of the manse, looking at the skies and the stars, and thinking of the wonders of time and eternity.

It was a blessed night; and the calm air as holy as if the breath of the spirit of peace had been shed abroad in its serenity. The heavens I thought higher and vaster than common; and the numberless stars as the lamps of the new Jerusalem, and lights in the dwellings of the angels. A religious solemnity was spread over the whole earth, and my thoughts were lifted up.

While standing in this sacred trance, wondering why the all-wise Creator had thought of making such a thing as the world, with that weak entity of presumption, man, to domineer in it, I heard the brushing of a foot in the grass; and, soon after, the weight of a man's hand was laid on my shoulder. Whereupon I turned round, and there was Mr Ettles; behind him, on the gravel before the door, the dark likeness of a stranger loomed in the glimmering—for it could not then be said to be night, but only a thin shadow of the twilight.

Blithe was I to see him, and to shake hands again with one who had so nestled in my remembrance. We then went to the other man, whom he introduced to me as a friend he was much interested in.

"Mr Roslin," said he, "came over with me in the same ship. He is a native of the east country, and, being an orphan when he went abroad, is not very sure which way to go till I am at liberty to go with him. As he has no other particular friend, I have brought him to you—though myself, in intercourse with you, but almost a stranger; confident that you will make him welcome for a short time till I look about me."

This introduction was more remarkable for the terms in which it was made, than in itself; though, in that respect, I thought it by common. I said, however, that I was well pleased to see and to entertain anybody Mr Ettles brought; and then remembering what he said about looking about him, I made a conjecture to myself that he was again drifting on the wide world. But I said nothing; only invited them both into the manse, where for a time we had a curious discourse about the foreign land they had come from; and I made a thanksgiving for their safe return; after which we retired to our several places of rest.

Chapter VI

I never closed an eye that night; for I was sorely troubled in mind about Mr Ettles; as I thought him, by what he had said, a young man ordained for disasters. Yet, saving this inadvertency about looking about him, he had given me no reason to think that adversity had in any shape meddled with him.

In the morning, we had a jocose breakfast, somewhat early, as Mr Ettles intended to go by the second boat across the ferry, meaning to travel to Glasgow that day; which he did, leaving Mr Roslin to bide with me till he could return.

This Mr Roslin was an elderly man, with a bald head, a contented countenance, and peering eyes, that denoted an inquisitive spirit. After Mr Ettles went away, we walked forth to the hills together, and had a very instructive conversation concerning many things, and especially of the uncertainty that hovered in life. But, though he was not overly orthodox, there was a solid ingredient of Christianity in much of what he did say, pleasant to hear; and he preaching resignation and contentment, like an apostle or a gospel minister.

From Mr Roslin, I learned, with a dismayed heart, that the bad luck which kythed to Mr Ettles in his green years, had been permitted to pursue him up and down, and that he was but little better in a worldly sense than when he left his native land. He likewise told me that, finding he was traffiking to little purpose, and the hope of brightening growing dimmer as he grew older, he had come to a resolution to pull in his horns, and make, as Mr Roslin called it, his orbit of a narrower scope. " Which," he added, " I was sorry to hear; for a man that changes his conduct on resolution undergoes no change at all, though to himself the change seem great. Poor Ettles will be still the same, and the world will think so too. He will reap only the pains of perseverance; and find out, when too late, the original sin of thinking he could make himself wiser than he was created."

This led me to remark, in reply, that the early observance of a predominance of resolution in the mind of Mr Ettles knit him to my affections and anxieties; for his barren bridal with Miss Graham was of that nature—taking, as it were, a security from Providence that she should be his wife.

Mr Roslin had never heard of that pitiful disappointment, and was very concerned when I told him the particulars; saying—" However, it was but a foretaste of what Ettles has experienced; for, although, of all men I ever saw, he is the least given to rashness, yet he meditates in secret of his purposes, and decides on adopting what he does, in a manner that surprises his best friends. When he has wrought himself into a resolution, the little good will be beggared, and yet not have turned him. He seems as pliant as a rush in the breeze: as pliant he is; but, once broken, he can never grow whole again."

I cannot explain the impression which the conversation with Mr Roslin in that first walk had upon me. It deepened into the very quick every recollection of Mr Ettles traced upon my memory, from the evening of the mystical marriage; and, without even a show of any reason, made me think of him with more solicitude. However, little passed afterwards about him, while Mr Roslin staid at the manse, which was fully three weeks; but I pondered a great deal on what had passed; for, in the town of a country parish, a misfortunate man is a great unco, and I could not but think Mr Ettles was one, though he was still young, with the air and promise of prosperity. But I have seen the apple tree with all its flourishes cut down in the spring, and said in my heart, "Wherefore were those blossoms?"

When Mr Ettles returned to take Mr Roslin away, he was persuaded by me to stop a few days at the manse, during which I hoped to discern something of that change which I thought must be visible upon him; but I saw none—only he never went to see Mrs Graham, nor minted a syllable of her daughter. On the morning, however, before he went away, seeing me taking my morning stray in the glebe, he came to me alone, and we had a few weighty words together. I say weighty; for what Mr Roslin had told me of the nature of his resolutions, when cooled and chrystalized, made me very acute.

TRIBULATIONS OF THE

Chapter VII

"Well, Mr Ettles," quo' I, as he came towards me, "so you are resolved to go to-day; but you have not said a word about when I am to see you again."

"It is because I do not know myself. If wishes were of any avail, it would not be long; for I am wearying for rest, and I think the bed for it is in a manse—or the kirkyard; but the machinery of Providence is very self-willed, and our inclinations can seldom influence its movements."

"Never," said I, seriously: "we but think we do, when we see the wheels going the way we wish; but excuse me, Mr Ettles, if I inquire, with the freedom of an old friend, have you come to any determination?"

He looked at me for a short time, thoughtfully—at last, smiling, said, "Mr Roslin has been talking then about me?" And he added, briskly—"I do not think I have met with much very uncommon; but, even little as it may be thought, it begets suggestions which those who know it not cannot imagine. It makes one sharp to see and keenly to feel; but the hypocrisy is ineffectual, for the world will not allow that there can be any change. It will still judge by the estimate it made of one in youth, without experience: few understand that alteration of which a man is himself conscious."

As he said this, I thought of what Mr Roslin had remarked concerning resolutions, and the obduracy of his: but I made no reply, for he speedily continued—

" I had a high and beautiful hope. It was soon quenched; but another, almost as bright and fair, arose. It was, in appearance, perhaps, as brilliant, but it failed to excite that desire which is the life of ambition. At last it was obscured, and tarried dimly in a watery cloud. Much of the charm of life soon vanished; and I could only ask, 'What is to be our recompense for having been born at all? ' No, Sir, the vanity of life is over—I have abandoned and forsworn the pursuit of its gauds. I will never more think of aspiring to rise; and I have resolved not to fall lower than—death."

I shuddered at the expression, and sighed with much sorrow.

" Most people," he resumed, " set a false value on the best things in life: I have accustomed myself to think of the worst familiarly;—suffering is but for a few days."

" Mr Ettles," said I, slowly, to make a deep impression, " you have not thought of disgrace."

" Perhaps not," was his reply, after a pensive pause; and then he added hurriedly, " but death can extinguish the sense of it."

" Your words are wild," was my answer. " In the name of God, what have you resolved to do? "

" To live—to do the best I can."

Just then, one of the serving lasses came to the door and made a signal to us that breakfast was ready. So we hastened back to the manse, our conversation being so interrupted.

After breakfast, and a hurried morning exercise, was

over, we walked all three to the ferry, where I bade them adieu in a cordial manner. But, as they stepped into the boat, Mr Roslin gave me a significant look, which shewed he had made a conjecture anent what had passed between me and Mr Ettles in the glebe. Then the boat rowed away, and I returned home in an unaccountable perplexity.

There surely was no earthly reason why I should be so concerned about Mr Ettles. What was he to me? Neither kith nor kin; and although I was, maybe, art and part in his romantical marriage with Miss Graham, that was an old story, and, by rights of time, should have been forgotten.

Then I thought of his familiarity with me, and how he took enfeoffment of my regards from the very first; for he was then a blithe birky, with Miss Graham at his side, who was indeed a lily of a young lady, that ought not to have died; but her Maker had use for her in his mansions—blessed be the name of the Lord!

All that day I was in a manner demented, and it was lucky for me that Miss Becky, my sister, was throng in the kitchen, with her jellies or her jams—I forget which, for my mind was in a state of anarchy and confusion—and she saw not what made me dismal. Towards tea-time, however, we had visiters—salt-water folk—to whom I was bound to be civil, as they had come across the loch to see me.

Being obliged to make an exertion, I was, by the time of their departure, in my usual; but ever and anon the thought of Mr Ettles came uppermost, although I had nothing more to do with him than a common Christian man has with a fellow creature that lays a rightful cess on our sympathy.

CHAPTER VIII

It might be a month after Mr Ettles went away, taking Mr Roslin with him, that I was sitting on my usual seat on the mossy stone near the shore, thinking of the wonderful plenishment of the earth, my thoughts solaced by the benevolence that then invested all around with peacefulness. Miss Becky had gone over the ferry in the morning, to buy something, and to bide all night with the Rev. Dr Dozent and his sister—a woman of a fashious kind, that I did not like, or I would have gone too,

Sitting there by myself, in a meditating posture, the ferry lad came towards me with a letter in his hand, seeking payment of the postage, which, by its heaviness, I knew had come from London.

Not having a sufficiency in my pouch, I rose and went back with him, to get the needful at the manse; for it was pactioned with my sister, that, whenever she went afield, she should leave some change always for outfalls, ready in a stroupless teapot that we keepit for the purpose.

When I had settled with Hector for the price, I then opened the letter, and, lo and behold! it was from Mr Ettles! But what he said may be gotten from his own penmanship better than from any precise I can make thereof.

"London.

"My Dear Friend,—I am *yet* vain enough to think you will be glad to hear of me; and I write this to let you know that I have carried my resolution, to remain sequestered from the busy world, into effect. A distant relation, desirous of retiring, has been induced to dispose of the good-will of his moderate business to me; and last week I was installed in his shop—

"'The world forgetting, by the world forgot.'

"My next object will be to find a suitable wife as soon as possible. The only obstacle, indeed, to my final settlement, is the want of sufficient means to make some provision for her in the event of my death; for I regard this as indispensable:—without it, marriage, in my eyes, loses all its sanctity. It will probably be soon settled; for my hopes of happiness are beneath the ground.

"I do not intend to be very chary either as to beauty or accomplishments: the walk I have now entered does not require that I should. Respectability is all I shall look for; but I shall marry like a prince—for policy. To you I need not say more—the grass grows green on the reason which influences me.

"Mr Roslin is still with me, and sends his best respects to you and the kind Miss Becky.

"Believe me, truly yours,

"Alex. Ettles.

"N.B.—It will oblige me if you could find time to

say what you think, now that I am fixed, of the course I have adopted."

The letter was short; but, coming from whom it did, it was to me full of matter.

First and foremost, a letter from Mr Ettles, and all the way from London, was a thing that never entered my head to expect; and I could not but jalouse that there was something in it more than met the ear. Then, what had I to do with his getting good-wills of businesses? He was in a manner a stranger to me; and how could he think I would care to hear of it?

But, for all the indifferency that I would fain have cherished, the tidings to my heart were not gospel, nor fraught with gladness; in short, I became very sad, and said, as it were, with an inspiration in which I had no volition—" So this is the end of him that seemed fashioned for great purposes! " And I shed a tear, thinking of buds that are blasted.

When I had meditated long on the first clause, I then took up the second. I hope there is no wrong in saying that I thought it overly worldly; for what would become of the command to increase and multiply, if every man put off his marriage till he was in a condition to make a settlement? I disapproved of it; and so I meant to tell him, and to say that the crows are wily and far-casting, but wha ever heard of them, or any of God's creatures, making marriage-settlements?

The third paragraph seemed to me, as it were, gritty

—a tear mingled with sand; and had it not been for the green-grass reason, which was eloquent to the heart of one that had seen Miss Graham, I would have been evendown angry with him.

But the postscript was mystical over all; for it seemed to me to say that he was not well satisfied with himself, or he would not have thought of asking for my approval; for it needs not the whole wisdom of the General Assembly to teach me that, when a man has done a turn, and seeks an opinion of it afterwards, he wants but to hear approbation, being doubtful himself if he has done right. And so I told him in my answer, but in a gentle and far-off way; for when I rose in the morning, his letter only inspired pity and compassion. I was, indeed, much cast down, and the reason of it was to myself a mystery.

Chapter IX

For more than twelve months, I heard nothing of Mr Ettles; and I began to think he had maybe taken it ill that I had been so free with him; still, somehow, I could not imagine how he might do that; for what I said was in sincerity, and my real sentiments, well folded up in Christian delicacy. However, about the end of a year, I got two letters by one post from London. The one was from Mr Ettles—just a bit line, telling me he was that day married to a woman; and the other was in a frank from Mr Roslin, anent the same job, giving me all the particulars. Of Mr Ettles' letter of notification I shall say nothing; but Mr Roslin's was well deserving of being recorded; and here it is :—

"London.

My Dear Sir,—Although I have been long of writing you, I have ever retained a very warm remembrance of the apostolic simplicity of your character. Perhaps, however, I might not yet have had this pleasure; but a friend has given me a frank, by which I can let you know, without cost, of an event which took place this morning, in which, I am sure, you will be interested.

"Our friend Ettles, in pursuance of a *resolution*, has been married. His choice seems, as far as connexions are concerned, to have been judicious.

"The lady has been bred, perhaps, too retired for him. She talks, however, very wisely; but I think that I have seen that she does not act quite so discreetly as might be expected from the tenor of her conversation; being a little like Charles the Second—

" 'Who never said a foolish thing, and never did a wise one.'

"I speak to you frankly; because I am sure that whatever affects his happiness is very dear to you; and I remain, respectfully yours,

"James Roslin."

This, it must be allowed by every one, was a curt epistle; and it caused me to have divers reflections, which, as always is the case in similar instances, were not to the advantage of the writer. This jealousy, as I must acknowledge it was, came not, however, of my nature, but was learned at college with my other learning; it, therefore, soon passed, like the shadow of the summer cloud on the face of the loch; and I was soon restored to myself again, but, in a manner, obligated to put several questions to my own mind respecting Mr Roslin.

Who is he?—how comes it that he takes such an interest in what pertains to Mr Ettles?—and what could make him so very explanatory about the disagreeables of the bride? For what he said was not opiatical to my anxieties; not that he was evendown with his condemnation, but it was very plain he had a sediment of anxiety in his bosom that Mr Ettles had been more governed in his choice by a resolution to settle himself, than by judgment, or taste, or a consideration for his own habitudes.

. When I had pondered some time—it might be the best part of the afternoon, for the ferry-boat comes over at one, post meridian, and I was still sitting, in my inward soliloquy, when my sister said that the tea was ready—not having exchanged words with her at dinner, but only saying the grace at it. I drank none, however, but rose and walked abroad, to refresh my spirit, as my wont was, in trouble of mind, with a sober communing with the mountains; the staid aspect of which, like that of grey-headed elders, never failed to conjure me into composure, if I needed it. Only for that, as well as for other mysteries, were the hills of the Highlands fashioned in the palms of the hands of divine wisdom.

Wherefore I was so vexed, after having come to a conclusion that Mr Roslin was a discreet, decent man, is not to be told; far less how I was so affected with the blithesome news of a wedding, betokening a fulfilment of the early command concerning the plenishing of the earth; but so it was—the news of that day were not to me blithesmeat, and yet I could not say the cause thereof.

After a season, and in the hallowed tranquillity of the twilight, I returned home, and told Becky—who had seen I was fashed at somcthing—that our friend, Mr Ettles, was again married, and that I had a letter from Mr Roslin; without saying anything to her of what it was about. She remarked, however, that I had visibly gotten a drug that had sickened me.

In time, the wound I had received—for I can call it no better—skinned over, though the part was aye tender; for never could I bear to think that a putting on of the conjugal yoke upon resolution, was according to Scripture, or could kythe in better than heart-burning and affliction.

Chapter X

For several months, nothing particular happened—only, it being known to the Presbytery that the dining-room in the manse needed painting, I was, of course, chosen to go into the General Assembly while it was doing; being subject, at times, when I took a cold, to a shortness of breath, for which the smell of the paint was not a condiment. And, going into Edinburgh on the solemn business of the Church, who should I meet with there but Mr Roslin? who, having nothing upon his hands, had come down from London to see how the Assembly was conducted.

He was most glad to see me; and we had more than two words about Mr Ettles, whom, he told me, he hoped was happy. I did not like to hear of that hope, for it seemed to intimate a fear. Moreover, he agreed with me that a marriage on resolution was not on a proper principle; adding—for he was an auld-headed man—that, although Mr Ettles was able for all things, it was not easy to say what he was fit for; being overly obdurate in sticking to his own opinion, even when most complaisant to that of others.

"It is a sore pity that he is so," quo' Mr Roslin; "for his wife is as obdurate as he is; and in every house and state there must be a head: the rule and power must either be with the wife or the man—it cannot abide with both. However, ye will be able shortly to judge for yourself; for Mr and Mrs Ettles are coming to Scotland, and I know he intends to visit you, for whom he cherishes a regard as sincerely as if he really hated you, and had resolved to love you."

The expectation of seeing Mr Ettles was as the spring time; and I walked every blessed morning to the pier of Leith, to inquire, at the smacks, if he was yet come; but he came not—and, when the General Assembly broke up, I returned to my own parish, with the sense of a cold in at my heart, being the sense of a disappointment. The complaint did not, however, afflict me long; for, in the month of August after, he and his wife came to the manse, soakit with rain. In coming over the ferry, a desperate thunder-plump fell from the heavens, and they were caught in the jaw of it, to which an evendown pour was a moderation. I mind it very well; for it was so inordinate, that it caused me, before they came, to put up an ejaculation for the poor beasts of the field, and the birds of the air, in which the dumb fish of the deep sea were not forgotten.

After they had shifted themselves—for they were past drying—we had some mutual conversation; gay it was, but not of a satisfactory solidity. I could discern, however, with the tail of my eye, that my sister was greatly taken with Mrs Ettles, who, she said privately to me in her transports, in the course of the evening, "was a most delightful creature." In conscience, however, I could not go so far; though I will not positively deny that she was void of merit. But I thought of Miss Graham, with a shaking head, and I looked at Mr Ettles, still in his promising years, saying to myself—"Verily, Providence clotheth itself in a mantle of perplexities."

As they took us at an unawares, we had not a by-ordinar' dinner that day; for everybody knows that a well-ordered manse is no a galravitching hotel in Edinburgh. But, after dinner, the ladies went away; and, as I heard afterwards, Mrs Ettles unpacked her trunk to see that nothing was wet, and shewed Becky such paraphernauls as she had no notion of. Mr Ettles sat with me, and we had some neighbour-like discourse together; but the upshot of it darkened my spirit; for I could see that much of his winsomeness, when here with Miss Graham, had taken the wings of the morning; and, though he might be glegger, he was an altered man, with a ponderosity, now and then, in what he said, that I could only think was diseased wisdom.

After a this and that, of no particularity, he began to tell me he did not think it was ordained that man or woman could ever love more than once; but I told him that I knew many most sensible and discreet persons who married three times. " Ay," said he—" I don't doubt it; but once for love, and twice for expediency "—by which we were led on, by a circumbendibus, to speak of himself; when he made an observation most astounding.

" Love," said he, " is an instinct implanted by the Creator: but resolution is the offspring of human reason, the flavour of the forbidden fruit. When we obey instincts, we earn happiness; but when we listen to reason, we are allured into suffering and sorrow, for reason is but the use of our knowledge of good and evil."

No more then passed; for, the ladies coming in, we were obligated to be jocose; but his words dwelt on my remembrance.

REV. COWAL KILMUN

Chapter XI

In the course of time, on that night when Mr Ettles and his new wife came to see us, we all went to bed; but, before I left Becky, she began to tell me what a pleasant woman the lady was, and what a fortune her father had settled on her to make them comfortable.

I did not like to hear this, and recollected how Mr Roslin had likened her, in his letter, to the runagate king; thinking she surely was at a loss for discourse, to speak even to anybody, of what her father had done or could do; and I went away sorrowful.

I could not help thinking that there was something in the indiscretion of Mrs Ettles that could not be very agreeable to the proud heart of her husband, if he knew it; for, although it was plain he had married on resolution, he was not such a sordid character as was ever likely to marry for the lucre of gain: and I thought it was a warning, though I could not say why, to all young women, to take good care never to put it in their husbands' power to suspect that it was possible for them to imagine that they had only married them for money; for man is a proud animal, and does not like, whatever may be his faults, to be thought meanly of.

From the little I knew of Mr Ettles, and the less I did of his wife, this bragging of her fortune was an omen that boded no augmentation to their happiness; for, though, no doubt, marriages have been made both by men and women for settlements, there has generally been something more looked to than mere money; and I was sure that Mr Ettles had another spoke in the wheel of his matrimony than it. However, I fell asleep, resolving to have my eyes open when I awoke, and to wise on the conversation to a disclosure; for now I began to think something was on the mind of Mr Ettles, which, perhaps, could be explained.

Next morning, the lift was bright and the earth all glittering, in so much that, although I did not forget my intention to probe the gathering visible in the bosom of Mr Ettles, my heart was not so set on it as it was in the watches of the night; and therefore I postponed my resolution to a more convenient season. Thus it came to pass that I did not trouble him at all with my scrupulosities; for the weather grew better, and the two days of his visitation were given to enjoyment—only there was one thing most touching, which fell out on the afternoon afore the day of his departure with the woman he had married.

When me and him had solaced ourselves with a tumbler after dinner, he proposed, as the day without was most enticing, that we should take a walk. Accordingly, as I am a man always for temperance, we went forth; and, in our easy, leisurely manner, talking of many things, and nothing important, I found ourselves on the road to Mrs Graham's dwelling, that had been. Thinking he might be minded to call there, for auld langsyne,

I said to him, stopping suddenly—"Mr Ettles," quo' I, "I jalouse ye are no acquaint with what has happened!"

"No," replied he; "what has?"

"Mrs Graham," said I, with a melancholious voice, "was removed last Lammas, and now sleeps with her daughter. We should lay it to heart."

He made no answer for some time; but I saw there was a going-on in his breast that could not be very pleasant. By and by, however, he spoke, saying—"No matter, we can go to the churchyard." And he walked forward, I following, really a dejected object; for I could not but think of one that had been most dear to him, and the blight which had early fallen on all his prospects.

In all the way to the kirkyard, which was then a long mile from the spot where I had corrected him, he never opened his lips, and I had nothing to say; for, though it was then the eye of summer, there was the shadow of a cloud still on my spirit, and I wondered of what would ensue; for he was then a married man, and I had some doubt if it wasna just right, meditating among the tombs when he had a living wife, though maybe she was not worthy to hold the candle to her who was the bride that bedded with the worm.

When we reached the kirkyard, the yett was shut, which obligated us to clamber over the dyke; in the doing whereof, I mind that the left knee of a new pair of black breeks, that I had put on for an honesty that day, was torn; and that I fell among burs and nettles, which grew hard by, seemingly of as little use as heritors, who are permitted to be for a fashion, and might be well weeded away without detriment to parish ministers, especially when dining-rooms in manses need painting.

Chapter XII

Being, after my calamity, over the dyke, we walked sedately to where Mrs Graham and her daughter were laired in cold and silence; and when I had shewn him the graves, I left him to his soliloquies; telling him, in order that there might be no mistakes, "That highest and greenest of the twa hillocks was the last hap of the old lady. The other grave," said I, "is a monumental emblem of the memory of man: it's in a state of obliteration, as the image of her that slumbers beneath it is in the minds of those who are yet of this world."

I then left him, and went about among the headstones, reading the epitaphs on many a frail memorial erected nigh; which, for the most part, were no doubt penned with a regard to veracity. One, however, I did meet with, which in conscience I could not approve; for how could the schoolmaster, who penned the same, tell what virtue and seemliness, as he said, were about the man whom he had never known in this life, nor heard even his name mentioned after death, as the sprose on the stone shewed forth. The fact was, that, one morning in winter, after a midnight mixture and jumbling of the winds and the waves, the drowned body of a genteel man, with a gold watch, and money in his purse, was found upon the shore; which, as it behoved the parish to bury, was done in a Christian-like manner. The valuables were given to me to keep till an inheritor would cast-up; but, after two years, none appeared, and Mr Beta, the schoolmaster, then proposed that his son, who was just out of his time as a mason, should make a headstone, as there was a fund to come and go on. To this I could see no reasonable objection. Accordingly, a very shapely headstone was hewn; but, before setting it up, the young man pointed out to me that it would be daftlike to have a monument without an inscription; so I told him to get his father to write one. The old dominie thought, however, that, as the stranger was unknown, a plain, simple headstone was quite suitable; and, consulting me, I was of the same opinion; but Tom, the mason, said that there never was such a thing heard of as a monument saying nothing—in short, it would be just a masonic dumbie, to put it up as it was; adding that, as there were plenty of funds in my hands, there could be no reason that the headstone should be a nonentity. So, to keep quiet in the land, I authorized his father to indite a becoming epitaph; and Tom engraved it, grumbling, however, at the shortness of the job; for he was paid by the lettering.

Till that day, I had never seen what was on the stone; and well pleased I was not, when I read such evendown trash, and so much of it, as that graceless creature, Tom, persuaded his father to write for his benefit. Indeed, I was wroth at the havers, and determined on the spot to have the nonsense hewn out and extirpated utterly; but, somehow, one thing after another has come in the way, and the headstone is still standing there, a laughing-stock to everybody that happens to see it. Few, however, are guilty of going, in this life, to so melancholious a place as our kirkyard, either to the molestation of auld Peggy Rankine's cow, that feeds in it, or to moralize on the headstones.

When I had smoothed my birses, after the perusal of the dominie's paternoster anent the incognito virtues of the unknown man, I went back to Mr Ettles, to see if he was done; and, still without speaking, he took hold of me by the arm, and walked me to the dyke, over which we came into the highway, an accident I was greatly surprised at; for, if I had recollected it, there would have been no need for us to have clambered the wall, or to split the knee of my best breeks, to say nothing about falling among nettles and gulbroch, which is not pleasant, and far from being odoriferous herbage.

All the way back to the manse, Mr Ettles was still taciturn; in so much, that his wife noticed it when we were drinking our tea, and said, that she was none surprised to see him "so glum after looking at his old sweetheart's grave;" for, it seems, she had seen us in the kirkyard, while she was taking a walk on the croft with Becky, my sister; who would not let her disturb us, being a woman of a compassionate nature, and really not so idolatrous of Mrs Ettles as she had been at first, notwithstanding her proper style of the English language, and her beautiful silk gown, trimmed with orange ribands.

Chapter XIII

In the evening, after tea, me and Mr Ettles were sitting very soberly together by ourselves, having a solid conversation concerning the difference in the physiognomy of coming and going Time; no doubt the consequence of his rumination at the door of the narrow house of Miss Graham; and he said that nothing disturbed him so much as to see that the companions of his youth seemed to think, after all he had borne, that he was still the same whom they had formerly known.

" I know," said he, " that some think, with reason, when a man resolves to change, he does not change at all—and my friend Mr Roslin is of that opinion—but they forget that we are creatures of circumstances, and that a change of circumstances forces on a change of character. I agree that when a man resolves, of himself, to become different from what he was, it is very doubtful if any alteration can be effected; but when resolution comes in aid of new circumstances, the effect may be very great indeed:—such is the case with me. The morning of my life was bright—the flowers in my path, oh, so beautiful! Fortune seemed to beckon me on; and, without vanity, I may say, that a conscious activity spurred me into enterprise But the sun became soon clouded, the flowers withered, fickle fortune flew away; and the activity now is apt to fall into fits of absence, and forget the seeming destination that once stimulated its energy. I live no longer for the world—I but endure life."

This was very recondite to me; and I did not well know what to say; but, all things considered, I reflected that it could not be far wrong to observe, "I was sorry to think he was not just as happily married as he might have been."

He looked at me seriously for some time, and then said—

"The change had come upon me before I thought of marrying. It should, therefore, be regarded as a consequence of having abdicated ambition. The motives existed no longer which formerly influenced me, and could not enter into the considerations which induced me to submit to the conjugal yoke. However, to answer your remark more directly, I have only to complain of what I believe most married men do—namely, that perhaps my wife does not clearly enough see that her own happiness would be augmented, if she thought more of mine; but it would cause trouble to her to do so; and it is the nature of the female mind to act more from inclination than duty, though it always thinks its sense of duty is paramount. A man is a more dutiful animal than a woman; but he says less about it."

Much more of the like discourse passed between us, and what Mr Ettles said was less intelligible to me; but two things increased my perplexity.

First, How he, Ettles, came to make me such a depositary of his secret feelings, who was, in a manner, a stranger to him. And,

Second, How I came to be so constrained against my will to be entangled with his tribulations; for, after that visit, they multiplied, and I thought of them the more and more.

It was plain that both me and Mr Roslin were in the mist concerning him; and so, when he and Mrs Ettles went away to England next day, I resolved to keep a gleg watch upon his fate and courses, he being a phenomenon such as the pastor of a country parish has it not at all times in his power to contemplate. His wife, I saw, was a mere woman; but he was a curious engine in the arsenal of Providence, of which the use was not yet discerned. Surely, indeed, it was a matter to suggest reflection, that a living man should account himself an implement of no use; and much and often I thought of that circumstance, saying, with reverence, that whoever has worldly functions left, has visibly worldly tasks to perform.

Upon the whole, the visit from Mr and Mrs Ettles was a visitation; and I was some time, many days, after their departure, no just myself, by thinking about them; wondering how folk that seemed so like the rest of the world, could have that within which was so different,

Of the wife, however, I did not cogitate much; for she was—what my sister said in her jocosity—a broth-and-beef character; whereas he was—as she likened also—a Pace-and-Yule dainty, whereof the ingredients could not be bought in every grocery shop, and, in the cooking, needed mair cunning than his leddy had power, she feared, to put forth.

CHAPTER XIV

It was fully the best part of half-a-year, from the time Mr and Mrs Ettles were with us, that, one wintry morning, Mr Roslin, who was in no sort of manner more than an acquaintance, and no an intimate one, came across the ferry to see me. Well do I mind the weather; for, although it might be then past the dead of the year, the winter was not, for weeks after, out of the dead thraws. The morning was bleak and the blast easterly, and there was a sprinkling of snow and hail on the tops of the hills, that betokened more of wind and wet than a solid rigour. In short, it was just as if winter were angry to think that spring was coming, and gowled her away.

Mr Roslin, it seems, had been detained at Greenock for some time, by a foul south-west wind; and everybody knows that Greenock, which is dreadfully addicted to south-westers, is, when they soak, a most wearisome place. He was then going back to the Americas—the stramash having ended in their independence; and, having nothing to do, thought he would come over to see me. But he paid dear for his pastime. The wind, which had been long squally from the south-west, changed into the easterly airt when he was in the ferry-boat; and when he left me to return to the ship in which he had taken his passage, she had availed herself of the easterly wind and sailed without him; which was surely a most hard thing, he having paid his passage. But no better could be expected; for the Yankees are not a people of a principle, not having an Establishment. It is hoped, however, that, in time, a candle will be lighted among them.

Mr Roslin, on his arrival at Greenock, finding he had missed his passage, was fair demented; and sent me a scrape of a pen, to let me know his condition, and how his trunks were gone, and with them all his money—which, I understood, was in a kind of foreign coin called the ready—begging me to lend him a small supply, till he could hear from London.

I cannot say that I was pleased with this; and Becky was most peremptory in saying he should have no money, knowing, as we did, so little of him; adding, likewise, that surely he had a stock of impudence to think of applying to the like of us. But, when I came to think of him, a forlorn stranger in such a metropolitan place as Greenock, the carnality of my heart softened, and I had some doubts if it would be just Christian to let him perish in the streets of that town for lack of a morsel. The upshot was, that I resolved to go to Greenock myself, and, if I found him in an extremity, to break the back of a guinea-note upon him. Becky, however, was of opinion that I should take no notice of his letter at all; for, she said, his writing to me was either an accident or offence, like those malefactions of which she read of in the newspapers, when she happened, now and then, to get the loan of one. Nevertheless, the more I thought of my duty, the more my feelings thawed; and, at last, out of a constraint of obligation, next day, I went to Greenock, so noted as it is for wet weather.

The mercy of Providence was very visible when I took my departure across the ferry; for the day was fine, and the lift as clear as a blithe lassie's glad blue eye. But nothing is steadfast in this howling wilderness.

As was to be expected, just as I got in sight of Greenock, it began to pour as if all the powers of the air had watering cans in their hands, watering, and the earth a hesp laid out to be bleached. In short, when I got to the inn where Mr Roslin put up, I was sorely steepit, all dripping—and, as I may say now in jocosity, no a roast of beef either. Umbrellas were not then created.

By the time I got to the inns, Mr Roslin had done with his dinner, and I catched him drinking wine out of a decanter, by himself; a thing I never evened my hand to, in the most disconsolate solitude.

He was glad to see me, however, as he said, and seemingly could not make enough of me; calling for a glass of brandy, which, he said, was better for my humidity than cold wine; and when I told him how I had come on purpose to temper, as it were, his affliction, he said that it was the very thing he thought I might do. Indeed, his gladness and sympathy, I'll never deny, put me on my guard; for the man, said I, inwardly, that makes ower muckle of you, has either cheated you or intends it;—so, notwithstanding, I was as jocose as could be with Mr Roslin, I joined, in the words of Scripture, trembling with my mirth.

When I had taken the brandy, dried myself, and got the residue, as Mr Roslin said, of his dinner—which might have been a reasonable banquet for the Duke and Sir Alexander—I opened the intent and purpose of my coming; the which, however, I must defer to another chapter.

CHAPTER XV

First and foremost, I began with a far-off moralizing anent the uncertainties of this life, and the troubles that man is born to, as the sparks fly upward; which Mr Roslin fully admitted was most true; adding, in a concerned way, that he had tasted the lot of human nature more acutely since his return to Scotland than he had ever thought to have done.

"All," said he, "that I formerly knew, when I went abroad more than fifty years ago, are gone. I was a stranger in the very settlement of my home—village I should call it; there was not one being that I ever heard of. The very minister, an old, venerable, grey-headed man, was removed, and two, successively after his death, had filled his place."

"That," I replied, "no doubt accounts for your destitute condition; all your friends being away, I really do not wonder at your dolorosity." But, although I spoke most sympathisingly, I girded my loins, and set a watch on the door of my lips, especially when he said—

"Now, this visit is most kind, and could not have been expected; and yet it is no more than what I thought might be. Something runs before me, that I am not to be long for this world; and, having nothing to do, waiting for your answer to my letter, I have been amusing myself in writing an outline of my will."

"That was very odd," quo' I, pushing my chair back.

"It was so; and here it is. Among other friends whom I have learned to esteem in life, you will find yourself mentioned for a small token of my regard."

He then read :—"And, in testimony of the impression which his apostolic simplicity has made upon me, I request the Rev. Cowal Kilmun to accept of one hundred dollars, to buy a ring, and to wear it as a memorial of one who believed him to be a pattern of honesty and truth."

I looked at his feet; but his shoes were like other people's; nevertheless, I thought, if he had cloots, he might hide them. Oh! I was feared; saying to myself, "Surely the devil can do no good."

We then diverged into a less particular subject; and, when it was about time to take a cup of tea, he ordered it in, and shook me cordially by the hand, saying, that, although he did wish I would visit him, it was a romance he had never expected to see fulfilled.

Afterwards, he became more like mortality; and my dread wore off, insomuch, that I thought him a very sensible man, especially when he mentioned that he did not intend to apply to me for any money, till he heard from London; by which I saw there would be time enough to meditate how best to jook him, before he calculated on being in need.

Thus, from one thing to another, till it was far in the night—the weather no mending, of course, for we were in Greenock—we grew into better acquaintance; and I had my doubts at last, if I had done him even scrimp justice.

Towards ten o'clock, we resolved to part for the night; and I was shewn to my bedroom, leaving him behind. About the small hours, I heard him also going to his room; and, soon after, I fell asleep, never thinking that anything could be amiss; for, although I was not at first content with him in my own breast, that dubiety had worn off towards the heel of the evening; and when I bade him good night, he really appeared to be a very wiselike, weel-doing man.

In the course of the night, however, or rather towards the morning, I was molested with a great ringing of bells; and, by and by, a waiter looked in on me, and cried that Mr Roslin was on the floor, in the jaws of death; bidding me get up and come, which I was not long of doing; and there was he lying in an apoplexy, with the complexion of a bandana pocket-napkin. Was not that very extraordinary?

But, not to summer and winter on the catastrophe, the long and the short of it was that he departed this life in a short time—less than an hour; and I was left with the dead body on my hands, not knowing what to do with it, being demented with consternation. Before, however, I proceed to relate the terrible things which ensued, it behoves me to make a few words of improvement on what had come to pass; for as much will, no doubt, be expected from a person like me, whose duty it is, by his vocation, to turn the calamities of life to a profit.

First, then, it cannot be denied that Mr Roslin dying suddenly in the hands of strangers, was an event to make an impression on the hearts of professing Christians; and,

Second, That his leaving, on so slight an acquaintanceship, a sum of money to me, to buy a mourning ring, was a most uncommon thing; for the which there was, no doubt, a purpose, though he was taken away before that purpose was revealed.

The uncertainty of life was visible in his death; and the wonders that come upon us like seeming chances, kythed in the provisions of his will; of which I will have to be more particular when I describe what happened after his interment. But it was a stang in the vitals to think how I, a quiet country minister, dwelling in the peacefulness of my manse, should have been innocently drawn into such a slough of despond; and shews, in a most edifying manner, that we know not what a day may bring forth.

Chapter XVI

After the breath of life was out of the body, and the folk of the inn had, in a most creditable manner—they could not have done better in a manse—got the remains straighted, I went again to my bed, fashed with what had come to pass, and soon after fell into a dover, that slippit into a sleep. In the morning, being awoke, I rose, and all the time I was eating my breakfast, had disconsolate thoughts; for I pondered how I was to get the dead buried; because he dying in an inn, which is a public, assoilyied the magistrates from the obligation of granting me an indemnification for the cost; and where was the justice of taxing me for the interment of a stranger? To let a dead corpse lie in the house for ever, it was not reasonable to expect the landlord would allow:—who then was to be at the expense of the removal?

Then I considered well that a lair was to be had—who was to be at the outlay for one?—for it was well known that Sir Michael made the toun council pay for the burying ground; and how could they be reimbursed, if every grave was to be free gratis?—besides, who was to pay the betherel for howking it? In short, the more I reflected on the bearings of the case—as an elder, who was an advocate, in the General Assembly, said—I was the more constipated; but out of my perplexities I got, in a sense, by the landlord coming into the room.

" Sir," said he, " this is a sad affair; for I understand from the waiter that the dead gentleman, was, in a manner, an utter stranger to you, and that you had some reason to suspect he was left by the Yankee vessel in straitened circumstances. What is to be done? "

" That is just what I think—what *is* to be done? "

" Has he no friends? "

" He left the east country many years ago, a perfect orphan, and he found the land of his birth a desolation."

" Very bad! I wish he had not died in my house. Had he no friend but you? "

" It could not be lawfully said that I am sib to him, either as kith or kin."

" Well, but who else was he known to? "

" I fear that your trust is a broken reed: he came to me with Mr Ettles, who, more than a dozen of years ago was a merchant, and perished the pack with his uncle."

I made this answer, for I was terrified for a responsibility, and thought it best to be guarded.

" I see how it is," answered the landlord. " I must, in the first instance, risk the outlay; but do me the favour to superintend the funeral, to see that no unnecessary expense is incurred; and write to Mr Ettles concerning what has happened."

This I agreed to; and, in the course of the day, I was

visited by several gospel-hearted persons, who condoled with me. The ministers of the town make it a point never to visit strangers in affliction; for, in a sea-port, that might be very troublesome.

Then, with the advice of the landlord, I set about the funeral, which I was for having with more frugality than him; but he said Mr Roslin came to his house and lived in it like a gentleman, and he could not be answerable to himself or the world if he sent him out of it as anything less; so we had a most decent ploy—everything creditable and no waste.

By the time, on the day of the burial, that we came back from the new kirkyard—as the Greenock folk call their burying-ground, though there was then no kirk near it, but only a Relief hobbleshow—there came a letter from London, directed for Mr Roslin; which the landlord, contrary to my solid advice, opened in presence of witnesses. However, this letter was from Mr Ettles, saying, he had invested the money agreeably to orders, and wishing him a pleasant meeting with all their friends in the other world; which, to hear, made my heart loup to my lips—it was so like blasphemy; for Mr Roslin was but minded to go to America, and had no thoughts of another world, though making his will. The landlord said, however, that there was a daybreak in the letter, which I did not well see, and took upon himself to correspond with Mr Ettles; but added—" Before I write, there is a desk which must be examined, that I may tell what is in it."

Accordingly, we had the desk brought down by a waiter lad, and found a key that opened it in the pocket of the waistcoat that the deceased had worn on the day before his departal. But what was in the desk need not be rehearsed—only there was found in it a will which he had penned after I had left him; and we all held up our hands in wonderment at it; concerning the cause of which, I will relate in the next chapter.

CHAPTER XVII

The last will and testament of Mr Roslin was a very well-penned manuscript paper. No lawyer's instrument could have been more to the purpose; for it testified that he was a man of substance, and could very well afford all the legacies it set forth—the chief of which was five thousand dollars to me, because I was a worthy character, overflowing with simplicity and truth.

This was the only alteration made to the will by which he left the hundred dollars to buy the ring, and I would have been most unreasonable to have objected to the alteration. The residue of his fortune he left to Mr Ettles; who, in short, when all was done, was a well-pleased inheritor to a nest-egg that was not addled. But many things must, *à priori*, be rehearsed.

Thus, it came to pass, on the day after the interment, that I deemed it expedient to return to the manse and to my sister, who I thought could not be an easy woman because of my absence, she only knowing for cause that

I was detained by Mr Roslin, who had gone off in an apoplexy. But before I left the Tontine Inn, I wrote a particular letter to Mr Ettles, advising him to come (meaning, if he could afford it, for I remembered he had been a broken merchant) and see after the will and the residue; telling him how discreet the landlord had been, and how abstemious the ministers were obligated to be, by a sense of duty, as to giving consolation to strangers respecting whom they knew nothing.

When the porter of the inn, a Celt, said, comically enough, that he had postponed my letter, I took my stick in my hand and leisurely walked away to the ferry. The day, when I did so, was not bright, as was reasonable to be expected in a place of the well-known habitudes of Greenock; but it was dry then; and, accordingly, as I went along by myself, I had time for reflection. I had not, however, gone far, when the wind began to spit in my face; and, before I got to the end of my journey, me and a wet man were none different. Indeed, I could not go into the boat by reason of my wetness, and was obligated to bide in the ferry-house till my clothes were dried, putting on a petticoat-commodity of the landlady's till my own nether vestment was dried on a chair-back afore the fire.

At last, I was ready for the road, and, stepping into the ferry boat, got safe over, and in due season arrived at the manse; where that very attentive creature, sister Becky, had the kettle boiling, and made me as comfortable as could well be, considering.

When I had taken a dish of tea, which was very refreshing, I told my sister all that had come to pass; and more especially about the ring and the legacy. But she was clearly of opinion that I ought to have nothing to do with either, knowing so little as we did of Mr Roslin, who certainly could have no good intent in making what seemed a benison, in dollars, instead of pounds sterling—for a most uncertain coin is dollars. It was evidently a castle in the air, luring into a lawsuit.

My fears did not carry me so far as my sister's scrupulosities did her; but, nevertheless, a fyke fell upon me, and I wearied exceedingly for a response from Mr Ettles, walking much by myself, and meditating on the nothingness of this world.

At last, a letter came, of which I could make neither heads nor tails, farther than that Mr Ettles would soon be with me, and that Mr Roslin was reputed to be a rich man; giving me no reason, however, to think how, as my sister said, he could, by a possibility, leave me a legacy, which, if the dollar was no more than four-and-tenpence, as she had known it to be, would still be a happy godsend. Altogether, it is not to be told what we suffered at this time; for Becky, to increase my tribulations, had glimpses of visions and trances, wherein she thought she saw that I was doomed to receive a true legacy, and conjectured about buying many needful articles for the manse that we had never wanted till "the gowden brae seemed to shoot on us."

Seeing her, who was upon the whole a wiselike woman, falling into inordinate fits, I communed with myself, and resolved, until Mr Ettles came, to make no change in my own walk and conversation. Accordingly, I made a point of preaching, not a new sermon, but one that was well thumbed; and I baptized two children on the next Sabbath, as composedly as if nothing had come to pass. But, for all that, I did not repose on a bed of roses, as may well be supposed by those who have experienced similar vicissitudes. At last, we heard Mr Ettles was coming down to settle everything, and begging me to meet him at Edinburgh; which was far from my hand to do, for I really had no faith in the legacy, nor could I say that my sister had oftentimes brighter expectations, especially when she talked with a rational sobriety. However, from less to more, I was in the end persuaded to go to the tryst, whereof I have now to relate the particulars.

Chapter XVIII

To the " Guid Toun," it may be inferred from what is set forth in the foregoing chapter, I did go, and by the fly from Greenock to Glasgow, and thence to Edinburgh, all in one day; and who was at the coach door, but Mr Ettles, who was most extraordinary glad to see me.

After the usual *parley vous*, he took me to the inns where he himself was staying; and, as I had come well on to seventy miles that day, a scomfished man I surely was, in great need of a cordial drink of tea, which I soon had; and being greatly recruited by the same, we spent a very instructive evening.

From him I learned that Mr Roslin was a man who died in a well-doing circumstance—who having no near kindred that he knew of, had long intimated his intention of leaving Mr Ettles his heir, not jalousing, however, that he was so nigh unto his own latter end as this come to pass had made manifest. In short, when he told me of many ins and outs, I wrote my sister about it, in a line by the next post, to let her know that I had gotten well to Edinburgh, without an accident, and that there was a prospect, through Mr Ettles, that the legacy would be something more of a substantiality than the wind of the mouth.

In the morning after, Mr Ettles could not but see I was fashed; and inquired, in a most sympathizing manner, anent the occasion, which caused me to say to him that it was a certain loss to come into Edinburgh, if all I had for it was the prospect of him going over the sea, as he had told me, the bulk of Mr Roslin's gathering being there.

At first he gave me a sudden glower; but soon after, he relapsed into his ordinary, and said, to give myself no concern about him; adding, it was, at most, but a trip across the Atlantic, which he thought nothing of.

This, no doubt, was an ease of mind, especially when he mentioned that it was his intention to pay off all the legacies first and foremost, as plenty assets to do so were in this country; and then he could take his own will with the residue, he being, in the words of the king's law, residuary legatee.

Still, in all this, I could not discern for what he wanted me in Edinburgh, and so I asked him, even down, the reason; which he laughingly said was to see how I would comport myself under my good fortune—a very unsatisfactory answer, for not a preeing of good fortune had I yet gotten; and, notwithstanding all that he had told me, I could not but feel I had only a cold coal to blow at; and that the outlay on the incoming was sure, and no trifle. But, as no better could then be made o't, I submitted myself to a gospel resignation, resolving not to kick against the pricks.

By and by, however, it came out that he was a more searching man than I had supposed; for he had learnt that some needcessitous relations of Mr Roslin were about the closes of the Canongate; and he was minded, if he could find them out, to make a division among them, and had thought that I might be of use in assisting him in that Christian quest. This I was well pleased to hear, for it was just like him to do so, as I ever thought by what I had seen from the first when he came to the manse a wooer of Miss Silvia Graham, of whom I have made mention, and who certainly was the loveliest creature that ever my eyes set on. His second wife was but a coarse worsted commodity compared to yon silken negligee. But, before I rehearse the upshot of our inquisition of the closes and unsavoury nooks of the Cowgate, as well as all the Canongate, it is necessary to say something of the town of Edinburgh, which, among the best-informed of the inhabitants, has not its marrow on this side of the New Jerusalem, that is paved with precious stones.

Chapter XIX

From auld lang syne, I had made it a rule to make observes in every foreign place I went to, after I was placed; which accounts for the insight of the world in these pages. It is not, therefore, to be thought that I would go about in such a town as Edinburgh surely is, with my eyes shut; and so, the better to enlighten the reader as to what I have to tell, it behoves me firstly to make it plain what my notion is in general of our old Scottish capital, wherein the Court of Session and the General Assembly are still allowed, by the prelatic Parliament of England, to hold their sederunts.

Now, I mean to be as plain as I am pleasant; for there are things in which diffidence is no virtue; and if I should make some folks claw where it's no youky, the fault is not in me, but in their own position. First and verily, I do aver, without the possibility of a denial, that Edinburgh, to say no ill of it, is one of the most self-conceited Babels that ever the Lord put the breath of life into; and certain it is, among the residenters, there are some who would give more for a forebear in a stoury lead kist than for a living preacher of the gospel. But no to be overly salt upon them, I ought to make a Nota Bene, that maybe they are not utterly void of kindness —of the which, me and Mr Ettles had a large experience among his acquaintance; for what with them that had new silver plate work to shew, and others that were sleeping partners, no doubt, in wine concerns, and had many sample bottles to pree, we had, as I heard a Paddy's man on the top of the fly say, " a galoring of dinnering." But there is much new-fangled bravery yonder; and sure am I, for all their sprose, that a silver tea-pot of the godly days of John Knox and the Lords of the Congregation, is not to be found within the four walls of the place.

One thing bred me much consternation—for it was never well cleared up—and that was a notion I had gotten somehow at the Divinity Hall of Glasgow, that there were only swans to be seen among the poultry of Edinburgh. I can, however, safely affirm on my conscience that I never saw a swan there. Only very common gooses are to be met with at the best tables; and it's my sedate opinion, that not one of their Ordinary Lords would ken, in a sense, a goose from a swan, though he saw it gabbling on the floor of the Parliament House.

I am the more particular anent this, because I was nearly shot through the lights and vitals, by a look that a leddy threw at me when she asked me to be helped one day to a calf's head. " Na," quo' I, " that, madam, is no dainties; but I'll take a slice from the bosom of yon swan that's afore your guidman." "A swan!" quo' she. "Ay, a swan," quo' I—"isna all the Edinburgh gooses swans?" The which response raised a mighty shout of laughter; but I saw, with the tail of my eye, that some of the professors and other literary characters then present, were near hand guffawing with the wrong sides of their mouths. Oh, yon are comical folk! Gude keep me from their gooses' and calfs' heads!

Upon the whole, I'll no undertake to maintain that "Auld Reeky" is just the land of Canaan. It may be, however, no a desolation to them that can fen on their own pock nook; but they maun ca' canny; for the acting yonder's no in a way of moderation. Their wedding-like banquets are a sign that they are sometimes obligated to sup muslin kail as a consequence, as well as handle the drumsticks of poney cocks for a fortnight after.

But though this is in a manner holy writ, concerning the general carnality of the place, yet it's no a town without garnels of the Lord in by places, as I will have occasion to shew and testify when I come to set down many things of which me and Mr Ettles had a verification to our senses, when we came to explorify the closes. Indeed, my chief purpose in speaking of the upping of the garnish inhabitants was, that the courteous reader might discern how it happens that a portion of the decent people shrink into closes, and scogs in wynds.—It is because they cannot vie with those that are no better than themselves; for, having a right notion of Christianity, they do not put out their arms farther than their sleeves will let; which, in the vernacular, signifies, they live within their incomes. In short, I could see that a lord's living would not play pue to an Edinburgh writer, buying land with a wadset; and it belongs to me, seeing so much of the world as I have seen, by being at the head of a parish, to testify my displeasure against all sorts of the prevailing immorality.

Chapter XX

It becomes a man whose duty it is to shew how the hardships of this life may be softened to the sense, to make himself acquainted with the dens of depravity and the hiding-places of wo; for, although it would not be right nor just to say that crime and poverty are either sib or connected, it is well known that they are near neighbours: and me and Mr Ettles saw this, in our visitations to the purlieus of the Canongate and the Cowgate. There the thief and the beggar dwell in the same close; and ne'er-do-weel cutties in garret-rooms up dark unwashen turnpike stairs, where many a godly weanless widow is constrained, by the unaccountable dispensations of mercy, to read her Bible in solitude, and make her meal of resignation.

Considering the intent of his quest, and the weight that curiosity had with myself, to see the haunts of want and iniquity, that I might edify my own people with a true account of them when I returned home; I said to Mr Ettles that I would, if he were willing, much rather enter on our business at once, than go to any more dinners with corky-headed advocates; for really they did not agree with me, and were of a nature, by reason of the aloes and myrrh wherewith they were in a sense served, to make the plain fare of the manse seem wersh and unsavoury.

He agreed with me that they certainly had such a tendency, and likewise that we should not delay our search; but when I thought, afterwards, how a paid porter might have explorified as well as us, I was troubled in mind to think if he could be actuated by a wish to find Mr Roslin's cousin, or to see the ferlies which are in the dark and secret abysses of the lower orders. 'Deed, I need not disguise it, as it did seem sometimes to me, by what fell from him, that he was moved more by a wish to see how I would comport myself in the howffs of squalor, than to find either kith or kin of Mr Roslin's; for he often said that the innocence and peace of a country parish made it a garden of Eden, compared to this world of a metropolis. But, although I may not penetrate into the mysteries of his thoughts, they are nevertheless patent to One who will judge of them aright; not that I think it could be a real deadly sin to dive with inquisitive eyes into the subterranean regions of Edinburgh, which the wynds and closes are, and yon dreadful darksome stairs, the broken windows whereof are mended in a way, with old hats and the cast cla'es of beggary.

Having wrought Mr Ettles into a Christian frame, to go in search of Mr Roslin's cousin, that might be discovered needful of a legacy, somewhere adjacent to the Parliament House, we fixed on the morn's morning after, to set out together; but, although at first he seemed very instantaneous to go, yet I could discern in the end a growing reluctance, as if he jaloused no cousin was there to be found; and I said to him that, should it so be, we would nevertheless see those things which are not shewn to kings and the princes of the earth, and which give a value to the mercies that the greatest possess; an exhortation which incited him to come with me. In his compliance, however, I had my own think; for he it was that first clockit the project, and why he came afterwards to fall into the dubieties about it, was a wonder, needing interpretation. Altogether, though riper intimacy made me notice many things in Mr Ettles to knit him closer and closer to my regards, there began to kithe about him something which I did not well understand; and now and then I could see, or thought I saw, a predominance of superiority, as if I stood before him as in the presence of one that had a discerning spirit, and was loath to give it head-rope. This was the more mystical, as I was surely fully his equal; being a minister of the gospel, placed in a parish with a sufficiency of stipend; and he, to say the least of it, only a damaged mercantile, with the prospect of a legacy from an unco. But I am transgressing on what should not yet be told, until I have given a particular account of what befell us in the unclean receptacles and odoriferous nooks of Edinburgh.

Chapter XXI

Alas, when I think on what we saw in yon caverns of sorrow, never more can I doubt, even in the finest day, that this is not a world of sin and misery.

Our first pilgrimage was along Princes Street, and across the North Bridge; and, at the corner where it enters the High Street we halted, looking about us to discover where we should begin. Then Mr Ettles suggested that we ought to go up to the Castle Hill, and come down, close by close, so as to leave not one without an investigation, till we had reached the sanctified kennel of the Abbey. I thought so too; for, since we were on a search of discovery, we could not be too particular. Accordingly, we went towards the king's stronghold, and I have now to relate our adventures and observes.

The first place we went into was of a declivity nature, in a land of houses, with an outside stair, near the Castle Hill. It was not remarkable, and the inhabitants, chiefly of the female gender in a state of widowhood, were elderly and composed persons, all looking from their doors and windows at the sight of a minister, and a gentleman likewise in black, asking for one Archibald Junor; for it was a cousin by the mother's side that we were in quest of; which causes me to make mention that I think folk are naturally more addicted to their mother's friends than their father's; which is mystical, for, by rights of nature, fathers are nearer than mothers. No doubt, however, this is one of the blemishes to which the children of Adam became liable by the fall.

In that close, we could hear nothing, and we came away to the next; remarking that closes on the skirts of towns are more cleanly than those sinks of iniquity that are in the throng places, types of the sinfulness that is foul at the heart of man.

Then we entered another, a long entry leading to a place that led downwards; and I doubt if there innocence was thriving, for it was very dirty, and the ragged callans and bardy lassies were not overly civilized, nor their parents, I suspect, of the elect. There, too, our pains were abortive; only a fat woman, more indeed, for manners, like a trumpeter of dragoons than the wife of a douce man, gave me a slap on the shoulder, and nicheringly inquired if I wanted to spy the nakedness of the land; at the which Mr Ettles looked at her pawkily.

We then soberly daunered unto a third refuge of the destitute. Like its predecessor, but something more, it abounded in slovenly-dressed women, who might be single; some of them, I thought, might have had other tow to spin than to be standing with the keys of their garret-rooms in their hands, hearing and telling new things. When I saw these Edinburgh calamities, I thought of the Athenians.

But this close was not the wilderness of Marah; for, as we were coming away genty, a donsy creature said, with something like Christianity in her voice—

" Maybe ye're seeking for the poor man that's bed-fast aboon. I'll shew you his lodging; for he cannot be out of the need of an awmous."

We followed her, and she led us up a dark timber stair, and shewed us into a chamber that was no better than a wastage. There, on the floor, on a pickle straw, beneath the residue of an old carpet, lay a lamiter man, wearying, as he said, for death.

My heart filled full at the sight; and Mr Ettles gave the Mary Magdalene who guided us up, something out of his waistcoat pocket, saying to me, " The precious stone is bright on the dunghill."

" What are ye, honest man? " quo' I to the invalid; which caused him to look at me with a glittering eye of one in a sore fever; and drawing the bit rag over his head, as if to eschew our sight, he responded, with a sad sullenness—

" A man."

" So I see," was my compassionate answer; " but tell us what ye were? "

" A beggar, as long as I could; now illness has made me bankrupt—a bankrupt beggar—for I cannot stir from the pallet of starvation."

His words bespoke breeding; and I turned, in a very tender-hearted mood to Mr Ettles, and inquired what he thought: to which he replied—" He must be the

Archibald Junor we are in search of; " and looked at me with a sorrowful countenance; whereupon, the true nature of our errand to those uncomely places came, like the element of light into the darkness, on my simple ignorance; and I said, " No possible! "

The damsel was still standing by; and while we were thus speaking, she bended down and churmed something into the lug of the dying man. What he said to her we did not hear; but, as she raised herself, he drew his hap closer over him.

" For godsake, gentlemen," then said she, " first gie him help, and then talk."

I trow Mr Ettles did not need another instigation; he cried to her to run for a doctor, and to fetch cordials, giving her wherewithal to buy what was wanted. I must, however, reserve what ensued for another chapter.

Chapter XXII

The pitiful damsel vanished outright, as if the very rowels of the spur of charity were up to their heads in the side of her heart; and we were left with the man, that, till we came, had been helpless, not knowing what to say or do, but afflicted with a palsy of consternation.

When we had stood some time, looking down at him on his straw on the floor, he pulled the bit dirty carpet off his face, and casting up towards us the pale eyes of a passer from the world, requested me to give him a drink of water, which I saw in a porringer on the floor. In the room was neither seat nor table; but, to be sure, I was not long of handing and helping him to what he asked.

He drank as one that was very dry; but before I took the porringer from his lips, there was a visible alteration in his countenance, and in his throat a sound.

Me and Mr Ettles were both awed and silent; for the king of terrors was then plainly busy making a conquest. Presently, after drawing a long sigh, the summoned departed, and his mortal remains lay before us, stiffening and still—a lean morsel for the insatiable grave.

There was a fearful haste, as it were, in this come to pass, that took away any small presence of mind I possessed; and Mr Ettles cried, "Good God!"

Then we heard a foot coming up the dark timber stair, and angrily muttering, "Damnation!" the which word, to hear at that time, struck me as a blasphemy or a doom. But I had not long to ruminate; for in came the doctor that the lass had sent, who, in coming up the stair, had met with a difficulty.

He was a young man, smelling of lavender water; and he looked about the room, when he entered, as if the air of it was unsavoury. Then he gave a glance at the mort, and said, "The man is dead—it was of no use to send for me."

Hearing him so hale-hearted, and seeing the dejection of Mr Ettles, I felt my corruption rise; but, before I could put a few words of smeddum together, he walked away, and left us standing in postures of grief.

Not long after, the ministering maiden returned, with

a black choppin bottle, without a cork, in her hand; and falling on her knees beside the corpse, she lifted the porringer, which I had been using, and poured into it from the bottle as much as a glass of whisky, which she held to the lips of that which had been man.

" It's too late, my leddy," said I—" he's done now with the bitters and the sweets of this life."

Whereupon she rose from her kneeling; and Mr Ettles, bidding her get what was necessary done, and he would pay for it, took me by the arm, and led me, without speaking, down into the Lawnmarket, where he said—

" This is more than I had bargained for; but the scene could not be uncommon, for many mendicants are in the world, and some of them must daily die."

He then fell into a reverie, and as we walked back to the inns, was evidently, as might be expected, inwardly troubled. As for me, I was filled with thankfulness and resignation for my lot having been cast in a lown manse, afar from the spectacles wherewith a sinful world abounds.

In the course of the afternoon, he thawed into more composity, and said, sedately, that he feared I had much reason to be displeased with him; telling me that, by the friendship of Mr Roslin, finding himself much farther aboon the world than he ever expected to be, and the whole scheme of his being again changed,he had thought he might, by my means, gain an insight that would, at least to himself, be edifying; for, said he—

" Though I have met with many possessed of great

knowledge of the world—of that knowledge by which men know how they may swindle with respectability—I never saw a man like you, who so unconsciously read the heart, and yet practised so little or had so little of that suspicion which is the basis of the world's craft. But what we have seen to-day has changed my purpose; I will pay you at once the legacy, and lead you no more to such sights of distress; for, verily, it cannot be wise to look at the sad side of things."

There was something in this that caused me to ponder; but still I could not away with what we had witnessed, and I thought the legacy a heavy handful, for exposing me to such trials as we had come through that day, especially the upshot.

Chapter XXIII

Oh, humanity! frail, ever-erring, inconsistent thing! But first let me tell what happened; for maybe the bare recital of it will, of itself, be a sufficient morality.

In the evening, after drinking our tea, being very dolorous and down-hearted about the worldly condition of sinful man, and communing of the awful sight me and Mr Ettles had seen in the forenoon, we were sitting in the inns—no singing, I am sure, the spring of " O'er the bogie"—when the waiter lad came in, with a jokefellow-like smirk, and said to me, that two ladies were in the street, wishing a word o' me; and, turning round, he added, to Mr Ettles, in a hauflin whisper, but loud enough for me to hear, that he durst not bring them into the house.

Mr Ettles *instanter* rose and left his seat and the room, leaving me all alone with the waiter, who did not seem to be too douce. But I inquired of him wherefore the leddies that wanted me durst not come into the house, saying—" For no doubt, if they wanted a word in secret, it would be more decent in-doors than out in the thoroughfare."

" So it would," replied he, with a havrel chuckle; adding that, as I was a minister, maybe, if I spoke to the master, he would let me bring them in.

Mr Ettles having gone away, I then sent the lad to ask the landlord; jalousing that his house, for an inns, being a sober sojourn, and the leddies maybe a wee quiscoskos in character, might be the reason of the prohibition. I told him also what a gast we had met with, that he might inform the master it was to a moral certainty the leddies had come about the dead man.

The news were as a miracle wrought upon the publican and sinner; for the landlord not only consented to let the leddies come in to me, but the poor lad, with his libertine nicher, was converted into as awful a thing as an elder at the brod, in the eyes of a wean that lays its first bawbee in the plate; which, by the by, in our kirk does not often happen, for the parish is in the country, and we only make a collection at the Occasion. But to proceed.

As I was going to say, the waiter had not been long on his errand, till back he came, shewing in the two scuffed women.

One of them was she that had played the part of Mary Magdalene, with the bottle and the porringer, as I have rehearsed; the other demosle—for I can call her nothing else—seemed to be a new recruit to the clan-jamphry.

They had both glistening eyes and bleezy faces. I had my doubts—gude forgie me if I blaspheme her good name!—that the strange woman was the waur of liquor; for, when she sat down on a chair, she swayed hither and yon, and was so coggly that I had my fears of a catastrophe on the floor.

When they had been some time sederunt, the one I had foregathered with in the house of mourning said that she had been advised, by her friend, Miss Gills, there, to let me know that all was sorted, and she was sure, to my liking; and to invite me up at the guessing time of the gloaming, to see that she did not dankle the truth.

"We have gotten a coffin from the session," said she, "and Mrs Farls has spoken for the shortbread to Mr Daigh, the baxter; only, as the outlay has been great, we'll need a replenishment to buy the wine, which, Miss Gills thinks, considering how you were present at the dead-ill, cannot, in Christianity, be dispensed with; for you know the ministers of the city will, no doubt, be invited by you to partake of the burial. As for the ministers, however, I'm not for them; for they are prideful creatures; and, if they gaed to beggars' late-wakes, they might not have time to make sermons for the gentlefolks."

I cannot but say that I was dumbfoundered so to hear her speak, and would have been at a loss what to say, had not Miss Gills, at that very moment, given a great hiccup, and no being in an elbow chair, coupit off with a circumbendibus, which caused me—no used to pull bells—to give a great alarm, and brought in the landlord, Mr Ettles, and the waiter, who all had surely been just at the door when the fracas happened.

Chapter XXIV

It is not to be told what ensued from Miss Gills' accident; but the upshot was that the poor donsy leddies were sent away with a flea in their lug. I could not, however, approve of the way the waiter conducted himself towards them; for he was desperate venomous, and ranted at them as if they had been tinselers, and he himself one of a moral principle. As for Mr Ettles, he said nothing, but looked pitiful, and the landlord sympathised with what I suffered; for, oh, yon was a humbling sight! far waur to the eye of the spirit than the starvation of the beggar man, in which the hand of a just Lord was visibly laid on for sins and iniquities he had seen; but with the poor outcasts, there was only a kithing of the original guilt of our fallen nature. So, although I might have been righteously very angry at them, I was sorrowful unto a sickness of the heart, and soon after retired to my room, to have an investigation of my own unworthiness.

At supper-time, when I came down stairs, I found Mr Ettles sitting by himself in a pondering posture; and he said—

"It is too late now for me to experiment with characters. The friendship of Mr Roslin renewed for a time, as it were, my youth, and I fancied that I might revive old tastes and predilections; but years and vicissitudes have wrought a change, of which till this day I was insensible."

He then looked at me with a concerned eye, and, after a space, subjoined—

"I am sure you will pardon me:—I but thought the poor entitled to a portion of the legacy left me, and had recourse to the stratagem which I practised with you to see their dwellings. There was no such person as that Junor whom we went in quest of; and I ask your pardon for having made you see sights that must have scalded with anguish your heart. But the last remaining dream of youth is now over; and the remainder of a life that has not been all sunshine, shall be spent in the usages of other men."

Upon reflection, I was not content to think he had invited me to visit yon abominable corners of Edinburgh, because maybe he thought I could afford it out of the legacy which he had wised in a sense to me; but there was about him, at that time, a something which fell heavy upon me, even like sadness; for really Mr Ettles had from the first seemed a man by ordinar: though making his bread by merchandising, he was, as I would say, created and born to be a philosopher. I never saw his marrow, nor one who had his will in such subjection to his own management. Not, however, to summer and winter more about him, I have only to mention that, next day, he paid me to the utmost farthing my bequest, and while I returned to the manse, made the best of his way to London.

Thus concluded that sore thing which occasioned me to indite this writing; and Becky, my sister, had no cause to be ill-pleased at the upshot, though sometimes a woman no overly content with the dispensations of Providence. Mr Ettles bought and sent to her by me a most grand silver tea-pot; having heard her once say that a manse with such a utensil was a match for a Highland gentleman's tappy-tourock dwelling.

Tait's Edinburgh Magazine,
November 1835–January 1836.

III

MY LANDLADY AND HER LODGERS

JOHN GALT, *from a drawing by* DANIEL MACLISE.

MY LANDLADY AND HER LODGERS

CHAPTER I

THE first time I had occasion to visit London was in the spring of 1804. I arrived in the York mail early on a fine May morning.

My journey had been uncomfortable. I had left home for the first time, I was about to engage in the warfare of business, and, partly arising from fatigue, and partly from the crisis of my circumstances, there was an altogetherness of dissatisfaction with myself, " the world, and my hostel," the inn where I alighted.

Being weary, sleepy, and annoyed when I got my luggage disembarked from the coach, I was shown, by request, to a bedchamber. It opened from one of the upper galleries of the quadrangle of the inn, and seemed to me, on entering, a strange and unsafe commonage, compared with the quiet propriety of my father's house. The floor was damp—the piece of carpet round the bed ragged—the curtains mean—and the aspect of the room and furniture gave no assurance of repose; nevertheless, I slept soundly, to which three days' hard journey specially invited.

It was eleven o'clock before I awoke, but although refreshed, the noise in the yard, and the cataract-like sound in the streets, were yet not calculated to alleviate the feelings of distaste with which I had been affected on my arrival.

Having dressed myself, I descended to breakfast in the coffee-room. Here every thing was still more disagreeable. The floor was coarsely sprinkled with sand, which grated beneath my tread—breakfast was slovenly served—the eggs were of course bad—and, by way of consolation, after I had tapped the end of the second batch, the waiter assured me that all bad eggs came from Scotland. Instead of the rural cream to which I had been accustomed, the milk was pale and lachrymal.

Before leaving home, I had been advised by some of my friends who had recently visited the metropolis, to take up my abode in one or other of certain genteelly frequented coffee-houses; but the manner in which I felt affected that morning, made me shudder at the idea of attempting to figure so openly on the stage of public life.

Having finished my breakfast, I went in search of a sober street for apartments, in which, for eight or ten days before delivering my letters of introduction, I might have time to determine where my permanent domicile could be best established. Accordingly, I walked into Newgate Street. The crowd passing from the east and west induced me to pause. I thought that on the one side a popular preacher had surely but just dismissed his congregation, and on the other, that either a riot or a patriotic election had been dissolved.

I stepped into a shop until the streams should subside, but after waiting, and remarking upon the subject to the shopman, I was civilly informed, that the commingling tides were daily customary, and would continue to flow until the business and diurnal vocations of men were ended by night.

This, the first fact which impressed me with a sensible notion of the magnitude of London, smote my heart, and admonished me of the helpless, the defenceless, and the powerless condition of a stranger in that great vortex of interests and passions.

I left the shop elbowing my way to the westward, and though many bills on windows invited me to look at lodgings, I yet passed down Skinner Street, then just becoming habitable, up Holborn-Hill into Hatton-Garden, and the Lord knows by what other turnings and windings, as it then seemed to me, until I reached Mortimer Street, Cavendish Square.

It has often struck me since as curious, that I should have traversed so wide an extent of the dormitory of London, without discovering a haven. But when I recall to mind the circumstances which led me to pass from house to house, and from street to street, I can scarcely suppress a smile.

In Hatton-Garden, I was deterred from applying at one house, because the door was newly painted, and the bill in the window, " Apartments to let," was wafered to the pane with three wafers of divers colours, and a slake of starch. It was impossible that neatness could be within, or aught of the order and prepared decorum so essential to comfort and tranquillity.

In Theobald's Road I saw in a window a lodging bill seemingly of beautiful penmanship. It was inscribed on the glass, in elegant characters, simple, tasteful, and alluring. I entered—I enquired—I inhaled an odour, and returned hastily into the street, exclaiming, How deceitful are appearances! The inscription on the glass of the window was permanent; it was the *chef d'œuvre* of the apprentice, an embryo genius.

I have another memorable reminiscence of that morning's perambulation. In Charlotte Street, Fitzroy Square, possibly in London or Howland Streets, but certainly in one of the three, I saw the ordinary placard. I knocked at the door, and was answerd by a Cinderella. I requested to look at the apartments; she shewed me into the parlour. Soon after came a matron with a masque of rouge, a handsome shawl, and a dirty morning gown. She assured me that her house was of the most respectable order, but to the veracity of which assurance, the paint on her cheek gave a blushing denial. I forget in what way I contrived to bid her good-morning, without ascertaining the state of any of her apartments.

Columbus-like, steering still my course westward, I at last came to a neat house in Mortimer Street, next door to an upholsterer. In its appearance were symptoms of cleanliness and compactness. A vine spread up between the two parlour windows—the sashes were painted for the season—the door, too, had put on a new verdure. It was a house, indeed, which, for its size, indicated pretensions to more consideration than such a size would have seemed to justify. It was respectable rather than genteel, and yet it had about it an air of gentility; for, instead of gaudy-painted calico, suggesting atrocious imagery of cathedrals, or of abbeys, the lower part of the parlour windows was screened with Venetian blinds. The knocker of the door was of a ponderosity that bespoke an expectation of guests not ashamed to demand entrance; and the bill in the window was written evidently by a female hand not practised in romantic literature.

I knocked at the door, and after a reasonable time it was opened by a loose-haired damsel of the north, who enquired my will and pleasure; I explained to her the quest upon which I had come, and, without reply, she shewed me into a small back parlour, and retired. Soon after Mrs Winsom, her mistress, came to me.

Mrs Winsom was, properly speaking, rather beyond what might be called a matronly age. She was declined into the vale of years, and the style of her dress, without being old or obsolete, evinced that she herself possessed a distinct knowledge of her age. She appeared to be just in her right station, and yet her look betokened a degree of intelligence greater than her station required. As I have remarked, she was not decidedly aged, but her manner, her dress, her look and deportment, indicated that she classed herself among the old.

A single glance at her person and appearance, persuaded me that in her house I should find a home; and accordingly, without reflecting on the silliness of the observation, I told her that I was come to take her lodgings.

"In which of the floors," said she, calmly, with a Scottish accent, but yet not exactly in the tone of a Scottish landlady.

I was disconcerted by her question, and still more by her penetrating look. However, I mustered self-possession to reply,

"I have been in search all the morning of comfortable apartments, and I have seen no house I like so well as yours."

She made no answer for some time, but looked at me curiously, and then she asked, "What part of my house do you think you could afford to take?"

This discomposed me still more, and I knew not wherefore. It seemed as if the question were impertinent, and yet there was an accent of kindness which changed the effect entirely, especially as she immediately subjoined, "I discern, young gentleman, ye're a stranger in London, and a novice in a certain sense to its delusions. But my parlour floor's a guinea a-week—my first floor two guineas—my second floor is a five-and-twenty shilling—and for the attics, I keep them for mysell and Babby, that we may not be brought into tribulation with the lower order of lodgers, the like o' them that dwell in garret-rooms. As for the parlour floor, that is in occupation by a most discreet gentleman that has a concern in the Parliament frae Embro'—and the first floor—the drawing room, which is very handsomely furnished, is bespoken for a family expected in town. But the second floor, which is the most comfortable of the three, and has a chamber bell which rings in Babby's room, just behind my bed-head, is at your convenience."

Our negotiation was soon concluded, and it was agreed that I should bring my luggage in the evening, and that Mrs Winsom should have the room prepared for my reception, and a cake of Windsor soap, as suggested by herself, on the wash-hand stand, as I had not provided myself with such an indispensable.

We had some further conversation on various topics, but it was chiefly on her side. She appeared to search as it were the objects of my visit to London. This inquest put me, I think, inordinately on my guard, and I replied to her dryly, and, like all young Scotchmen, drew myself up into the full stature of all the consequence I could assume.

" I hope," said she, as I was leaving the house to return to the coach inn, " I hope you have not provided yourself in coming to London, like many other thoughtless young men, with new clothes? "

I assured her I had not. " Then," replied she, " you are, no doubt, recommended to a fashionable tailor—what's his name? "

I gave her at once that of my ever since and present indulgent creditor, Mr Stitches. " I thank you," said

Mrs Winsom, " for it's a rule with me to gang for a character rather to a young gentleman's tailor, than to his high friends and fine connexions."

CHAPTER II

After leaving Mrs Winsom's house, I felt as if I had established a home, and, although I wandered in my way back to the coach-inn, it was without anxiety. I knew, when tired, I had only to go into the first coffee-house and order a coach. Such is the effect of having a local habitation. I have, however, discovered, that without the precaution of going into a coffee-house, a coach may be obtained by hailing in the street.

When I had thus, aimless and purposeless, spent three or four hours in a desultory transit from street to street, I found myself at last, about dinner-time, near Charing-cross. I knew not then the place, but I recollect well that it was there I first was sensible of the total insignificance of an individual in London. In passing from Pall-Mall down to Whitehall, I met a gentleman of a superior appearance, walking with a little red-nosed personage. It was the Prince of Wales and Colonel Macmahon. No one seemed to notice His Royal Highness except a young man of a mechanical appearance, with a paper cap. He paused and pointed out the Prince to another, seemingly a country lad, and I was amused at the astonishment with which the latter looked back on a phenomenon so ordinary and so familiar as His Royal Highness appeared to be.

I am not sure that any single incident ever gave me so much instruction as this one. It plucked from me the feathers of vanity, and taught me that in London a man was to be valued only for himself. I was disturbed by the discovery, for I had brought with me a whole mail of recommendatory letters—many of them were to the wise and high, the rich and renowned. I paused, and for a moment hesitated. I then said to myself, What claim have I upon the patronage of those?—none. I will put my letters into the fire, and see what fortune has prepared for me, by luck or endeavour, in the circumstances into which I may be cast.

The savoury steam of the Spring-garden coffee-house, at this juncture, invitingly addressed my olfactory nerves. I looked at the low, mean, kitchen-like apertures from which the fume was ascending. I conjectured, by the dull, numerous windows of the coffee-house above, that appetite might be appeased there, so I went in and ordered dinner.

While it was preparing, I examined the features of the apartment. They did not seem much superior to the triste and gritty appliances of the coach-inn. They were neater certainly, and, when the dinner was served, there was an unnecessary show of plate. It was manifest that I was in a different atmosphere from that of the neighbourhood of Newgate-street. The other guests in the coffee-room were spruce and trim, talked loud, and spoke curiously, hereby shewing themselves a different race indeed from the unshaven and coach-rid travellers of the Bull and Mouth.

My first day's visit to London was, as may well be supposed, unsatisfactory. My accustomed habits were shaken. I was not taught that they had been wrong, but I was convinced that the world had no respect for individual feelings. I would have smiled at my own foolishness in attaching importance to the looks and bills of lodging-houses, but, somehow, it was impossible to divest myself of the persuasion, that in those things there were at once admonition and information. I was come into a sphere over the movements of which I could have manifestly no control, and yet my thoughts occasionally reverted to the peculiarities and motherly manners of Mrs Winsom, and in driving in the hackney-coach which took me to the inn in the evening to bring my luggage from thence to her house, I resolved, old woman as she was, to win from her some of the results of her experience; for, in the course of our interview she had impressed me with a high idea of her discernment and prudence.

When I reached Mortimer Street, Mrs Winsom had gone out, but her handmaid, Babby, was in expectation of my arrival. The apartments were prepared, candles set, and the appearance of my sitting-room had an air of homeliness and comfort, in pleasant contrast to that strange combination of solitude and bustle which is at once the charm and annoyance of a coffee-house in London.

Babby made some thriftless excuse for the absence of her mistress, which perhaps would have passed unnoticed had she not said,

"Puir body, it's a pity she's sic a compassionate woman, for her hainings just gang like chaff before the wind amang them that hae been her lodgers, and hae but sma' claim or cause for a godsend frae her. Howsomever, it's no an ill faut that comes o' kindness, and I maun thole wi' her indiscretions, though she wiled me frae my parentage in the shire of Ayr, wi' the vision o' an inheritance—holding out to me, to say in the words o' the Presbytery, that, being her cousin, I was to be helper and successor. But gude kens where the succession will come frae if all's gien awa' and naething be retained for an honesty."

I did not very well understand this commentary, but I concluded that Mrs Winsom was a good, kind-hearted body, and that something in the history of a previous lodger had drawn upon her charity.

This surmise, with the favourable impression of her appearance, led me to think, when I retired for the night, that I had fallen into the chances of some adventure.

In the morning I found Babby busy in my sitting-room, preparing breakfast.

"Will you give my compliments to your mistress," said I, "and say I would be glad of her company to breakfast?"

"Na," replied Babby, "I would think shame to do the like o' that, for what would my mistress think o' a young gentleman inveeting her to his forlorn breakfast? She has ne'er done the like o' that."

But, notwithstanding Babby's protest, I again requested her to invite Mrs Winsom. Some circumstance, however, unexplained at the time, prevented my invitation from being accepted, but in the evening, after having dined again in a coffee-house, when I returned home, I found candles and the tea equipage set on my table, with two cups on the tray. Babby lighted the candles, and soon after her mistress came into the room.

"It would," said she, "have put me to an inconvenience to have troubled you with my society at breakfast, though it was at your own request; but I thought you might have a leisureliness at tea-time, for I jalouse you're of an inquisitive nature, and you have been thinking I could tell you something of the town. Now, sir, for that reason I have come of my own accord to drink my tea with you, though, on so scrimp an acquaintance, sic familiarity may no beget for me a great respect. But when we have few friends, we're fain of companions; and maybe I have an examplar and a lesson to teach worth an inexperienced young man's attention. You hear that I'm a woman of your own country, but you know not what has made me to fix the pole of my tent in a foreign land."

By this time Babby had arranged the material of the tea, and Mrs Winsom having, after blowing into the spout of the teapot, determined that all was right and proper, proceeded to sip and chat, until from less to more she gave me the following sketch of her life.

Chapter III

" My father," said Mrs Winsom, " was an Antiburgher minister, with a narrow stipend, and a small family of cleven children, whereof only five came to the years of discretion, and I was the youngest of them. He was a worthy good man, and held in great respect by the minister of the establishment, Doctor Drumlie, whose wife was a perfect lady, and took upon her my edication, which was the cause of its coming to pass that I grew into a superiority above the rest of my father's daughters.

" Being of a sedate and methodical turn, Mrs Drumlie thought when I was grown up, that I would make an excellent housekeeper till her brother the Laird of Kirkland, whose leddy was in a weakly way, and his house for that because in great need of redding. His servants were neglectful, and everything about him had fallen into a sort of decay and wastery. So, to make a long tale short, after writing letters and getting back answers, and talking a great deal of the good fortune that awaited me, I left my father's house, like Christian in "The Pilgrim's Progress," with a burden on my back. I trow it was not, like his, a burden of sin, but what the folk in Scotland call 'gude hamert-made claes.'

"The house of Kirkland was an auncient building, some thought it was the work of the Peghts, but the Laird himself, a man of edificial knowledge, was of a different conceit, and maintained it was of the time of the Reformation.

"The lady of the house of Kirkland being, as I have said, an ailing woman and of a frail condition, was sitting, when I was shewn into her, in an easy chair, on the lee side of the dining-room fire. I saw that she was prejinct and genteel, and that if she had been in a state to herd her householdry, there would have been nae need of the like of me.

"When she had judged of me by some questions, she bade me to sit down, and put me under a strict examine concerning what I knew; but I had been so well brought up by her sister-in-law, Mrs Drumlie, that she was pleased to commend me as just such a young woman as she had long wanted. Thus it came to pass, that I espoused my fortune as housekeeper in the house of Kirkland; and verily it was a great charge, for the Laird had his fykes and was ill to please, being a sort of an astronomer, greatly addicted to big auld-fashioned books. His book-room was just a confusion. I made a trial on an occasion one morning to set it in order, but Oh! the whirlwind of passion that he was in when he saw what I had been doing! so I was debarred from that time frae putting my foot within the door of that chamber. As for the Leddy's sickliness, it had nae doubt helped to make her silly, and not being able, by reason of rheumatics in her legs, to go about the house, the ordering of her own room and the room she sat in was her day's darg. But though she was a thought malcontent, I must do her the justice to bear testimony, that if she was fashed with trifles, she yet could reward merit and eydencie.

"My time, notwithstanding the Laird's fykes and the Leddy's fashes, would have bowled away pleasantly enough, but to get the upperhand of the neglectful servants was not an easy task. However, what by parting with one and ruling with moderation the rest, before a year was done, I had conquered the regency of the house, and it was spread far and wide that I had wrought a meeracle at Kirkland.

"My name being so spread, it was thought throughout the country side, that I would make a wonderful wife; and thus it came to pass in the course of nature, that Zachary Winsom, who was then butler at Guzzleton Castle, as Jenny sings in the sang, 'cam a-courting to me.'

"He had saved money, was held in great respect, and though rather too well stricken in years, he was yet a blythe and portly man, with a pleasant rosy look and powthered hair, and he had a jocose and taking way with him, so that, from less to more, after acquaintanceship had quickened into affection, we were married; and a vacancy being at the time in Guzzleton, by the death of the housekeeper, Mrs Pickles, I was translated into her capacity. But there was an unca difference between the household charge of my new situation, and the faculties o' my duty at Corncraiks. However, I gave satisfaction to the family, and when Sir Alexander died, which was in the third year of my servitude, he left a brave legacy to my husband, and leaving a legacy to him I was not forgotten, so we thought o' coming into Edinburgh, and taking up a house o' lodging for the genteeler order of Colleegeners. But after a short trial, we soon saw that it was a trade would never answer; the young gentlemen were often outstraplaes, which was a way of life and manner that did not accord with the orderliness of my habit and repute; and, moreover, they had no reverence for Mr Winsom, but made light o' his weel-bred manners, and jeered at some o' his wee conceities; for although he was a man o' a thousand, I'll no deny that he had his particularities. But they were innocent infirmities, and had won for him both civility and solid testimonies of favour from the gentlemen and friends of our late honoured master. We, therefore, after due deliberation, made a resolve that we would give up our house in Edinburgh, and before entering on a new sphere of life, would take a jaunt to see the world.

"Accordingly, in the summer, when the college broke up, and our lodgers had gone home to their fathers' houses, we packed up a trunk, and having gotten it on board a Berwick smack at the pier of Leith, we sailed for London, where, after a pleasing passage of four days, we were brought in good health, much the better of our voyage to this town, where Mr Winsom having a cousin in a most prosperous way, living in Bury Street, St James's, letting lodgings to government members of Parliament, and nabobs with the liver complaint from India, whereby he was making a power of money; and making a power of money, it so fell out that Mr Pickingwell (for that was the name of our cousin) invited us to stay with him and his wife, they having at the time a room unlet. Well, ye see, speaking with them of what we had come through with our lodgers, they gave us some insight how they managed with theirs; and when we had been with them the better part of a week, seeing shows and other fairlies, me and Mr Winsom had a secret consultation about settling ourselves in London, and setting up genteel dry lodgings like Mr Pickingwell's. This led to a confabulatory discourse between the men, while I sounded Mrs Pickingwell, who was just transported to hear of our project; a thing, when I considered we were to be rivals, was very liberal, indeed, on her part.

"When the ice had been thus broken, it was agreed among us, that until we had got some experience in the way of management, we should set up for a doucer kind of lodgers; and so it came to pass, that after looking about us for a house, we came by an accidence to hear of this one, and having bought the lease, Mr Winsom went to Scotland and brought our furniture, I staying in the meantime getting insight with Mrs Pickingwell. And it was just extraordinar to see what a profit they had on their weekly bills. But it was not ordained for me and Mr Winsom to fall into the way of such good fortune; for, although this house is worth twa of the house that Mr Pickingwell had, yet the folk that come here are for the most part of an economical nature, though I'll allow they're to the full as genteel, being in a certain sense men of stated incomes of their own, but no sae free as those wha hae the handling of public money, or the rooking of Hindoo Rajays. But for all that, if our gains were less, we led a quieter life, and for the first three years we lived in the land of Caanaun, till one evening Mr Winsom having the gout in his toe, felt it come into his stomach, whereby he was, before break of day, (though we had the best of doctors) removed into Abraham's bosom, and left me a disconsolate and forlorn widow, in my seven-and-thirtieth year. Maybe I might have retired, for I'll no misca' the blessing by denying that I had a competency sufficient to have maintained me with decorum among my friends in Scotland; but usage to the business, and the liking I had to see things in order, enticed me to remain where I was, and thus, from less to more, day by day, and year by year, I have come to the verge of age, seeing but small cause to repine at my portion in this world, when I compare the sober passage of my life with the haste and hurries that I hae witnessed in the fortunes of many of my lodgers."

The old lady having finished her narrative, I could not but applaud the tranquil respectability in which she had spent her days; and her concluding remark led me to say, that although her sphere had been narrow, it would yet seem that it had not been without interesting events. She acknowledged that this was the case, and added, that a lodging-house is "a wee kingdom, wi' different orders and degrees of inhabitants, all subject to many changes. Maybe had it been less so, I would have wearied and gone home to my friends; but whenever I had a hankering o' that sort, something was sure to befall my lodgers that led me to take a part in their concerns, and detained me here. No farther gone than the present spring, I had come to a resolve to dispose of my lease, and, for that purpose, I had the house newly done up and beautified; but before I could find a purchaser, a lady and a gentleman took the first floor; and they were not long with me till I found myself fastened to them by the enchantment of an unaccountable curiosity,—not that there was anything remarkable in their manners, or that I had any cause to suspect their conduct was wrong, but still there was a mystery about them; they were visited by nobody, and the lady was often, when alone, seemingly in deep distress. They remained with me about a month, and suddenly left the house. I could discover no cause to induce them to remove; but still their determination was so hastily adopted, that I could not but think some unexpected and unforseen event had wised them. In the course of a fortnight they came back, but the apartments were occupied, and I could not then receive them. Yesterday, a short time before you called, they came again, and, at the lady's request, I went to see her this morning in the lodgings where they now reside. I am still, however, as much in the dark as ever respecting them. It may be very true, as the gentlewoman says, that she prefers my house to that where they are at present accommodated; but that throws no light on the cause of their abrupt departure, nor on the distress which she so carefully conceals from her husband, if he be indeed her husband."

This incident, so casually mentioned, induced me to express a desire to hear something of those lodgers who had on other occasions attracted her particular attention, and she promised to gratify me when I had a leisure half hour to hear her; for the night was by this time too far advanced for her to enter upon any new topic.

Chapter IV

On the following evening I was engaged abroad, and did not return home till late. On entering the house, I perceived that some change had taken place, and Babby, in lighting me upstairs, told me by way of news, that the lady and gentleman who had taken the first floor had arrived, and that her mistress, being fatigued by the bustle of receiving them, had retired for the night.

There was nothing in this communication calculated to excite any degree of surprise; but Babby, after lighting my candles, instead of taking up her own and leaving the room, took a pin from her girdle, and trimming the wick, looked as if she had something important to tell me.

" I dinna think," said she, having replaced the pin, and lifted her candle, " I dinna think the folk we hae gotten will bide lang, and that we'll soon hae back the sweet afflicted young creature that sae often made my mistress sorrowful; I'm sure though I maun allow that she is a sweet young creature, that she's but a daffodil after all; and if I was in Mrs Winsom's place, I would ken what sort of commodity she is before I would take her a second time into my house. But my mistress may do as she pleases, only she'll no lang please me. I wasna to be brought from my father's house with the hope of gathering gold in gowpens here, and the prospect of a fat legacy hereafter, to see the property wasted awa' and thrown to the dogs and donaguids. Do ye ken, sir, that she hasna ta'en plack or bawbee frae that Miss Mournful and her gudeman, if he be her gudeman, the whole tot of the time they stayed with us, and that was mair than a month? and then they gaed aff in the cloud o' night in a terrification as if they were fleeing frae a hue and cry. If she take them back, I'll let Mrs Winsom soon see the breadth of my back, so I will."

I was little disposed at that time to encourage the loquacity of Babby; but she had laid open a new trait in the character of my worthy landlady, and I repaired to my pillow ruminating on the strange mixture of qualities in characters.

Mrs Winsom was so evidently in the station for which she was designed, that it was impossible to conceive she could have filled any other better. All about her house partook of the neatness and good order of her own appearance—an impress of method and propriety was visible over all; and in the little history of her life she had alluded to no circumstances which might have led me to suspect her of a generosity so indiscreet and general as that of which her kinswoman and handmaid accused her. Finally I began to fancy that she was more interesting herself than any of the personages of whose history she intended to speak. Full of this notion I fell asleep, and when I awoke in the morning, and entered my sitting-room to ring for breakfast, I found her seated there with a book in her hand waiting for my appearance. It was Sunday morning, and the weather extremely wet. " You will be surprised to see me here, sir," said she, " but I am very anxious to speak to you. In such a wet day ye'll no can go out unless it clear up, and nobody will come to you while such an evendown pour continues, so we are not like to be molested."

I shall pass over the little preliminaries which constituted the overture to her conversation, and relate only the more interesting passages.

" I promised you," said she, " to give you some account of the most memorable of my lodgers, and last night a very wonderful thing has happened. The lady and gentleman for whom the first floor was engaged by a friend of theirs, have proved very old acquaintances; the gentleman being no other than the identical first lodger me and Mr Winsom had after taking up house here. He was then a bare young lad, come to push his fortune in London. The lady is the daughter of Squire Retford, who with her mother lived in our drawing-room floor. It was a thing amaist contrary to nature that that rich and proud old Squire's daughter should ever have been allowed to marry Mr Melbourn, and yet it came to pass, and not by any cause or providence arising out of their meeting in my house. But the most curious thing of all is, that now when they are old, they should come without premeditation here. Their object in being in London, is to seek for their only daughter, who has run away with a young gentleman whom they had ordained her to marry, but whom she mistook for his brother."

"The occurrence is remarkable enough," said I; "but what were the circumstances which induced you to think the marriage of Mr Melbourn and Miss Retford so improbable?"

"I will tell you—he was not a man likely to win favour with a fair lady, and he was poor. His father, like my own, had been a minister, but not of the Antiburgher persuasion. He was of the Church of England. It coudna, however, be said of him, honest man, that he was a fat wallower in the troughs of her abundance, being only a curate, whose lean cheeks and white haffits shewed that he held but a barren communion with her feast of fat things. Mr Melbourn was his only son, and as I learned afterwards, had come to London to get some preferment from Government, and while he was staying with us his father came twice to visit him. The first time the old gentleman came, his thin face was bright and gladdened. He had come to introduce his son to a great man. They went out together, rejoicing in their hopes, and counting the sheaves of the harvest before the seed was sown. When they returned it was with longer faces. The old gentleman himself told me that their reception had been vastly polite, but that the Earl had offered his son no place.

"'Did you ask him for any?' 'No,' said the good simple man. 'I was afraid he might think us intrusive if we did.' In short, it appeared that both father and son had come in the fond expectation of obtaining the friendship and favour of a statesman, without having any means of return. For as I told him, tho' nae doubt his son was possessed of a talent, yet he wasna like, from what I had seen, to put it out to usury. We then had some further discourse when the young Mr Melbourn was present, and I depicted to him how he should indite a pitiful letter to the Earl, and move him, if he could, to let him have a nook in a government office; for I had heard that this was a way to rise in the world. But the young man was proud and the old man was simple, so that between them nothing was at that time done, and the father went back to the country—no doubt with a heavy heart.

"Some short time afterwards, both Mr Winsom and me, for he was then living, began to discern, as we thought, a straitness in the mouth of the young gentleman's purse, and he lived with such a scrupulous penury that we often made naething on his weekly bills, which caused us to cogitate and repine, and to wish that he would leave the house; for being then but new in the business, we coudna discern how with such customers we ever could make the twa ends meet. About this time the worthy old man paid his second visit, and we both remarked, that though his valise was heavy, his countenance was downcast.

"After he had been some time with his son, I took occasion to seek for something in the room where they were sitting, and seeking for something there, I saw they were very disconsolate, and it was manifest that their hope was sickly and drooping to decay. In my fear, for there were more than five weekly bills unpaid, I told Mr Winsom that I jaloused our debt was in a bad way, and argued with him that he should speak for a settlement. But this he was loth and reluctant to do, for we had both a great regard for young Mr Melbourn, and the old man was so pale, and lowly, and meek in his demeanour, that we felt it would have been profane to have craved him for money, when we were in our hearts satisfied that he had none to give.

"In the course of the same evening the old gentleman came into our parlour with an ill-put-on pleasantry of manner, and said to Mr Winsom and me, that he had brought with him some old useless trinkum-trankums of silver plate, that he wished to dispose of, begging that we would tell him the name of some silversmith who would give him the best price. His nether lip quivered as he spoke, I saw the tear shoot into his eye, and I felt great remorse in my own breast for what I had been urging Mr Winsom to do. However, we put on the best face we could, and Mr Winsom, in the end, took him that same night to an honest dealer in silver in the Strand, and the plate was sold. Next morning our bill was paid, and in the afternoon the father and son left the house, and we never heard for many a day where they went, or what had become of the young gentleman.

"As I was telling you, Miss Retford, with her father and mother, were then lodging with us. She was a lively light-hearted Miss, and Melbourn, being a long lean defective-looking young man, was often a subject of her merriment between her and the Squire. One day, after I had overheard her so scornfully lightlying him, I took occasion to let her know that tho' he couldna help his looks, yet that he was a man of more worth than many who were praised for their comeliness, and I told her the story of the honest sacrifice that had been made to pay our bill. But then she was bold-hearted, and overly proud of her prospects and her pedigree. My words were as water spilt on the ground, and I couldna help telling her that I thought she was an ungracious damsel, that would rue the day she ever jeered the hidden grief of honest poverty. And so in the upshot of time this has surely come to pass, for she's the now, the very wedded wife of that same Mr Melbourn.

" But I am not yet done with his story. Some time late in the summer after, me and Mr Winsom went to take a stroll in the fields; and strolling in the fields, we came at last to a pleasant tea-garden, which was then situate behind the Foundling Hospital, and we went in, and Mr Winsom thought, seeing we were by ourselves, that we would have a half a pint of wine, the which was brought in a cruet with two glasses, and while we were taking our wine, talking of the pleasures of the season, and making ourselves agreeable, who should come into the gardens and sit down in the alcove next to ours, but Mr Melbourn and his father. They didna see us, and we didna like to speak to them. But we could hear what they said to one another, and you may well guess what I thought when I heard the young gentleman rehearsing the difficulties he had come through, after the money was all gone which had been received for the plate. But the dark does not endure for ever; while he was reduced to great need, the dawn began to appear. Providence brought him in the street to an old schoolfellow, whose father was a city merchant or alderman in a great way. Beset with his need, Melbourn told his old companion of his sad estate, and so, to make a long tale short, a place was found for him in a counting-house, and, by little and little, he grew to be the toppingest man of all the town.

" It's true that he was not so at the time he came into the tea-garden, for he then had been but a few days in his situation. Nevertheless, the guileless old man, his father, was so transported with the change in his prospects, that had he been Lord Mayor of London, he couldna have been so overcome with a fulness of thankfulness. Indeed, he spoke in such a manner, that he filled my eyes with tears, and softened the heart of Mr Winsom to such a degree, that he called for a whole bottle of wine, and invited the two gentlemen to partake of it.

" Out of this renewed acquaintance, a friendship began that has never since been broken. But I must now tell you how it was ordained that the saucy heart of that pert lassie Miss Retford came to be softened to the fulfilment of fate."

Chapter V

The conversation, the substance of which is related in the foregoing chapter, occupied the time during which we took breakfast; and when Mrs Winsom had made an end, I could not but compliment her as an observant woman.

" It's no for me," she replied, " to object to any kind of approbation; but if I had the power to observe, I have never had the authority to do, so that the things of which I may have to speak have passed before me, and passed away without hinderance, or let, or stay."

She then added, abruptly, " But the wisdom of commendation does not belong to me, so we'll leave off remarking, and I'll tell you how it came to pass. Proud

Squire Retford's daughter was brought under a humiliation, and taught, that though gold was good, worth was better.

"This Squire Retford, you see, was a man of great popularity and substance; his estate was so wide that I would go far wrong were I to undertake to talk of cubits and of furlongs concerning it; and then he was a man of an ancient family—he had a scutcheon in his coat-of-arms, and a family vault to hold his ancestors. From all I heard concerning him from his servants, there were few like him in England, whether it was for wealth, pride, or pedigree. So out of the contraries of the time, just when the French were beginning their stramash, he was set up to be made a Member of Parliament. Poor man! what he would have done in Parliament has been a perplexity to me, unless it had been to get an act for the country gentlemen, and other such-like squires, to hang poachers on the next tree!—But I'll no blaspheme.

"Well, being set up on the leet for Parliamenting, he drew, and others pulled; and, what with riding of horses and drawing of chariots, and horsemen horsing on their horses, he was made a member and a ruined man. Then came borrowing money—mortgages and heritable bonds—and after another season, his lady having departed this life, he came to London, and brought with him his daughter Miss;—Oh! but she was an altered young woman! They came back to our house, and though I did every thing to make them comfortable, the old gentleman yammered from morning to night, till his daughter grew as patient as an effigy, or a tomb in Westminster Abbey. Though I couldna say I ever had a right sort of regard, I began to pity her; and as she was often left by herself, I invited her to drink tea with me, my excellent husband, Mr Winsom, being by this time no more.

"Now ye see, Mrs Retford being dead and gone, and Miss being left, by her father's Parliamentary needcessities, in a certain sense disjaskit and forlorn, she was glad on the nights of great debates, or when there was a call of the House, as it was called, to spend her evenings with me. And young Mr Melbourn dropping in at these times, he made an acquaintance, and as he was now rising in the world, he was growing courageous,—so that, to make a lang tale short, he began to speak saft words and gentle tidings to Miss Retford; and she being an abstract creature, with few friends or acquaintances, on account of her father's ruin, began to incline her ear to such effect, that when the Parliament was over, she was fain to make a downset by marrying Mr Melbourn. Her father, however, was a contumacious old man, and couldna bide the thought of his daughter taking up with a merchantable fortune. I was, however, very sorry at the marriage on Mr Melbourn's account, because I could discern that she took him for a convenience. I'll no say that all was freewill and free-gratis love on his part, more than on hers. For when his father came to be at the wedding, there was more talk about good connexions, and ancient families, than was needed to have been said of a matrimony founded and built on a right affection. Howsever, married they were, and if it wasna slanderous, I would say poor Mr Melbourn soon began to see the value of his bargain.

" For some four or five months after the wedding I saw nothing of him; but the winter coming on, he suddenly, on a wet evening, dropped in and besought me to make him a cup of tea. I have told you he wasna a man of temptation in his appearance, for he was lean, and of a dislocated anatomy; but for all that, he had a kind and gentle look, and if his face bore no beauty, it kythed of great goodness. Twice, it may be three times, he came to see me, in that docile, though thoughtful and familiar way, and I thought, on more than one occasion, there was a something in his mind for the which he wanted sympathizing; but he declared nothing, and I could only guess, wondering how a man that all the world reputed so prosperous, should have any secret cause of discontent with his lot. But before the next summer he grew an altered man. I saw nothing of him, though I heard a great deal; he was wonderful in the newspapers, and an organ of wisdom at public meetings for the King and Constitution, and at charitable dinners for the benefit of posterity.

" In process of time, no doubt, we might have worn out of acquaintance, he having become a national ornament, while I remained the humble mistress of a lodging house here in Mortimer Street. But there was at the bottom of his heart a solid matter of sterling worth, and though there was no intercourse between us, he often sent to me lodgers who could well afford to pay, thereby testifying that he had a memorial of friendship in his heart. But not to dwell on his particular case, or to say more concerning the great bruit he made in the world, there chanced to befall, out of one of his recommendations, an accident that might have been the means of great trouble."

Chapter VI

"I would not advise you to be of opinion," resumed Mrs Winsom, "that my apartments were always habitable to every one that applied, even when, as in September or October, they were of a necessity empty, that we might get the beautification done properly before the beginning of the next season. I tell you this, sir, with a particularity, for one day, it was the 27th day of August, all my lodgers for the time having, like other birds of passage, flown away, there came to me, rather at an indiscreet hour in the morning, an elderly gentleman from Ibbitson's Hotel, telling me that he was a stranger in London, to whom my house had been recommended by his friend and correspondent, Mr Melbourn, and requesting me to take him for a week or two.

"He was a most genteel-loooking man for his years, but whether they were sixty or three-score and ten, would have been a kittle question to those who had no knowledge of the fact. I think he was between the two. It was plain to see he had come from a foreign land, his hair being no grey, but white, like a fringe of cotton on the selvages of his bald head. His eyes were quick, glancing and glimmering, lively and sharp—very much so indeed; his brow was fair, broad, and bright, with here and there a small red spot; it was, however, a brow that had not been much exposed to the temper of changeful weather; it was a genteel indoor brow, shewing a great and long trust in officiality; his cheeks were very red, but it was not a coarse, weather-beaten red, nor was it a bunckled crimson, like old gentlemen given to debauch; it had but little of the port wine about it; it was pink, pleasant, and popular, such as became a man that had long been at the head of good fellowship among the better order of doctors and lawyers, and other professional intellectuals.

" The appearance of Mr Flowerfield was really most inviting; he was to a certainty, at the first glance, a man that had been in consideration. His ruffles were of delightful French cambric, but the body of his shirt was of that Glasgow duplicity for linen commonly called calico, but which every sensible and frugal woman better knows by the name of steam-factory flimsy.

" I told him that I was not just then prepared to let my apartments; but he spoke extraordinarily kindly; by which I was moved to let him have my first floor at three guineas a-week; the common price was two guineas and a half; but he made a stipulation that I was to take no other lodger into the house but himself, and his blackamoor man Jugurtha, and that I was to make no alteration by white-washing, painting, or otherwise, while he staid.

" Considering the time of the year, and the effigy of wealth that was about the old gentleman, I thought this a godsend, that I should in thankfulness acknowledge, by accommodating him with every kind of civility. The same night his blackamoor man, Jugurtha, brought his trunk and baggage home; but Mr Flowerfield himself did not come till after breakfast next morning, being, as he said, loath to disturb such a well-regulated family as mine he was sure was, by the motherliness visible in the house.

" This was most polite of him; and I hope that every body who knows me, and with what credit to myself and comfort to my lodgers I have so long kept this house, will be in no astonishment that I should endeavour to render the situation of such a genteel man satisfactory.

" It came to pass in the course of a few days, that the morning being wet, keeping all Christian people within doors, he began to speak to me concerning his fortune and affairs.

" ' Well, Mrs Winsome,' said he, ' here am I, after three and forty years broiling in the sun of Jamaica, come home to enjoy myself among old friends, and the scenes of my youth,—and I should have the enjoyment, for I have endured many a cloud and storm since I left them. But I begin to be afraid that, although neither the world nor I have been standing still, we have not been going at the same rate, or rather that we have been moving in different directions. I had never been in this great town till the day before I called at your house, though I have seen much of the world, having traversed the Atlantic,—been a book-keeper on a sugar estate,—an overseer on another,—and the proprietor of a coffee penn, in the parish of Hanover, in Jamaica;—besides having been twice a member of the house of Assembly, and on jocose terms with his Excellency the Governor. In short, Mrs Winsom, this city of London is not what I thought it was. It's either a place for a young man of great upset, or for an old one of an ancient family. I doubt that we, of Jamaica, and the West Indies in general, are but halflin sort of folk here; and for the last two days I have just been a fish out of the water. Thanks to your kindness, and to the friendliness of old correspondents, I need not fear that I may not get every thing that's dainty and agreeable; but it's a very dull place to a man who has had authority over several gangs of niggers, and been of the same consequence in the island of Jamaica that I was.

"'With your leave, Mrs Winsom, as I am going to Scotland, to see old things and old friends, I would wish my trunks to remain with you till I come back; and really, though it may cost me something, I would be glad you would keep your rooms for me till I send you a countermand.'

"Whether it was something in the dull, drowsy, dribbling, drizzly day that had saddened my spirit, or that there was the melancholious melody of disappointment in the voice of Mr Flowerfield, I cannot tell; but what he said was not so worldly as might have been expected from a heretofore dealer and driver in the hard labour of slavery. There was in it the boom of a far-off spirit of an innocent humanity; and though he said nothing to cause the remembrance of my father's frugal hearth, and pious evening exercise, to come upon me, I thought of both as he spoke.

" 'London,' he continued, 'is no place for me; I am too old for its pleasures, and too ignorant of the way to reach them; but I hope, as I have long hoped, that in the sunny village of my young days I may find a pillow and a friend. But I'll not disguise, that a few days have taught me that even this is doubtful. However, I will go and see, and the worst that can happen, after all, is to go back to Jamaica.'

" After this conversation, we made a paction that I was to keep the house for him until he came back, and that the blackamoor, Jugurtha, should be put upon board wages. Poor unchristened creature! if ever I committed a sin in my life, it was in consenting to such a simplicity; for what was to be expected of a black boy from the slavery of Jamaica, in the corruptions of London, but a colonial rebellion?

" Not, however, to dwell on what was the upshot of leaving the misguided creature to himself, in the course of two days Mr Flowerfield went off in the mail-coach for the north, I saying to him at the eleventh hour, 'It's true that he should—had it only been for a bravery—have taken Jugurtha with him.'—'But no,' said he, 'I am going to visit simple folk and homely scenes; and it would be looked upon perhaps as a pretence, were I to be seen otherwise among them than as I have, in many a reverie, long desired to be.'

"By and by, in less than a month, Mr Flowerfield came back, an altered man. The pleasant ruby of his countenance was faded into a yellow hue—the sparkling of his little sharp blue eyes was become dim—and though his hair was similar to what it had been, there was about him a look of disease, and a cast of peevishness touched with sorrow. For all that, he was greatly rejoiced to see me, shaking my hands like an old friend, saying, 'I have come home to you again.'

"But he never let wot that he had spoken to me of what he had hoped for in his journey. I saw him, however, often sitting in a disconsolate posture. I fain would have enquired what was the matter with him, but there was no symptom of sickness to justify the inquisition. On the contrary, it was plain that the heart-ill was upon him, and that with all his fortune, his niggers, and the great man he had been with the Governor, were proofs to make him feel the nothingness of the course of his life.

"At long and last, having well noted his dejection, I one Sabbath evening spoke to him of the effectual consolations of the Rev. Mr Greatsound's preachings. 'But,' said he, 'it is not the thoughts of the world to come that molest me—it is for the world which is gone that I am so grieved. I went abroad in early life, like many of my countrymen, to make a fortune, with which I might return, and gladden the little theatre of my first pleasures and cares. Through all my endeavours and difficulties, this thought was the pillar of cloud by day, and the pillar of fire by night, that cheered me on in the wilderness, and my heart always continued young. But it is not by the sense of my unfitness for London that I have been taught the unsubstantial nature of the phantom by which I was allured. Those scenes where I expected to find the treasure which my perseverance struggled to earn with such constancy, and for so long a period, have proved more changed than all the world. Where I expected beauty, I shuddered to find decrepitude, and many of those vices which make poverty itself almost a vice. The things that I have worshipped in the secret orisons of my heart, were all changed. The eternal face of nature, though unaltered in features, was no longer the same in complexion to me; all had suffered by the withering touch of age, or by the inconstancy of fortune; where aught of stability in character and affection could be discovered, all its pristine worth was alloyed with some base, sordid, and crawling interest!'

"In this sort of forlorn despondency did that worthy man for some time croon, knowing not in a right sense wherefore he should be so despondent. He was purposeless, and growing, if I might use the word, not sleepy, but deathy. His will was at an end—he had no intents, motive, or cause of action—but, like a weary baby, he laid his head on his sofa, or on his hand, for many an hour, fretful that sleep would not come."

Chapter VII

"That same night after the conversation I have just told you of," said Mrs Winsom, "Jugurtha, the now corrupted creature, came home in the twilight ree with drink, his face shining like a carved mahogany head varnished, and his white eyes rolling audaciously. But as he was in the main a good-natured thing, he was more an object of derision than of anger.

"He had not well sat down at the kitchen fire, till he began to sing, in a very odd way, the song of 'Rule, Britannia—Britons never will be slaves;' and every now and then he rose and rampauged through the kitchen, giving a stamp with his foot that made the whole house dirl, crying out, 'Don't care d—n for Massa—me Massa now—Massa floggee me—me floggee now Massa—Rule, Britannia—Britons eber will be slave!'

"'Jugurtha,' said I, in a kind and composing manner, 'be advised by me, and sit down soberly, and tell us what all this outstrapolousness means.'

"'Missee,' replied he, 'me free—me no black man, nigger—me Briton, me heart of oak—me drub 'em—old Massa pay me shall wage for time me come to old England—

"Me gentleman of England,
Dat lib from home at seas."'

" 'Well, well, Jugurtha,' was my sedate observation, 'no doubt ye are a gentleman. It may be seen ye are, just by looking at ye; but what's to become of this Maroon war that we have heard so much about, and how bloodhounds were brought from Santamingo to hunt the runaway niggers? Surely ye're no turned a Maroon?'

" 'No, Missee—no, Missee—me fire out de clearing-house round de door, when 'em d—n Maroon would kill Massa.'

" At this moment Mr Flowerfield, who had heard the uproar, and something of what was going on, came down stairs, and cried, 'You black rascal!'

" The sound of his voice cowed Jugurtha, the intoxicated emancipator, causing him to retire slinking towards his seat at the fire-side, rebuked and subdued. But it was only for a short duration, for the drink was in his head; he became most dreadful; starting from his seat, looking awful with his white teeth, and crying, as it were with a roar, 'Me no black rascal—me free man —my soul buckra soul.'

" 'And who washed the Ethiopian?' said Mr Flowerfield, looking round the kitchen, as I thought, for some weapon to inflict law and justice for such contumacy. Jugurtha snapped his fingers at the old gentleman, who had, by this time, caught hold of the hearth-brush, and who, without saying a word, knocked him down in a most methodical manner. I thought he was murdered, and Babby thought he was dead; and so, to see such a black act as the slaying of a nigger in our house, caused us both at once to cry out in desperation, 'Murder and help—help!'

"It just then happened that the watchman, or the patrol, I'll not undertake to say which, was going his rounds, and passing our door at that critical conjuncture, and hearing our terrification of murder, knocked at the door. Babby and me, no having the presence of mind to answer, he sprung his rattle, and presently a mob gathered round the door, and broke it open like an egg-shell, so that, in the twinkling of an eye, an auld carle was amongst us, with a diver hat, a beggarly drab-coloured big coat, with an old Barcelona round his neck, a horn bouet and a club stick in one hand. He grippet Mr Flowerfield, with the other, by the throat. A siclike, but of a more juvenile nature, took hold of me—the uncircumcised Philistine! He was an Irishman—and begged my pardon in asking me to take a pleasant walk with him to the watch-house. Two others, of a like gruesome countenance, had by this time laid hands on our Babby, for she had gone demented, and was drumming with her heels, and cymballing with her knuckles, like mad. She thought Jugurtha was a murdered man, and was yelling in a fantasy, as if we were all already at the gallows-foot for the deed. Meanwhile Jugurtha, drunken ne'er-do-weel! was lying on the floor, and another of the watchmen took him by the cuff of the neck, and raising his head, and holding his lantern to his face, said, 'Poor fellow! are you dead?'—'No, but me d—n bad,' said Jugurtha, giving at the same time, an unseemly hiccup in the watchman's face.

"'Tossicated, by the holy poker!' cried the watchman; whereupon the outrageous hands that had been laid on me and Babby were removed, and the crowd that had gathered began to laugh.

"But that night's sport was no laughing to me, for while the riot was raging in the kitchen, the street door having been left open, a gang of thieves and pocket-pickers got into the parlour, and carried off every commodity of value that was on the sideboard and mantel-piece. Among other things, I was ravished of three tea-spoons, a beautiful new plated bedroom candlestick, and a most valuable conch-shell which Mr Flowerfield had given me, a curiosity from Savannah-la-Mar.

"But all this was nothing to the after come-to-pass. The watchmen, ye see, saw that me and Babby and Mr Flowerfield were in a state of perfect sobriety; and that being the case, they lifted up Jugurtha, and carried him off to the watch-house. Oh, but Mr Flowerfield was in a true and earnest passion when the house was calm. He made a vow that he would spend a thousand doubloons to make an example, for the benefit of the other slaves, and the protection of the planters and overseers.

"To be sure, it was most natural he should think of punishing such an insurrection, especially of a nigger who had been born on his own penn of Coffeehill, and who was the natural son of the gentleman from whom he had purchased the property,—' than whom,' said Mr Flowerfield, ' was never a more humane man, or one who had clearer ideas on the danger of altering the condition of the slaves.'

" When the house was restored to its propriety, and Mr Flowerfield had finished his accustomed tosy, we all went to bed. I did not sleep well, and Babby was in a jeopardy till break of day with the nightmare. As for the old gentleman, he was like the last man, and declared that the ruin of England was evident, and that all we held here was in a bad way.—Truly he had cause to say so; for before he had well finished his breakfast next morning, in came a lawyer's claw, claiming forthwith payment of wages, at a most extortionate rate, in the name of Jugurtha, from the day of the ' black rascal's ' arrival in England.

" Mr Flowerfield of course broke out into a hurricane at this, and shook the man by the lapel of his coat, for such an insult and imposition. Notwithstanding, the man calmly expounded that he had not come to take him up, but only to make a demand. This dumbfoundered Mr Flowerfield, who, being naturally very courteous, calmed, and considering that the first loss was often the least loss, he referred the demand to his friend Mr Melbourn, in the city, giving, at the same time, a genteel solatium to the man for what had happened.

" Scarcely had that man quitted the house, when, lo and behold, an officer came with a warrant to take Mr Flowerfield to the police-office, for having 'saulted and battered the ne'er-do-weel Jugurtha, and both me and Babby were obligated to be of the party to bear witness. There, after a deal of argol-bargolling to no manner of purpose, Mr Flowerfield was found guilty to stand trial, and put to the extortionate necessity of sending for two of his respectable correspondents to give bail for him.

"Never did I see a man so distressed in mind as the good old gentleman was at this legal injustice. 'The ruin of England,' said he, 'is too manifest. No nation can long stand where niggers are so encouraged to insult their masters. But the sooner I get out of it, and back to Coffeehill penn, the better.'

"Accordingly, that morning he began to prepare, and having confided the law-plea to the management of Mr Melbourn, he sailed by the packet from Falmouth in less than a month after, behaving to me, on taking his departal, in the most genteel and satisfactory manner; nor did he forget me when he got back to Jamaica, for he sent me, by one of Mr Melbourn's ships, next year, a bag of coffee beans that weighed no less than a hundred and fifteen weight, a barrel of the most beautiful raw sugar, and a lovely parrot, that could speak every word, though neither Babby nor me understood it, for it was a Spanish parrot, and conversed in no other language; and he continued his tribute of sugar and coffee regularly every year, till his death, when he remembered me in his will as 'that most kind and sensible lady Mrs Winsom, with whom he staid in Mortimer Street,' bequeathing to me a legacy of fifty guineas, to buy a ring or a silver teapot."

MY LANDLADY AND HER LODGERS

Chapter VIII

Some two or three days elapsed before I had an opportunity of renewing my conversation with Mrs Winsom; but at last another wet Sunday morning came to pass, when she was kind enough to favour me with her company. After some preliminary reminiscences touching Mr Flowerfield's case and the Melbourns, she began upon a new subject.

"I'm sure," said she, "I have good cause to bear in mind, brighter and above many events, the pleasantries of a visit which Bailie Seeston and his wife made, to view the particularities of London, during which they were lodgers with me. They came from Paisley, and were bein, thriving bodies, who had made, some years before, a power of money, by a certain beautiful pawtron silk gauze, as Mrs Seeston herself told me. They called it the Princess Elizabeth's soufflé; and the year before they thought of their jaunt, they had again been coining money by something of the same sort, which was the special encouragement that allowed them to come to London: —their business being, as the Bailie said, to take the benefit of God's blessing; adding, that a sight of the great world was good for trade, as well as for sore eyes. He was, by this time, learning to speak high English.

"Having but few fashionable acquaintance in London—for how could it be expected that Paisley folk could be overladen with siclike?—me and Mrs Seeston made ourselves most agreeable to one another;—and she was pleased to say, after observing something by ordinar about my manner, that she had an apprehension I was a lady that had seen better days.

" It would not have been discreet of me to have gainsaid ony thing detrimental to so polite a judgment—so I replied nought; but in sincerity I'll own to you, I had the day before bought another hundred in the three per cents, by the which I was more than five hundred better than when dear Mr Winsom departed this life.

" Well, you see, Mrs Seeston and me growing condisciples, and having a right understanding with one another, neither her nor the Bailie would gang a foot a-field without linking me with them,—by which I got more edification concerning the sights of London, than falls to the lot of most single women of character.

" But I should speak the truth, for in this there was a great, though a silent and inward, triumphing on my part. When the Bailie and his leddy first came to the house, it was to be seen that they intended to be mighty and grand. The mistress was civil, for she was of a blithe and warm-hearted naturality; nor could I object to the Bailie, for he too was courtly and condescending; but it was plain that they thought themselves something better than their landlady. I had seen the like pretences before, and so they were free to take the length of their tether.

" Mrs Seeston was, I must confess, not of a genteel

habit of body, being short, and of a protuberant corpulency, bearing a burden of many fine things, without knowing how to wear them. She was, on the second morning after they came to town, going out to walk a-shopping in Oxford Street, in white satin shoes, had I not laid my hands upon her, and told her in a whisper, before the Bailie, what she might be thought of. She kicket them off at hearing that, and nearly faintit.

"This was the beginning of our conjuction. The Bailie—he was really a worthy body—might be a degree farther over the hill height than the mistress; but he had a guess, as he said himself, of what glamour was —aboon the lady. In short, he was slee and sleeky, with a pawkie whirly in the corner of his eye, that shewed, if he wasna a sinner, he kent what a pleasant thing sin might be.

"I'll no say he was a fat man, for he being of stature low, that might be a question; but I have had a Glasgow provost of a jimper capacity, and likewise a Dumfries dean o' guild that, in the measurement of girth, would hae buckled within his belt, to an owercome of a nail and quarter. But for all that, Bailie Seeston was a capital man—jocose, and knowing the difference between meconomy and nabalness; what he waurt upon us, in our ploys, was truly spent wi' the spirit o' hospitality.

"At the Talbot Inn at Richmond, on a Sunday, though the bill for eels, a duck with green peas, and a grosette tart, was enough to make the hair on the head of any man to stand on end, far more that of a Bailie, who is reputed to get his dainties from the common stock, he was wonderful facetious, and treated us with a bottle of claret wine on the occasion, which Mrs Seeston said, and I thought, was some trash. The Bailie himself, however, acknowledged that he had once tasted better at Lord Glasgow's, at the Halket-head, where, to be sure, every thing was of the first quality.

" It would, however, be overly long for me to summer and winter on the diversions we had thegither, going to Vauxhall, and even to see the execution of a forger; for, as Mrs Seeston said, if it was not sae dreadful a thing as a murderer's, yet it was an edifying curiosity of its kind.

" The only drawback that I had by the Bailie and Mrs Seeston was their inordinate passion for pawtrons, especially in Ludgate Hill; where, as the lady very truly made the observe, there was more of a fine taste for the better sort of goods than even in Bond Street itself: not, however, that they were intent only about gauze and flounces; for, to say what is only true, they were diverting themselves, and but took up the shop windows in walking along, in the way of pastime.

" At last they began to turn the eyes of their understanding homeward, or, as Mrs Seeston said,—' She was beginning to be wearyiet wi' the gaieties and gallantings of London.'—So out of that weariness grew a resolve of departal. And no gentleman or leddy could behave genteeler than they did to me, on account of my helping them so well to the sights and curiosities. The Bailie gie'd me, in courtesy, a very handsome garnet-coloured piece of silk, eight yards, which I sold to Mrs Flounce, the dress-maker in Queen Anne's Street, for five and three-pence the yard; and Mrs Seeston bought me a lace bonnet, the twin of one she bought for herself;—and they paid their bill without a question,—very unlike the Scotch in general. So that, if I couldna in conscience uphold the Paisley Bailie for a courtier, I am bound to maintain he was friendly, jocose, and of a furthy liberality, that's worth mair, in a sterling point of view, than all the congees of Edinburgh—not that I have ever had cause to complain of the inhabitants of that very respectable town; for such of them as have lodged with me have always proved themselves genteel to a nicety, though some of them have been a thought hampered with scrupulosity. And here I would make an observe, which is, that the folks from the West of Scotland, who are not people of pedigree, are most liberal and genteel; whereas those from the East, and especially from Edinburgh, who are, for the most part, the offspring or the ancestors of lords and kings, are of a narrow, contracted meconomy; the cause of which, to account for, would not be easy in philosophy.

" About two years after the visit of Bailie Seeston and his leddy, I had a letter from them, telling me that they intended to be in London soon, and hoping, if my apartments were not engaged, that I would keep them for a week or two, for they would not grudge the rent, to be again so comfortable as they had been with me. By this I could guess the Bailie had made another great year; but in the course of three or four posts after, I received a line from Mrs Seeston herself, to let me know that they would not want the rooms, for the gudeman had made a great mistake in making up his accounts, by adding the year of the Lord as a sum in his profits."

Chapter IX

After a short pause, Mrs Winsom resumed her narrative, saying—

"But ye're no to think a lodging-house is free from calamities, for I can assure you, that soon after the jocose days I had with the Lustrons, I met with a sore trial. It came of the misfortune of a sweet young miss, who was beguiled from her parents by a dragoon officer—one of your prodigals that defy the Ten Commandments and the laws of man, with mustophas on their upper lips—no that he was to be objected to on account of his visiognomy, for in truth he was an Absalom of beauty, and had a tongue to wile the bird from the tree. Indeed, after I saw him, I almost thought the poor maiden was but lightly to blame; and I never could satisfy myself how so brave a gallant—so free-hearted and fair-spoken,—could be a perjured wretch; but, for all my womanly indulgence, he was so, and I was condemned to acknowledge it by my conscience, as I crooned in the watches of the night,

"'Men are deceivers ever.'

"Miss Fatima Camomile was one of the seven daughters of the Reverend Dr Camomile, by his third wife, who, according to the most authentic accounts, had fewer children than either of the two who were her ancestors in his bosom.

"The Doctor keepit a school for select young gentlemen, ordained for a classical way of life;—and out of it came to pass, that when Captain Rampant was a bit laddie, he was sent by his doers to learn Greek and Latin with the worthy Doctor, who surely was a most superior man.

"Miss Fatima and the Captain, when they were playing bairns—he a birky laddie, and she a bardy lassie—fell into love, according to the fashion of teens and nonage, and betrothed vows of everlasting perdition if they proved false to one another.

"But it came to pass, as in course of nature it was to be looked for, that his friends took him from the Doctor's school, and placed him in the army, where, as might have been expected, he grew, being a handsome young man, and a great ne'er-do-weel. After some five or six years, his regimentals were quartered in a town contiguous to the village where Miss Fatima lived with her father and the multitude of her sisters, in the enjoyment of every comfort, and the pleasant innocence of a classical academy.

"Out of this accidence, the Captain—or, as I should call him, the Hornet, for he was as yet not farther promoted, repaired his old acquaintance with the Doctor, and renewed his familiars with Miss Fatima, until off they came in a chaise-and-four, making a loupment into my first floor, as if they had been a real man and wife, according to the Gospels of the Bishops of London, or the Archbishop of Canterbury.

"Well, you see, being in my house, I began to have my doubts o' the sincerity of their marriage. I couldna tell how such doubts arose—that was impossible; but I thought they were overly fond to be by themselves—nobody came nigh them—and one Sabbath night I said to myself, Is't no wonderful that never a young leddy comes to speir for Mrs Rampant, if it were only to get insight into the nature of matrimony? In short, before Monday morning I was worked into a persuasion that Mrs Rampant was not a creditable lodger. Young, lovely, and lamenting—for she was often in tears—I discerned there was a doubt; and what would have become o' me and my valuable property in this house, had I no made a testification?

"Let no man, or woman either, say that I was moved thereunto by an expiscatory curiosity. No! I had a dread upon me; I thought my house might inherit a blemish from that thoughtless and friendless pair, and therefore was I stirred, by an obligation of duty, to look into the young lady's affair. What a discovery was mine! The salt tears rin into my eyes when I think of her story. Oh, the natural perfidiousness of man!

"She told me with what innocence, like two babes in the wood, when he was at her father's school, they had loved one another. How often, while yet neither knew the meaning of their words, he promised to marry her, and how fondly she had reckoned on being Mrs Rampant. It was very pathetical. 'Often when he was gone,' said the poor young lady, 'I have walked into the fields, having no companion but the holy moon, and those witnessing stars which had their light purified by the simplicity of our fondness, calling upon them to bear testimony to the truth of my love. There was a spell upon my heart, which assured me he would come back, and that our happiness would yet be fulfilled. I never thought of any other love; when the lily bloomed, I worshipped the sign, because I knew my weak heart taught me to believe so, that when he saw the blossom, he would dearly think of me, we had so often in our young years admired its fragrance and its spotlessness together.

"'He came at last,—and, though no longer the merry madcap boy, who had been both in gladness and in sadness the companion of my sweetest hours, he was the same being, but with a richer stock of manhood and cheerful bearing. Still he was so much the same, I could not love him less than I had ever done. Alas! I soon began to feel I loved him more. Nor did his passion seem diminished; and I was pleased it should be so, for who could think that there was any guile in Harry Rampant?

"'He had been, it is true, five years in the world, and I had been always at home; nor could I imagine what five years' transmutation in barracks, and the licence of young soldiership, could effect on the heart of man. He seemed to me all I desired; where was truth, if he was not true? In that soft, that fearful, and confiding time, in which I felt myself to be more in fault than he was, I could not doubt the faithfulness of his honour.'

" I thought," said Mrs Winsom, resuming her natural tone, " when I learnt this, that it would be a hard thing to hurry the young man before the session after such a disclosure; and I reasoned with Miss Fatima, for I would no longer adorn her with the tittle of Mrs Rampant, telling her that she had been an overly fond cutty, and was much to blame.

" But notwithstanding, though my words were surgical knives, removing proud flesh, I yet told her for a comfort, that I would speak to Captain Rampant, and with God's help would end her misery. Poor thing! she was by this time most disconsolate to behold! Her fair eyes were waxing wide—the gracious beauty of her cheeks was become pale—her mouth had lost the swirl of dimples that made it gayer than smiles, and she rose from her chair with a heaviness as if there was about her a burden or a shame.

" That same night, after she had been long abed, the Captain came home from one of his parties—she never went to any. I sat up on purpose to meet him. He was not ree, but gay—his wits were all about him; but they were sparkling.

" ' Captain,' quo' I, when I had let him in, ' come into the parlour, for I would fain have a discourse with you—Mrs Rampant, as ye call her, is very bad '——

" 'Who dares to say so? ' cried he.

" 'Captain, Captain,' was my reply, 'dinna ye be contrarie; there's a fault somewhere, and the sooner it's owned the better—She's ill, I should have said.'

" He had been in Scotland, and knew what owning a fault meant in a Christian country; so of course he began to make an equivocal of a ridiculous kind with me; but a power was then given to me, and verily I have thought that I was surely fortified and inspired with the spirit of truth and seriousness.

" 'Oh, Captain,' was my answer to his light-hearted ribaldry, 'ye're due a great debt—ye hae a great sum of sin to answer for. Here was a young lady, rosy and sweet, blooming upon her native bush, though it may have been thorny. The dear and kind enchantments of auld lang syne were around her paternal sanctuary—and gentle Memory was ready with her golden key to open the tower to you when you returned.'

" He looked clouded as I said this—his mirth was departed; but for all that I persevered, saying,

" 'And what, Captain, have ye earned by your deceitfulness?—a withered flower and a broken heart. Oh, sir, where was fine feeling when ye brought the harlot thoughts of camps and barracks into the defenceless and innocent bowers of love and confidence—where was bravery, when the silly blandishments of a simple maiden won you to forget the virtue wherewith remembrance had sanctified the scenes wherein she fell—and where is your honour, knowing that what was won was given in the faithfulness of youthful constancy, that you refuse still to redeem the pledge of fidelity?'

"I spoke like my father in the pulpit; and, by the pith of what I said, so daunted the worldly audacity of the Captain, that he sat silent, and made no answer. Seeing him thus in a sort of penitential meditation, I pressed upon him further—I bade him compare what the unfortunate lady was, with what she might, but for him, have been. It was a depicting that made my own heart melt with sorrow, and my eyes to overflow with tears.

"I inscribed upon his conscience, how, before her ruin, she went bloomingly and gay to her father's church, the bells ringing in unison with her happy fancies. I spoke of the worthy young men who then eyed her with love and admiration, but whose advances she repelled, because she thought only of him; and then I shewed him what he had made of her—a destitute creature, scorned by all who knew her in her blameless time, being in a stranger's house, fearful to visit the streets; and my corruption rising, I cried with vehemence, 'Reprobate! she was beloved and honoured, and you have made her a light woman!'

"He said nothing to me; but he rose, and, putting on his hat with an emphasis, as my father would have called it, left the house.

"Next morning, Miss Fatima had a letter from him; but what was in it she never did reveal, for she read it over to herself. It contained a bank-note for a hundred pounds—which was a large sum, considering my bill was not then above eleven—and she read it again, and began to moan and mourn from the depths of her spirit. Then she gave me the bank-note with a melancholy smile, and said she thought it was enough—and she pressed my hand kindly, and added, she had overheard all I had spoken to the Captain. In the same moment she started up, and, shaking her hands towards the holy skies, she cried, 'It is so—I am such; and it shall be done.'

"I was amazed and terrified at her vehemence. I feared, but could not guess, what her intent was; but she soon after put on a countenance of calmness—yet it was a calm without quiet. Her pale cheek, which had long lost its flower, became of a clayey deadliness—her eyes glittered as if they saw not—her voice had a far-off, hollow, tomblike sound—and there was a horror in her smile, that made me suffer as if the world of the dead had been disclosed before me.

"Such she was for some four or five days—it might have been a whole week—I'll not dispute that, for I was in a manner myself demented; but a change at last began to manifest itself—and such a change!"

Chapter X

Mrs Winsom was deeply affected by what she had related, and she told it with so much dramatic propriety, that I wondered at the talent she displayed. I have, however, since often observed the same singular faculty in other illiterate persons, and have seen them rising in the course of a narration to the supposed beautiful eloquence of the higher minds of whom they discoursed. I ought, however, to acknowledge that I was melted with more than ordinary sympathy for the doom of the unfortunate lady, which the motherly zeal of my worthy landlady had evidently precipitated; and my curiosity was so excited, that I could not repress the desire to be informed of the sequel of a story so tragical.

"When," resumed Mrs Winson, "when the desolated creature came to a true sense of her forlorn situation—for in her panic she was too wild to have a right discernment—it was freezing to hear how she lamented; she didna plead that she had been a resisting victim; nor did she take all the blame upon herself. There was a flattery in her heart that she had been betrayed by the condition of her father's house more than by her own weakness, or that the accomplisher of her ruin had a premeditated purpose. Still, however, she wept and wailed until her hopelessness became incurable.

"It was soon manifest that Death had laid his cold hand upon her, in defiance of all medicine and doctor's skill.

"From morning to night she sat by herself on the sofa, her one hand on the other resting on her knee, and her eyes reading, as it were, the leaf of a curious page of vacuity in the threads and pawtron of the carpet. She thought of nothing but of time.

" When I went into her room in the morning, she would say, ' Is not this Wednesday, or Friday?' as it might chance to be. And as often as I went again during the rest of the day, she would ask the hour. It was melancholy to see her despondency, and how pleased she was when the time had seemed to have run a little faster than she expected. How patient and how beautiful she was in all this; but oh! how plainly her heart was breaking.

" When more than eight mournful months had come and gone, seeing that, by the course of nature, she was soon to become a mother, I thought it my duty, in a far-off way, to remind her that it was needful to prepare for a stranger.

" She looked at me, I thought reproachfully, but her eyes were full of tears, and she answered, ' No. I have here, within, a conviction that my sin and shame will pass from this world together. I dreamt last night that I beheld my venerable grandfather—he was a holy and religious man—standing at a gate to which I had come with a baby at my bosom, and he took me by the hand and led me in, and made me known to all my ancestors, even to Adam and Eve. No; the life that should be, is not—it becomes my condition—a husbandless wife—a childless mother! '

" I reasoned against her despair, and entreated her to be of good cheer, but she smote her bosom, and said, ' How can that be? ' adding, ' I am not guiltless; but there was no other but only himself, in all the world, by whom I could have been undone. Stars of light and purity—eyes and oracles of heaven, ye know my chastity! But how can he believe it? Oh! scorned by him, what is left?—where now is my place in the world?—The grave.'

"After a season of some days, the wild lamentings and continual cries of a spirit in agony began to moderate into sighs and low heart-murmurings. I entreated her to let me send for her father, or for one of her sisters; but she was absolute, and would not have them. At last the mother's time arrived, and she became, as she foretold, a mother without a child.

"'Place,' she cried, 'the mute witness of my infirmity before me. It was not in sin, but in the confidence of faithful love, that this monument of frailty hath had being.'

"We placed accordingly the dead-born baby upon a pillow, covered with one of my best damask servits, on a chair by the bedside. It was punishment enough for many a sin to see what then ensued.

"She raised herself on her elbow, and studied the beautiful thing as if it had been an alabaster image of curious handicraft. What was in her thoughts no one could tell, but ever and anon she cast her eyes upwards, and smiled as if she had discovered some pleasing similitude, and once she said, 'How lovely and how like!'

"She then laid herself down, and seemed to be communing in prayer. After a season she raised herself again, and covering the body with the servit, she made a sign for it to be laid on her bosom, which I did with my own hands.

" At that crisis the door opened, and the Captain appeared at the bedfoot; flustered he was, and of a wild look—she saw him, and stretched out her hands lovingly towards him, but they fell on the innocent corpse, and in the same instant she was no more.

" The Captain, as ye may well suppose, was a most demented man. He called himself by all the ill names that contrition could find, and, to a surety, none of them were too bad. But as I told him, despair was then out of season, and it behoved us to think of sending for an undertaker. The upholsterer over the way being a moderate and respectable tradesman, I accordingly sent for him, and after a decent time was allowed to pass, the funeral was performed in a very genteel manner. But, alas! how the curse of Heaven will sometimes work!

" The Captain, being melancholious with what had happened, was enticed, on the night after the burial, to go for a pastime with a friend to see how the doctors make atomies, and that same night he came rushing to my door like a ghost in a whirlwind. His senses were gone—he raved of a sight he had seen, and of a deed that had been done.

" His friend, with certain others, came flying after him, and, dreadful to tell, one of them described the vision of vengeance he had seen. From that hour he became mad with a frightful shout of laughter—it was such laughter as the dead would laugh—if that could be—and he died in the course of a year after in a Hoxton Bedlam."

CHAPTER XI

When Mrs Winsom had finished the sad story of the unhappy Fatima, we naturally fell into conversation concerning the other mysterious young lady and gentleman who had come to her house in the same clandestine manner, and had left it so suddenly, without explanation. For some time she appeared a little averse to enter upon the subject; but when I happened to say, I should be none surprised if the lady proved to be the lost daughter of her old friends, Mr and Mrs Melbourn, she gave me a significant nod and a smile.

" 'Deed," said she, " ye have made a true guess; but I promised no to speak of it; for now all, by the help of my agency, is put to rights, and to-morrow the whole party are to return to Mr Melbourn's country-seat, to hold a celebration of the marriage, as becomes their fortune. A good laugh has been raised at the expense of Miss for her romancing, though it is allowed on all hands that she shewed both a right pride and delicacy in concealing from her husband the sorrow and remorse she suffered for the indiscretion she had committed, owing to the esteem in which she held his affection. However, as both the old folk and the young are anxious that as little should be heard about the matter as possible, we'll make a passover of this case, and I'll relate to you some comical doings I had with a Mr Kenneth Macquirkie, who was recommended to my house by Mr Melbourn, some years ago.

"This Kenneth Macquirkie, Esq., W.S., as he put upon his cards (which W.S. signifies a writer to the signet, some sort of a lawyer in Edinburgh), was doer for a tawny bairn of a planter, who, like Mr Flowerfield, was one of Mr Melbourn's West Indy correspondents. This bairn had a mulatto mother, who left a good gathering by will in full to her, but which it was thought would make it necessary to put her into the Court of Chancery, or, what was the same thing, make her a dreeping roast to Mr Macquirkie. Now, ye see, as I had an inkling of this, and had, moreover, heard that he was to be allowed a sappy fee for coming to London, I thought it was but reasonable to deal with him accordingly, the more especially as he had engaged the first floor, and was to have cooking done for him at home—the which is a covenant of works that, turned to a proper use, should be advantageous and comfortable to the keeper of a lodging-house. But oh! such a trouble as I had with that man at the settling of our weekly bills on the Monday morning! for he was of a short memory, and a brittle temper, and, over and above, he was as greedy as a trap, and as gair as a smiddy vice. But, as I had been well recommended to him, and he had, moreover, some reason to wish to stand in a favourable light with Mr Melbourn, he was fain to bear, though he couldna thole without complaining.

" One night he had been at the playhouse of Covent Garden with a friend that he brought home with him to eat a lobster, and drink porter, and talk of playactors and authors, in the Edinburgh fashion; for in all the time that I have kept a lodging-house, I never have met with folk so beside themselves about genius, and promise, and the freshness of young talents, as the Edinburgh lawyers. Indeed, it's most extraordinar to hear them, and wonderful how men of the law should have time to think of such phantasmagory. As a mathematical lodger and friend of mine, from Cambridge, once said, 'I wonder,' said he, ' how it is, that men of cases and precedents, quotations and instances, can afford to learn such mythologies; but the effect is seen on their business—they are constantly coming to London appealing against the sentences of their judges, and are as often sent back to make a revision—a proof,' said he, ' how little general knowledge is of an advantage in legalities.'

" Well, this Macquirkie, as ye may discern, being a most troublesome man, the lobster was gotten for him, and the pot of porter, and he and his friend began to crack the shell, and to speak about the pathos of a play-actoring lady that they had that night seen; and it turned out that one lobster was an insufficient supper for the two, so Babby was desired to get them another; and being desired to get another, and not finding one that she thought big enough, she brought two. Hereupon, on the Monday morning following, arose a most kittle question. Mr Macquirkie contested the charge on my bill, saying that he had given orders for only one lobster that would serve two.

" As he was a dinnering-at-home customer, I submitted to let the affair pass for that time. But, shortly after, he would have a dinner for two friends, and, accordingly, I was duly authorized to make all proper preparation. You may be sure I got him one of the best of dinners; but when the bill came to be presented, it's an impossibility to describe how he stormed; for he thought, being, like the Edinburghers, ignorant of our politer ways of the world here in the South, that I would just have made a charge per head for the three, like a coffee-house keeper; but that wasna my trade; so, notwithstanding his tempest, I just charged him dish and dish, with a reasonable consideration for extra trouble, not forgetting the contested lobster. Oh, but an Edinbro' W.S. is a most severe customer! But at last I got the right way of managing Mr Macquirkie; for whenever he made on objection to what he called an overcharge, I subdued him by saying, that it was wonderful how such a genteel people as usually came from the Athens of the North, as they called Auld Reekie, should make a controversy about candle-ends and cheese-parings, as if they had been habituated to live at home in a straitened circumstance.

" Having thus got into the right way of managing him, he grew so pliable, that I might have twisted him round my finger, and in the end did me a world of good, as I shall presently tell you."

MY LANDLADY AND HER LODGERS

CHAPTER XII

" About the time Mr Macquirkie went home," continued Mrs Winsom, " there arose in a certain town in the west of Scotland, called Blackbirch, an inordinate passion for begetting acts of Parliament. What he had to do in the business it would ill become me to pretend to expound; but that he was art and part in the mystery I was well assured was plain to be seen and clear to be understood. In short, he was fee'd to become a counsellor to the bailies and other bodies of the town, besides the feuars and subfeuars.

" Among other things, it seems in talking law with them over their toddy, he set forth, among other great discoveries he had made in London, the vast comfort and economy he had enjoyed in my house, with the skilful manner in which he managed me. From this it came to pass that the Blackbirch folk, having bethought themselves of a necessity of getting a new act of Parliament, sent one of their Bailies for that purpose to London, and he brought with him a most civilized two lines from Mr Macquirkie to me, commending him in a most special manner to my attentions. Thus I became, as it were, standing Landlady, as you shall hear, to the Blackbirch folk. For the Bailie, after some prigging, took my first floor for a month; and he was not well in, when I was constrained, in a sense, to take in a delegate from the malcontents who were opposed to the Bailie's Bill.

"The way of it was this. The Bailie, like all other magistrates, was greatly versed in the knowledge of human nature, as he told me himself, winking cunningly at the same time, to let me know that he was a man of the world; and then he began to give me a hint anent the great business which had brought him to London, and of the bad spirits who had risen in opposition to the just and necessary measure, which he and his colleagues had undertaken for the good of the town, and all that was dear to it.

"I hope ye'll no think I was so forward as to offer my advice to a Bailie—a Blackbirch Bailie, too—although I could not discern, even after he had explained the whole matter to me, wherefore it was that the feuars and subfeuars of the town, together with the magistrates and town council, were so eager to make themselves statutes.

"But when the delegate explained to me his view of the subject, it seemed quite manifest that the Bailie and his party were conspiring to impose little less than the yoke of an arbitrary government on the necks of the poor defenceless inhabitants of the unfortunate town of Blackbirch. Then he enlarged on the freedom of trade, and proved to my satisfaction that certain things which the bill was intended to put down, such as the crying of London candy, was a lawful calling, and that if it were put down by constraint of law, what would thrifty families do with all their old brass, cracked crystal, and broken buckles? In short, as it were in despite of my understanding, I was seduced to take the popularity side, and to do all that I could to help the cause of the delegate, though he was but a parlour-floor lodger, and the Bailie was paying for the drawing-rooms two guineas and an half a-week,—a rent, ye'll allow, was moderate, considering that a whole town was paying it.

" Well, to make short of a long story, the Bailie and the delegate, after divers days of going out in the morning couthy friends, and coming back at night from the House of Commons argol-bargling like tigers, it came to pass that the Bill, as the Bailie's measure was called, was read a second time. I thought, when I heard so, of the great patience of Parliament, for it was a book almost as big as a Family Bible, and to read it through in one night, after having spent a night at it before, was most extraordinary.

" Truly the Bailie on that night was a jocose man, triumphing and shouting as if he had overcome the Philistines. But his transportations, like every other earthly felicity, were, worthy man, of short duration; for it seems there was a thing they called a Committee, that took hold of his Bill and tore it all to pieces, as the delegate told me himself, with much sobriety. He did not clap his hands and make a joyful noise like the Bailie, but spoke of his conquest like a man of sense, as all the Blackbirch folk shew themselves to be, and in naething mair than their great love for law and interlocutors.

" By this time, ye see, I had been deep in their councils; and seeing the Bailie, by what the Committee had done, dejected, I began to take pity upon him, and to devise a possibility of a reconciliation with his adversary, who, though a popularity man, had a smeddum of satiricalness that increased with his prospect of gaining his ends, and was very afflicting, I must allow, to the Bailie. But in what way that reconciliation was to be brought to a come-to-pass cost me no little thought. I had, however, discerned, that often in their controversies they spoke of Port Punchtown, and I saw that, however disastrous their opinions were on all other subjects, they perfectly agreed that it was a place that ought not to be—especially as it was swallowing up their trade, the people thereof being much cleverer in all matters of maritime business than those of Blackbirch. To be sure, neither the Bailie nor the delegate ever acknowledged the fact of this superiority, but, on the contrary, cordially agreed that the inhabitants of Port Punchtown to a man were the riddlings of mankind, and not fit to tie the latch of a shoe in Blackbirch.

"Having meditated in the watches of the night on all I had heard them say, next morning I said to my friend the delegate, that it was a great pity to waste his town's money for such fasherie as the Bailie's Bill, and that it would be far better, seeing there was an obligation on every true-hearted Blackbircher to put his heel on the neck of the presumptuous place, Port Punchtown, to contrive a way of extinguishing it for ever. I never saw a man better pleased in my life than he was to hear me. But as I have told you, he was of a composed and controlled nature, and did not expose his inward satisfaction with any inordinate outward demonstration. However, I had inoculated him, and at night he brought home with him Mr Tedious, his law man; and shortly after, the Bailie being in, they rang the bell and requested me—for I answered it—to ask him to come down and take a glass of toddy with them. I saw by their countenances that they were baith big with something;—so, when I had delivered the message, curiosity got the better of decorum, as it will sometimes do with other ladies as well as landladies, and I went into the bedroom, and put my ear to the keyhole, to hear their high treason against the devoted town of Port Punchtown.

"Mr Tedious began by condoling with the gentlemen on the unfortunate effects of their controversies; telling them, that the Bill had come out of the Committee a monument of insufficiency, and warily he worked till he brought the rival town upon the carpet.

"'It's a town,' said he, 'against which nature has manifestly set her face. It would long since have perished and been utterly undone, but for that energy and enterprising spirit which the inhabitants possess in so superior a degree.'

"Both the Bailie and the delegate protested, in a vehement manner, against this doctrine of superiority; and the Bailie assured Mr Tedious, that if Port Punchtown had not been a pet of the city of that name, it was naturally a place that no Blackbirch gentleman, in his greatest indignation against its upsetting, would condescend even to insult.

" The delegate explained, in his calm and methodical manner, that the world was quite wrong in supposing that Port Punchtown was a place of any respectability at all. As for the superiority of the inhabitants, they have not the capacity to make even a Bailie, but must just take any bogle that their parent city thinks fit to send them.

" Here the lawyer interposed, remarking, that it must be allowed they had, in their projects of improvements, made their town a rankling thorn in the side of Blackbirch.

" This the Bailie and the delegate denied.

" ' Be that, however, as it may,' said the lawyer, ' the clear policy of Blackbirch is, to put an extinguisher on her rival.'

" ' Rival! ' exclaimed the others; ' she is none to Blackbirch.'

" Then," said Mrs Winsom for herself, " I was just frying to hear such nothingness of an argument, and would fain have broken in upon them, when Mr Tedious giving a clap with his hands, cried, ' Gentlemen, I'll tell you what: it being admitted on all sides that the Blackbirch people must either have a law-plea or a bill in Parliament, I would recommend that your dissensions should be suspended and that you should unite in some great undertaking, either of the one kind or the other, to prove that you have a power when you choose to shew it. Now this bill, which, between your two parties, has cost the town already more than £1200, even were it carried as proposed, would not have given you any advantage over your rival.'

" 'Not rival!' exclaimed the Bailie and the delegate; 'we won't admit that.'

" 'I would therefore advise that, next session you apply for an act to enable your town to improve the harbour and town of Punchtown. How beautifully your disinterestedness could be set forth in your application to Parliament!'

" 'Improve Port Punchtown!' exclaimed the Bailie and the delegate, in an agony.

" 'Yes,' said Mr Tedious, emphatically, 'by bill. But when the bill shall have become an act, there will be no need to act on it. Thus you will have it in your power to stab your rival in the vitals.'

" 'And could we not, then,' said the Bailie, 'choke up the channel of the river with an old ship?'

" I could hear," said Mrs Winsom, " the lawyer rubbing his hands fidgetty fain, as he cried, 'By that means you will have both a contested bill, and a capital law-suit.' "

She then proceeded to tell me, that before the gentlemen left her house for Scotland, the whole business was arranged; and that out of this happy expedient for the overthrow of Port Punchtown grew such felicitous unanimity in the town of Blackbirch, as has seldom been equalled, never surpassed. At the next election of the magistrates, the delegate was chosen by the Whig interest to be the compeer of the Bailie, who represented the Tories; and it was mentioned in the newspapers, that such was the joy of the feuars and subfeuars on the union of parties in the town, that the two magistrates, in long procession, followed by all the feuars and subfeuars two and two, walked hand in hand on the day of that unanimous election, singing, " Together let us range the fields; " the bellman on the right, and the town-drummer on the left, proclaiming their praises.

Here I might have set worthy Mrs Winsom right as to these particulars; but on consideration, I thought the least said is soonest mended—for if the town of Blackbirch is not yet in that state of blessed unanimity, I am sure it ought to be.

Chapter XIII

I forget now the cause, which, for some time after the Blackbirch affair, interrupted my *tête-à-têtes* with Mrs Winsom, or, as her handmaid Babby called them, our crim. cons.; but the renewal, as I well recollect, took place on a Sunday evening. I had been the night before at the Opera to hear Catalani for the first time, who was then in all the plenitude of song and beauty. Having invited Mrs Winsom to make tea for me, after some disquisition concerning the performance, she began:—

" Experience has taught me that the lodging trade, like the generality of commercing, is not always of the same profitableness. So it came to pass in the course of time that my apartments were no to be let to the progenitors of the AA or the PP; that is to say, artists, authors, or actors, commonly called painters, poets, and players; and for a good and solid reason, as I shall make manifest to your hearing.

" Artists, though needing but small attendance, and being of a frugal nature, are yet of such ill-redd-up dispositions, that it is often no in the power of soap and water, besom or brush, to make a satisfactroy restoration after them, without the help of a char-woman—and she costs money.

" I once had a short-sighted, prejinct, pernicketty bodie of a minatour maker, who staid with me only three months; but it took such a length o' time to make a clearance o' his residues, that, besides the positive outlay for the white-washer and char-woman, I lost, before the rooms were again ready, a Glasgow magistrate, with a punch-bowl belly, whose very face, to any lodging-house, was as the sight of a dripping roast—for he was a dining-at-home customer.

" As for authors, one of them, for troublesomeness, is equal to two artists; and I verily think, that, according to the rule of three, if two poets be equal to one player, the whole nine Muses could not be worse than a single she-play-actor.

" For making a litter of paper, the authors are just tremendous; and then they are never ready for their meals, for they are of the kind that live at home, but have either a line to finish, or a sentence to conclude, at the very time the dishes are going to the table. Moreover, they are naturally crisp in their temper, and cannot abide to be told anything in a hurry, even when the case is necessitous; and they sit up to the dead hours of the night, and often frightening sober lodgers from the country with the dread of robbers, as they walk about romancing or mumbling their reasonless rhymes. In short, they are 'dividuals of a precarious humour, and neither profit nor pleasure is to be won at their hands.

"Then the players—Gude! put never another of thae things till me, especially of the feminine gender! But the vocality are the worst of all. About five years since, I was so misfortunate as to let my first floor to a leddy-player, who was reckoned very prime at Drury-lane Theter. Never was a creature in this world so void of understanding; she had hands and fingers too, that must be allowed, but they were as useless as the siclike of a heathen goddess, cut out in a marble statue—saving that she could jingle parley-voos on a pianoforte. Oh! such a drawing-room as she did keep! It was an anarchy and confusion—a French revolution compared to the shop-board with nine tailors sitting on it making clothes for three bridals and six burials that are to happen the morn's morning. And she had a guinea-pig whittering about her petticoats; a lap-dog would have been Christianity compared to such an abomination.

"'Miss Cymbal,' said I to her one day, 'I wonder how ye can demean yourself with such an uncircumcised thing. It's no right of you—It's a beast of prey, Miss Cymbal, and ought not to be allowed to live in a land of law and gospel.'

"'My beloved Porkettino!' said she, lifting it up—and she kissed it—as I am a living woman, she kissed it! The pig-faced leddy, from all I have heard of her, would never have done the like of that."

Here I deemed it advisable to arrest the garrulity of the worthy old lady, for by this time I had discovered, that when once set a-going on any topic affording scope for simile or illustration, she was apt to run a little too long, particularly when morals or manners were concerned.

"And what became of Miss Cymbal?" said I.

"What became of her! I'm just ashamed to tell—It's enough to sanctify concubinage as holier than wedlock! She was married to an old lord that's fond o' fiddling, an' she now gallants about the streets in her own carriage, as if she was a natural dignitary with a pedigree."

"But do you know what sort of wife she makes?"

"Wife! what could you expect of a woman that made a beloved of a grumphy? To be sure it was a small one, but that did not make the fault any less—as I told her. However, as I was going to tell you, from that time I could not look on her with complacency; and so I resolved to see her back to the door on the first convenient opportunity. But that did not come to pass quite so soon as I had hoped it would do, and I was obligated to thole with her for more than five weeks, when one night, instead of coming home from the theter, she whisked awa', with a heycockelorum, to the house of my Lord L——. I must, however, do her justice in one particularity; next morning, when both Babby and me were boiling with a resolution to ding the door in her face if she shewed herself at it, my Lord's own gentleman came to make an apology, which he did in a most well-bred manner, presenting me with a marriage favour, which, besides a very large slice of very excellent seed cake, and a knot of silver-ribbon, consisted of a fifty-pound note to clear her bill—I assure you it was one of the sappiest settlements I have ever had."

I was a good deal amused with this account of Miss Cymbal, and said to Mrs Winsom, that, besides her general objections to authors, she had doubtless met with some one of the remarkable among them.

"I think every one was more remarkable than another," said she—"But if ye'll allow me, as the tea is by this time well masket, I'll pour you out a cup."

Chapter XIV

While we were engaged with our tea, some of Mrs Winsom's friends happened to call, which obliged her to retire with them to her own apartment; and I had no opportunity, for several nights, of resuming the conversation. But at last, a favourable evening, the weather being very wet, came round, and as I had no temptation to go abroad, I sent her the customary invitation.

I had, during the forenoon, been visiting the improvements on the Bedford estate, at Russell Square; and opened the sitting by telling her where I was, and what I had seen.

" Yes," said she, " though London is London, and aye likely to be, at least for our time, yet being a world within itself, it is, to a surety, subject to world-like changes. Ye cannot well say in what it alters, but after a time ye can see where a change has taken place, just as I observed to Mrs Carroway, when I went with her for the second time to Margate.

" ' The rocks,' she observed, ' every body of a right frame of mind may tell, without a text of Scripture, are everlasting, and bear testimony to the nothingness of human life.' But I proved to her, though they were, in a sense, unchangeable, still they were ever changing, shewing to her, in divers places, how things were worn and mouldered away, while the generality of the cliffs were seemingly still the same; among others, a projectile of the works on which her nephew had carved our names only two years before; it was quite gone, obliterated, and no more.

" But, as I was saying, London being of the nature of a perpetual world, undergoes alterations in a way that, without making a visible change, is still a change. It came to pass that, one summer, the winter having been adjourned from June to October, for the convenience of

Parliament, my rooms were evacuated for a longer space of time than had ever happened before, from the time of Mr Winsom's departal, in so much, that I was beginning to dread a total desertion—for the French Revolution was then rampaging like a drunken man with a drawn sword; and I had nightly fears anent dethronements, and the casting forth of every man of substance, so that lodgers should come no more.

"Well, you see, there being a dearth of lodgers, and rent and taxes dreadful, I made a resolve in my own mind no to be so overly particular when the season was over; and thus it came to pass that, one Saturday, a most respectable-looking elderly gentlewoman came in a coach to the door. She had seen the bill on the window, and liking, as she was pleased to say, the appearance of my house, she had stopped to enquire, and was glad that I responded she could be accommodated.

"'I'll take the first floor,' said she, for all were empty, 'without taking the trouble to look at any of the other apartments.'

"I was greatly ta'en with this leddy, for she was motherly in her looks; her dress foretold she was a gentlewoman, and her countenance that she was by ordinary.

"I got for her, as ye may believe, a comfortable cup of tea, for she had come from off a long journey. She tasted it, and said it was excellent—and indeed it was a fine tea; but I could observe, while making it for her, that her heart often filled full, and was ready to burst, and that the tears shot into her eyes from some hidden source of sorrow.

" When she had composed and refreshed herself, she observed that the day was far spent, and said, with a sore sigh, ' It is too late this evening! ' She then returned into her bedchamber, leaving me to wonder what she could mean by saying, ' It is too late this evening.'

" Her room was below mine, for I slept that night in the second floor to keep the bed aired, which I regularly do when my rooms are empty; and all the live-long night I could hear she was restless, often moaning to herself, as with the anguish of a great agony.

" By the break of day she was up, and gone forth without giving a single direction about her breakfast, which, you will allow, was leaving me in a perplexity; and she did not return till the heel of the evening, which did not look well; and yet I could not say wherefore, as she was plainly a most decent matron, and had signs of a substantiality about her that were, to me, as good as securities for her bill.

" I could discern, however, that she had not been abroad gathering honey, for, though her countenance was composed, it was of a constrained composure, more of fortitude than calmness, and she was absent of mind, thanking me kindly—more so than need have been—for my civility.

" I saw she was troubled, and marvelled what could be the cause; but she was of a powerful endurance—

that was evident; and I had not courage to enquire into her misery.

" On the morrow it was with her as the yesterday; she was up, out, and gone at a most premature hour; and I was all day in a consternation concerning three particulars—whence had she come, what was her grief, and where did she go? But conjecture gave no satisfaction.

" Day after day the same thing was as regular a come-to-pass as a rising and the setting of the sun. But when she had been an inmate eight days, she came not back till very late at night—a Saturday night: a fearful night that was! Seven lamps in Cavendish Square were blown out of their places on their posts; a chimney-pot in Henrietta Street fractured the skull of an aged watchman; and in Portland Place arose a yell of fire frightful to hear. In such a night that mysterious lady, whose name was unrevealed, came home from Newgate. The Sessions were over.

" She said to me nothing of where she had so often been; but on this occasion her countenance was a darkened wonder. It was sad, but with a sadness in which there was no melancholy; her eyes were uplift and religious, and very piteous to behold; still she appeared serene, but it was manifest her heart was weeping—weeping blood. I let her in myself at the street door, and lighted her up stairs without speaking—her look smote me, so that I could not speak. As I set down the candle on the table till I could light her own, I found strength at last to say, ' I fear, madam, you have met with a sore trial? '

" ' Yes,' said she, ' but it is now over.' She then requested me to get her a glass of wine and a crust of bread; and when I had done so, and she had tasted the wine, she desired me to send for Mr Hatchment the undertaker, from the next street; which I did, and he came immediately.

" After they had been a season by themselves, I went into the room to enquire in what I could be serviceable, and found her weeping very bitterly. Mr Hatchment, had received his orders, and had then gone away; Babby opened the door to him as he went out, and she told me he was like a man that had seen a consternation.

" After the passion of her grief had in some measure abated, she said she hoped I would have no objection to receive the remains of a relation of hers——She could say no more, her sorrow returned with such violence. Judge what I felt; but I sympathized with her, and assured her I would do all I could to serve her.

" The next day being Sabbath, she moved not from her room till the gloaming, when she sent for a coach, and said she would not return before daylight. When she did return, there was a great change upon her. Her countenance was of a sedate solemnity, her tears were dried up, and there was more of melancholy and less of despair about her.

" All Monday she was hidden in her darkened room above; and there was such a dread—we could not tell the cause—on Babby and me, that we spoke to one another in whispers, and walked about the house on our tiptoes, as if the corpse was already come.

"Soon after dark Mr Hatchment arrived, and the door being opened, he said, 'It is coming,' and presently a hackney-coach stopped at the door, and out of it was brought a plain coffin, and the coach was sent off.

"Mr Hatchment's men bore the coffin into the parlour, and placed it on my big table, which was set out on purpose; and shortly after two other men came with a fine coffin, covered with crimson velvet, and adorned with gold ornaments, into which the beggarly box of criminality was set and screwed up;—at the same time a grand hearse came to the door.

"As the men were moving the pageant of mystery to the hearse, an old gentleman came in at the open door, pushed the grand coffin aside, and demanded to see the lady; at that moment a shrill scream from her told him where she was. He said but three words to Mr Hatchment, and hastened up stairs, crying in a wild and pathetical voice—'It is pardonable in a mother,—but must not be!'

"Mr Hatchment hurried off the hearse with its dismal load; and in the course of a few minutes after, a footman with a fine carriage came to the door, into which the old gentleman handed the lady, and took his place beside her, giving me a twenty-pound note, which was, I own, very handsome. But really it was a mysterious affair, and I was more than a month before I got the better of it."

MY LANDLADY AND HER LODGERS

CHAPTER XV

As my acquaintance increased in town, my leisure diminished, and I had gradually less and less time to spend at home. Still, as often as I could command an evening, I endeavoured to enjoy the company and stories of my Landlady. An accident, however, suddenly placed a little more time at my disposal than was quite agreeable—a bit of orange-peel on the pavement caused me one day to sprain my ankle, by which I was confined to the house upwards of a week. During that time Mrs Winsom told me several more of her stories; among others, the following of a Country Captain.

" Soon after the tragical mystery, of which I told you the particulars at our last sederunt, I was sitting by the fire when Babby came into the room with a great flaught, to tell me that a gentleman wished to look at the first-floor rooms.

" ' What like is he, bairn? ' said I. ' He's a most weel-far'd, sponsible-looking elderly man ' (he was little mair than fifty, but Babby was young). ' He speaks wi' a loud voice, as one having authority, and not as the scribes. I dinna think he's under the degree of a bawronet, or at least the master of a Dublin veshel.' So I hastily preent on my dress-mutch—which I was in the act of doing when Babby cam ben—and went to the gentleman.

"I, who have seen so much of the world—(as a second-floor lodger of mine, Lieutenant Splice, used to say; who had been at the four quarters of the world, and was thirteen years aboard ship without sleeping as many nights on shore)—as I was saying, I, who have seen so much of the world, am not easily deceived with appearances. I saw at a glance that Babby was wrong in some particulars. Bawronet he plainly was not, and he was as plainly of another sort than the skipper of a Dublin coal-bark sailing from Ayr. His age was on the more judicious side of fifty. He was as sun-burnt and swarthy as a Spaniard; frank, rattling, portly, and good-natured; but he did not leave me long in the conjecturals about him.

"After looking at the rooms, and being satisfied with their convenience, and, what was more pleasantly to the purpose, surprised at the moderation of the rent, he told me that he was a country captain in the East Indies, and commanded a vessel between the island of Bengal and Calcutta, and some of the other islands, of which I do not recollect the names; and then he informed me, with a friendly frankness very unlike a European, that he had made a little money, and had managed to remit a sackful of rupees wi' a vestment of silk and indigo, and that he was still half owner of the 'Babec Sahib' of Calcutta, the ship he had been the captain of.

"He agreed to take possession of his rooms next day; in the meantime, he behoved to go to the Jerusalem Coffee-house to meet a friend who had come home three years before, and with whom he was to spend the day at a snug Bungalow, on a reach of the river below the Isle of Dogs, in a pleasant airy situation between the coal-tar factory and the chain-cable smiddy.

" About mid-day of the day following, as agreed upon, he took possession, and soon after came a waggon from the East India docks, ' with,' as he said, ' what little baggage he would require in town.' The heavy baggage he had shipped in a Leith smack. What quantity there was of it I cannot say; but for light baggage no Christian ever saw sic a collection—kists as big as meal girnels, with brass locks and hinges, and baskets made of cane o' a' sorts and sizes. One of them, that might have held himsell, was fu' o' dirty claes; he afterwards gave it to me, for, being made of cane, I thought it better than a close kist to haud claes. Among other curiosities, he had a fine auld kind of Madeira, of which he left me half a dozen bottles; likewise he left me a bottle of Balairic rack, a cordial medicine, which had the taste of rum pushiont wi' tar.

" He had also a black, or rather a brown, servingman, in an Indian dress, and a turban like a puddock-stool;—an extraordinary well-bred thing it was, and it aye made a low boo, with its hands on its forehead, not only to me, but to Babby, and the lassock Sally we then had to help, for Babby was but newly come from Scotland, and had not properly learnt the English language.

" After dinner he invited me ben (for he was a home-faring lodger) to taste the fine auld Madeira; and being couthy and pleased, he began to recount to me his adventures. He came from the shire of Ayr, like mysell, and served his time to the sea oot o' Greenock, after which he was shipped for Calcutta, wi' seven-and-thirty young lads from the same kintra side, consigned to Messrs Warden, M'Fergus, and Co., a' kith or kin to the chief of the concern. The Captain, being the nearest relation of the whole tot, was soon made third mate of a vessel; and so, by interest and merit, he had risen to the command of the 'Babec Sahib,' and to be master of the lac of rupees.

" He told me that he had no family, but he had two natural daughters by a Hindoo woman, for whom he had well provided; and his plan of life was, after he had taken a cruize in London, to go down to Ayrshire and build a cottage near Ardrossan, which he had heard was a pleasant place, much frequented during the summer by the best of company from Glasgow and Paisley.

" He went out early for the theatre without taking tea, as he wished to see how they came on there, in comparison with the gentlemen who acted at Calcutta. Seeing he was innocent of the ways of London, I admonished him of the deceits practised by the slight-of-hand part of the audience; but he made light of them, and told me, that the pocket-pickers here were not worth a d—— (ye must not expect me to repeat all the whole word) compared with the thieves and reevers of China; and that though he had made many voyages to Canton, they ne'er were able to come over him.

" Weel, to the playhouse the Captain goes; and as he told me he would be home early, I had a bit of my own Dulap cheese ready toasted for him, with a bottle of Edinburgh ale for daintice. Neverwas a man come to so many years of discretion, so comical as he was on his return. The grandeur of the house was above all parabolics; but as for the players, they did not understand their trade at all compared with the Calcutta gentlemen, though he thought one Mr John Cammell, and a Mrs Siddons, might pass, too, at Calcutta.

" But, above all, he was most delighted with the civility of the company, especially with a most polite gentleman whom he had met at the pit door, and who warned him of the blackguards who invest that theatre. He told him the names of the players, and pointed out every thing most interesting, from the ladies in the boxes, to the beautiful chandelier, which cost a thousand pounds, in the ceiling. ' I promise myself great pleasure,' said he, ' from this acquaintance, and I have invited him to dine with me to-morrow; but he suddenly left me to join a friend he saw in one of the upper boxes.'

" By this time, as it was wearing late, the Captain thought of going to bed, and feeling for his watch to wind it up, lo and behold it was gone! and away also was his diamond breast-pin! Though I was sorry at his loss, I yet couldna but feel something like a satisfaction that he had found frost in no taking my advice; however, I counselled him to go to Bow Street and consult the magistrates. I trow he owed me a fee for that advice, for at the cost of no more, as he said, than ten guineas, both his new gold watch and diamond pin were recovered. But, poor man—we ought to be proud of nothing in this world—when the newspapers came in the day after, there was the whole story set forth in a most reprobate manner, under the title of, ' The misfortunes of a wise man of the East, or, doing a flat.' I need not add, that his polite and ceeveleezed frien' never came to dinner—You understand?

" While he was at Bow Street, a young woman, clothed in the rags of what had once been a silk dress, came into the office. She stated her case to the Magistrate in a most moving manner. She was the widow of an Ensign, who, in consequence of a quarrel with his commanding-officer—a tyrannical character—had been brought to a court-martial, and was deprived of his commission in the Island of St Kitts, where he immediately after died of the yellow fever, brought on by a broken heart. His brother officers, and other humane gentlemen, raised a subscription and sent her home; but on her landing at Chatham out of a transport, she fell sick, and all her little money was expended, and her clothes sold, before she was in a condition to come to London. The Magistrate was deeply affected by her tale of woe, and giving her a small sum for immediate relief, advised her to memorialeeze the Duke of York.

" Captain Monsoon said he never felt more for a poor creature in his life; but having, since his landing, been taken in before by a pitiful story, he was determined to be more cautious for the future; so, instead of giving her anything in the office, he took her address, and went next morning to the house,—a wretched shell, in a loathsome place,—and there, in a hideous garret, he beheld such a scene of misery and starvation as couldna be equalled. The poor creature was sitting in the midst of seven more than half-naked children, all huddling together to keep themselves warm, and the helpless orphans told him they had not tasted food for two days. His heart was so melted he could stand no more; so he put a five-pound note into their mother's hand, and promised to raise a subscription for her among his friends at the Jerusalem Coffee-house. Nor did he fail in his promise; some days after, having gathered upwards of fifty pounds, he came to me triumphing, saying he would make the widow's heart sing for joy; and he actually persuaded me to put on my pelisse—and I put on my best—to go with him to that house of mourning.

"Well, when we arrived, we could not get up the stairs, there was such a crowd of women assembled round the door, all speaking at once to a decent-looking, short, fatty, elderly man, with a curly brown wig. He was one of the Mendicity Society, come to enquire into the sorrowful tale; and, by putting different things thegither, he discovered that the afflicted madam was a second-hand country play-actress, and that the seven children were beggars' brats, hired by the week, at a shilling apiece, to make a scene. Did ye ever hear of such limmerhood? But the leddy was off and away, having eloped with a notour pocket-picker, after she had filled him fou the night before out of the five-pound note.

" It's no possible to describe the kippage the Captain was in at this discovery, nor what he said of the Londoners in general; but he gave me the fifty pounds to distribute in charity, charging me never to mention it, for if it reached the Jerusalem, he would never hear an end o't. And much good did that fifty pounds do to many a straitened Scotch family, who had not proved so fortunate as the generality of our country-folk in London.

"Soon after this another accidence befell the Captain. The Indian lad, his serving-man with the puddock-stool turban, was, along with our Sally, whom he engaged for a housemaid, sent off in a Leith smack, with a letter to his sister, a minister's widow, living in Edinburgh, that they might have a house ready for his reception, he himself intending in the meantime to take a tour by land to see the country, by the mail coach. But his first news was, that as soon as the two landed they got themselves married. How they courted, or how came to a love-paction, is past my fathoming; for no a word of English, or even of Scotch, could the lad speak; and it was no in nature that Sally could understand Hindoo, or any other dead language.

" But the Captain's tribulations were manifold, and some of them of a comical kind; for after he was so often taken in he grew just desperate, and would scarcely believe the sun was in the firmament on the sunniest day. To me, however, he proved a very worthy and discreet lodger; and I daresay in time, when his Indian vapours were properly evacuated, he sobered down into a good-hearted gentleman, with a competency of common sense, which is more than I can say of all my other Indian acquaintances."

Blackwood's Magazine, August-November 1829

GLOSSARY

aboon, *above.*
aff hand, *off hand.*
argol-bargolling, *disputation.*
arle, *earnest.*
art and part, *aiding and abetting.*
assoilyied, *acquitted.*
atomies, *skeletons.*
auld-farrant, *old-fashioned.*
auld-headed, *sagacious.*
awmous, *alms.*
ayont the dyke, *lit. beyond the wall.*

bardy, *bold.*
barmed, *worked.*
baxter, *baker.*
bein, *well-to-do.*
Beltane, 1*st of May.*
betherel, *sexton.*
bien, *thriving, comfortable.*
biggen, *grow big.*
bigging, *building.*
birky, *lively, young fellow.*
birses, *bristles.*
blate, *shy.*
blaw-thorough, *draughty place.*
bleezy, *fuddled.*
blithesmeat, *food provided at birth of a child.*
bodles, *coins, value twopence Scots.*
bogle, *scare-crow.*
boo, *bow.*
bouet, *lantern.*
bouks, *bulk.*
boun, *ready.*
boutger, *glutton.*
brittle, *uncertain.*
brod, *offertory plate.*
broo, *liking.*
buirdly, *stalwart.*
bunckled, *pimply.*
by common, *beyond the ordinary.*
by-ordinar, *extraordinary.*
by-set, *misfortune.*

callans, *lads.*
calm sough, *silence.*
cankery, cankry, *bad-tempered.*
canny, *cautious.*
carle, *old man.*
carlin, *old woman.*
cauk, *chalk.*
cauldrife, *chilly.*
cess, *tax.*
chack, *snack.*
chandler pins (on), *particularly nice.*
cheeping, *creaking.*
choppin, *quart.*
chucky-stone, *pebble.*
chumla lug, *fireside.*
churmed, *murmured.*
clachan, *village.*
clanjamphry, *riff-raff.*
claw, *scratch.*
clecking, *hatching.*
clockit, *hatched.*

cloots, clutes, *hooves.*
coggled, *shook, balanced uncomfortably.*
coggly, *unsteady.*
concosmentos, *compos mentis.*
conkesting, *acquisition.*
conneck, *connected.*
coomy, *grimy.*
corky-headed, *giddy.*
corruption, *temper.*
coupit, *tumbled.*
couthy, *agreeable, comfortable, kind, pleasant.*
craig, *throat.*
creeshy, *greasy.*
croon, *murmur.*
cruet, *decanter.*
crunkly, *rough.*
cutty, *jade, silly girl.*
cutty-crumb, *small, childish.*

daffin, *sport.*
dagon, *idol.*
daintice, *delicacy.*
dankle, *deviate from.*
darg, *work.*
daunered, *strolled.*
dauntoning, *terrifying.*
dauty, *darling.*
deacon, *adept.*
dead-ill, *last illness.*
dead thraws, *death agony.*
departal, *death.*
deval, *cease.*
dirl, *vibrate.*
disjaskit, *dejected.*
diver, *bankrupt.*
doers, *agents, guardians.*
donaguids, *good-for-nothings.*
donsy, *saucy.*
dooly, *grief.*
douce, *sedate, sober, respectable.*
dour, *stubborn.*
dover, *doze.*
dowie, *sad.*
down-draughts, *causes of depression.*
dreeping, *dripping.*
dreichly, *heavily.*
dress-mutch, *best cap.*
dumbfoundered, *amazed.*
dumbie, *dummy.*
dunting, *beating.*
dyke, *wall.*

eidency, eydencie, *diligence.*
eildens, *equal in age.*
errander, *messenger.*
ettering, *gathering.*
ettle, *purpose, effort, strive.*
evendown, *downright.*
evened, *demeaned.*
evening, *comparing.*
expiscatory, *fishing out by inquiry.*

faik, *abate.*
fain, *fond.*
fair, *completely.*
fairings, *comestibles.*
fairlies, *sights.*
fash, *trouble.*
fasherie, *troublesome matter.*
fashious, *troublesome.*
fause, *false.*
fen, *make a living.*
ferlies, *wonders.*

GLOSSARY

flaught, *bustle.*
flitting, *removal.*
forenent, *opposite.*
fou, *drunk.*
frush, *short.*
fu' kite, *full belly.*
functy offishy, *functus officio, having discharged his official duty.*
furthy, *forward, frank.*
fyke, *worry.*

gabbart, *lighter.*
gair, *thrifty, hard.*
gallantings, *rovings.*
galravitching, *riotous feasting.*
ganging a gey gait, *living in fast style.*
garnels, *granaries.*
gart, *made, caused to.*
gast, *fright*
gaunt, *yawn.*
gavalling, *merry-making.*
gawsy, *portly.*
genty, *genteel, trim.*
get, *offspring.*
girnels, *large chests.*
glaik, *gleam.*
gleg callan, *smart boy.*
gleg een, *sharp eyes.*
glegger, *sharper.*
glegness, *keenness.*
glunching, *frowning.*
go marrows, *unite.*
gotchard, *grandfather.*
gowled, *howled.*
gowpens, *handfuls.*
greened, *longed.*
grippet, *seized.*
grosette, *gooseberry.*
grumphy, *pig.*
gude hamert-made claes, *good home-made clothes.*
Guid Toun, *good town.*
gulbroch, *tansy, ragwort.*

haffits, *temples.*
hained, *saved.*
hainings, *savings.*
haivins, *manners.*
halflin, *half-grown.*
hameart, *homely.*
handwaled, *carefully selected.*
hap, *cover.*
hauflin, *half-grown.*
havrel, *silly.*
heck and manger, *free quarters.*
hempies, *rogues.*
herd, *tend.*
het, *hot.*
het and fu', *warm and full.*
hidling, *secret.*
hinder, *latter.*
hobbleshow, *rabble, tumult.*
hoggart, hogger, *stocking used as a purse.*
honesty, *respectability.*
houff, howff, *haunt, place of meeting.*
howking, *digging.*
hugger mugger, *speak privately.*

idleset, *idleness.*
ill-faured, *ill-favoured.*
ill-redd-up, *untidy.*
interlocutors, *legal judgments.*

GLOSSARY

jalouse, *suspect.*
jaw, *downpour.*
jimper, *more slender.*
jo, *sweetheart.*
jook, *evade.*
jouked, *dodged.*

kail-pot, *soup kettle.*
keckle, *chuckle.*
keek, *pry.*
kenna-what, *nondescript.*
kenspeckle, *conspicuous.*
kilfudyocking, *fireside disputing.*
kingcost, *whooping-cough.*
kink, *a choking.*
kippage, *rage.*
kirned, *mixed.*
kist, *coffin, chest.*
kite, *belly.*
kithe, *show.*
kithing, kything, *manifestation.*
kittle, *difficult, ticklish.*
kittled, *bred.*
kittling, *kitten, tickling.*
kythed, *showed.*

lair, *grave.*
lair, lear, *learning.*
laithron, *drab.*
lamiter, *cripple.*
land, *tenement.*
lanerly, *lonely.*
lassock, *little girl.*
late-wakes, *death watch.*
leet, *list of candidates.*
leeted, *selected.*
lift, *sky.*
lightlying, *disparaging.*
limmerhood, *deception.*
linking, *arm-in-arm.*
logive, *extravagant.*
loup, *leap.*
loupment, *elopement.*
loup-the-dyke, *runaway.*
lown, lowne, *serene, calm, quiet.*
lug, *ear.*
lums, *chimneys.*

marrow, *match.*
masket, *infused.*
mells, *meddles.*
mim, *demure.*
minted, *hinted.*
mort, *deceased.*
Mother's Carritches, *the Shorter Catechism.*
moulin, *crumb.*
mudging, *movement.*
muslin kail, *broth made without meat.*

nabalness, *meanness.*
nauby, *churl.*
nicher, *snigger.*
nicheringly, *laughingly.*
niffered, *bargained.*

Occasion, *dispensation of the Sacrament.*
oe, *grandchild.*
o'ercome, *burden.*
Ordinary Lords, *Judges*
outfalls, *accidents.*
outstraplaes, *obstreperous.*
overly dourly, *very hardly.*

owercome, *surplus.*

Pace - and - Yule, *Easter and Christmas.*
paction, *agreement.*
pactioned, *contracted.*
paraphernauls, perafarnals, *bride's property, possessions.*
pawtron, *pattern.*
peinor pig, *money-box, penurious.*
penny-fee, *wages.*
peoies, *conical fireworks of moistened gunpowder.*
perishes the pack, *wastes money.*
pernicketty, *particular.*
pickle, *little.*
plack, *fourpence Scots.*
plainstones, *pavement.*
play (the), *a holiday.*
playoc bairn, *playing child.*
pluffs, *flashes.*
pock, *bag.*
pocket napkin, *handkerchief.*
pockneuk, *bottom of the sack, resources.*
poney-cocks, *turkeys.*
powter, *poke.*
preeing, *taste.*
preent, *primed.*
prejinct, *neat.*
prigging, *haggling.*
provice, *provost.*
puddock, *frog.*
puddock-stool, *toad-stool.*
pue, *breath of wind.*
pushiont, *poisoned.*

quiscoskos, *queer, perplexing.*

rampauge, *romp, rage.*
ramplar, *roving.*
rax, *stretch.*
raxes, *andirons.*
redd, *advise.*
redding, *being set in order.*
ree, *crazy, drunk.*
rift, *wind.*
rifting, *belching.*
riping the ribs, *clearing the bars of a grate.*
rung, *staff.*

sair foot, *lit. sore foot, rainy day.*
sappy, *fat, profitable.*
scog, *hide, shelter.*
scomfished, *disgusted.*
scowry, *cold and showery.*
scrimp, *short, short measure, barely.*
scrimping, *niggardly.*
scuffed, *soiled.*
servits, *serviettes.*
session, *kirk-session.*
shanks' naggy, *one's own legs.*
shune, *shoes.*
sib, *akin.*
siccar, *secure.*
siclike, *same, similar persons.*
silly, *feeble.*
skailed, *dismissed.*
slaik, *smattering.*
slake, *smear.*
slee, *sly.*
sleeky, *cunning.*
sliddiness, *slipperiness.*
smeddum, *mettle, sharpness, spirit.*

smiddy, *blacksmith's shop.*
snodded, *tidied.*
snodness, *tidiness.*
sorrow, *wretch.*
sough, *rumour.*
souping, *sweeping.*
souter, *shoemaker.*
sowans, *dish made by steeping and boiling the siftings of oats.*
speer, speir, *inquire.*
speshy, kind.
sprose, *boast.*
spunk, *spark.*
stang, *sharp pain.*
staun, *booth.*
stends, *bruises.*
stey brae, *steep ascent.*
stoitering, *staggering.*
stots, *young bulls.*
stoury, *dusty.*
stramash, *uproar.*
stroupless, *spoutless.*
swatch, *sample.*
sweert, *reluctant.*

tappy-tourock, *top-knot, tower, turreted.*
tavert, *doted.*
teetle, *title.*
tent, *heed.*
thole, *endure.*
throng, *crowded, busy.*
tining, *losing.*
tinselers, *lost souls.*
toomed, *empty.*
topping, *leading.*
tosy, *drink.*
tot, *total.*
tow, *hemp.*
trinkum-trankums, *gewgaws.*
trintled, *trundled.*

unca, *strange.*
unco, *curiosity, novelty, stranger*
upsetting, *stuck-up.*

vekle, *carriage.*
virgos, *verjuice.*
vogie, *proud, merry.*

wadset, *mortgage.*
want, *mental defect.*
wared, waur'd, waurt, *spent.*
warsled, *struggled.*
weel-far'd, *good-looking.*
wersh, *tasteless.*
wersher, *weaker, lacking in flavour.*
whirly, *twinkle.*
whittering, *running aimlessly.*
wise, *lead.*
wised, *directed, induced.*
writers, *lawyers.*
wytes, *blames.*

yammered, *grumbled.*
yawp, *hungry.*
yett, *gate.*
youky, *itchy.*

Uniform with the present Volume

THE HOWDIE AND OTHER TALES

By JOHN GALT

Edited with an Introduction

By WILLIAM ROUGHEAD

INCLUDING:

I. THE HOWDIE
II. SAWNEY AT DONCASTER
III. THE AUNT IN VIRGINIA
IV. THE CHIEF: OR, THE GAEL AND THE SASSENACH
V. THE JOKE
VI. MY FATHER'S HOUSE
VII. THE GUDEWIFE
VIII. THE MEM
IX. THE METROPOLITAN EMIGRANT

T. N. FOULIS, LIMITED, LONDON & EDINBURGH

BOOKS BY WILLIAM ROUGHEAD

"Every page . . . is a sheer delight to the criminologist, the historian, or the more gentle reader."—*Scottish Historical Review.*

GLENGARRY'S WAY AND OTHER STUDIES

Price 10s. 6d.

CONTENTS

Glengarry's Way: a Footnote to "Waverley"—Plagium: a Footnote to "Guy Mannering"—Locusta in Scotland: a Familiar Survey of Poisoning, as practised in that Realm—Poison and Plagiary—The Strange Woman—The Last Tulzie—The Twenty-Seven Gods of Linlithgow—The Hard Case of Mr James Oliphant—The Hanging of James M'Kean: Lord Braxfield's Last Case—The Bi-Centenary of Lord Braxfield.

THE RIDDLE OF THE RUTHVENS AND OTHER STUDIES

Price 10s. 6d.

CONTENTS

The Riddle of the Ruthvens—The Real Braxfield—The Husband of Lady Grange—The Pack of the Travelling Merchant—Auld Auchindrayne—"Antique" Smith—The Abduction of Jean Kay—The Witches of North Berwick—Bargarran's Daughter—The Devil in Pittenweem—The Law and Mrs Yelverton—Nicol Muschet: His Crime and Cairn—The Master of Sinclair and the Fifteen—The Toll of the "Speedy Return"—The Adventures of David Haggart—Mackcoull and the Begbie Mystery—With Braxfield on the Bench—A Note on Robert Fergusson.

THE FATAL COUNTESS AND OTHER STUDIES

Price 10s. 6d.

CONTENTS

The Fatal Countess: a Footnote to "The Fortunes of Nigel"—Mr Kirkwood and the Kirk; or the Holy War—Laurel Water; or the Wicked Brother—"Indian Peter": an Old Edinburgh Portrait—The Ambiguities of Miss Smith: a Romantic Tale—The Secret of Ireland's Eye: a Detective Story—Physic and Forgery: a Study in Confidence—a Gossip on a Novel of Galt's.

W. GREEN & SON, LTD., ST GILES STREET, EDINBURGH